D1483310

OVERLORD

Volume 2: The Dark Warrior

Kugane Maruyama | Illustration by so-bin

NEW YORK

OVERLORD

VOLUME 2

KUGANE MARUYAMA

Translation by Emily Balistrieri
Cover art by so-bin

First published in Japan in 2012 by KADOKAWA CORPORATION ENTERBRAIN.
English translation rights arranged with KADOKAWA CORPORATION ENTERBRAIN,
through Tuttle-Mori Agency, Inc., Tokyo.

Yen On
1290 Avenue of the Americas
New York, NY 10104

Visit us at yenpress.com
facebook.com/yenpress
twitter.com/yenpress
yenpress.tumblr.com

First Yen On Edition: September 2016

Yen On is an imprint of Yen Press, LLC.
The Yen On name and logo are trademarks of Yen Press, LLC.

Library of Congress Cataloging-in-Publication Data

Names: Maruyama, Kugane, author. | So-bin, illustrator. | Balistrieri, Emily, translator.
Title: Overlord / Kugane Maruyama ; illustration by So-bin ; translation by Emily Balistrieri.
Other titles: Ōbārōdo. English
Description: First Yen On edition. | New York, NY : Yen On, 2016-
Identifiers: LCCN 2016000142 | ISBN 9780316272247 (v. 1 : hardback)
| ISBN 9780316363914 (v. 2 : hardback)
Subjects: LCSH: Alternate reality games—Fiction. | Internet games—Fiction. | Science fiction. |
BISAC: FICTION / Science Fiction / Adventure.
Classification: LCC PL873.A37 O2313 2016 | DDC 895.63/6—dc23 LC
record available at http://lccn.loc.gov/2016000142

ISBNs: 978-0-316-36391-4 (hardcover)
978-0-316-36392-1 (ebook)

10 9 8 7 6 5 4 3 2 1

RRD-C

Printed in the United States of America

Contents

OVERLORD

Prologue

The office of the highest ruler of the Great Tomb of Nazarick was a luxurious one. All the furnishings were elaborately ornate, giving the place an air of elegance and rarity. Soft, fluffy scarlet carpeting covered every inch of the floor and muffled any footsteps. Flags with various designs hung, crisscrossing over each other on the far back wall.

The desk in the room was made of dignified ebony. And the room's master sat in a black leather chair. This individual clad in a raven-black robe that seemed to suck light in could be described briefly as "the Dark Lord of Death."

His bare head had neither skin nor flesh—just bone. Red flames burned in his hollow eye sockets, with something black mixed in. He had once been called Momonga but now went by his guild's name, Ainz Ooal Gown.

Ainz folded his finger bones. His nine rings sparkled, reflecting the glow produced by the Continual Light spell. "Sheesh, what should I do now?"

Eight days had passed since the day the Dive Massively Multiplayer Online Role-Playing game *Yggdrasil* closed its servers and he was mysteriously transported—as his skeleton-like character—to another world. During that time he had checked the conditions of his castle, the Great Tomb of Nazarick, and his minions and learned that it wasn't so different from in the game, so he decided to make his next move.

"Everything will be as you wish, my lord." The gorgeous woman standing quietly by responded to Ainz's muttering. She was flawlessly, peerlessly beautiful, wearing a snow-white dress. Her smile was like that of a goddess. Her lustrous hair was a black the exact opposite of her dress and reached all the way to her waist. But she wasn't human.

She had golden irises with vertical slit pupils, and thick horns curled forward out of her temples like a ram's. Furthermore, black wings sprouted out of her back near her hips, arching around her such that they concealed her feet.

"Hmm. I'm glad to have your devotion, Albedo."

She was Albedo, captain of the Great Tomb of Nazarick's floor guardians. There were seven floor guardians, and she was the NPC who oversaw them.

Ainz and the other members of his guild had built the Great Tomb of Nazarick. Now the NPC servants they created had become self-aware and sworn allegiance to Ainz. He was pleased about that, but it was also a burden, since he used to be just an office worker. Acting like a master before his subordinates and making sure things were running smoothly—an absolute ruler had a lot of responsibilities.

The biggest problem was that their guild lacked information about the world outside.

"And the next report?"

"Here it is, Lord Ainz."

Ainz accepted the sheaf of papers and ran his eyes over the characters written in bold fountain-pen lines. It was a report from the guardian of the sixth level, Aura Bella Fiora.

Her report explained that so far they hadn't encountered any other *Yggdrasil* players like Ainz, nor seen any sign of them. She said that their survey of the forest near the Tomb was proceeding on schedule and that they had reached the lake at the foot of the mountains on the other side.

Ainz nodded. He was most concerned about running into other players, so he was relieved they hadn't. "Got it. Please tell Aura to proceed under her current orders."

"Underst—" There came a succession of quiet knocks on the door. Albedo looked at Ainz, and then, with a bow, went to answer it. Once she'd seen who it was, she announced, "Shalltear would like to see you."

"Shalltear? Sure, let her in."

With Ainz's permission, a girl of about fourteen wearing a raven-black ball gown with a full, wide skirt made a graceful entrance. She had almost waxy white skin, and "unparalleled" was the way to describe her shapely face. Her long silver hair bounced with every step she took, as did her chest, which was big for how old she looked. She was guardian of the first, second, and third levels, "True Vampire" Shalltear Bloodfallen.

"I hope you are well, Lord Ainz."

"You, too, Shalltear. What brings you to my quarters today?"

"I came to see your handsome face, of course."

Ainz's skull didn't change expressions, but instead the crimson flames deep in his orbits flickered. He was about to say, "Save the brownnosing," but decided against it—because he saw the smile on Albedo's face gradually change as she watched Shalltear's crimson pupils cloud over with lust out of the corner of her eye. Her subtle expression remained, and her beauty was unspoiled, but the smile was no longer a smile. It was the grimace of a jealous demon. But Ainz felt all right—the glare was directed at Shalltear, not himself.

"Then you're satisfied now, right, Shalltear? Lord Ainz and I are presently discussing the future of the Great Tomb of Nazarick. Could you not bother us? This is something important we need to do alone."

"It's basic politeness to greet someone before stating your business. Don't be so disagreeable, Ms. Over-the-Hill. What's your hurry? Are you past your expiration date?"

"Food so pumped full of preservatives it doesn't have an expiration date is no different from poison! I think I'm still on the safe side."

"...I wouldn't underestimate the bacteria that cause food poisoning. Some of them even cause contagious diseases."

"...Do you even have anything to eat over there? Your display is quite impressive, but when it comes to the goods...you know?"

"......'Display'?! I'm gonna kill you!"

"......So *who's* past her expiration date?"

Before Ainz stood two women whose facial expressions were difficult to describe; those looks could put an end to a hundred million–year romance. He quelled the impulse to hold his head in his hands and spoke up before an appallingly ferocious battle could break out. "Cut out the kids' stuff, you two."

They immediately answered in unison and beamed smiles at him. Instead of whatever horrors they had been moments before, two lovely, innocent maidens now stood there.

Women are terrifying... Or maybe it's just these two... Even Ainz, whose larger swings in emotion were suppressed since becoming undead, was a little freaked out when faced with such rapid adjustments of attitude.

The reason for their conflict was that they were rivals in love. Both Albedo and Shalltear had fallen for Ainz—i.e., he was loved by two incomparable beauties. What guy wouldn't be happy about that?

But Ainz couldn't just accept their feelings, especially when Shalltear the sticky-voiced necrophiliac came over to whisper, "You have great bone structure; it's as if you were modeled by a god," in his ear. Maybe to her they were words of love—or a compliment—but to Ainz, what had happened several days earlier would be remembered as a shock to his system: The first compliment ever paid to his appearance was as a skeleton.

He cleared the trivial matter from his mind and repeated his question. "I'll ask again: What is it, Shalltear?"

"My lord, I am going to join Sebas as you ordered. It seems like I won't be back to the Great Tomb of Nazarick for a while, so I came to say good-bye."

Ainz recalled the orders he had given her and nodded. "Got it. Stay sharp, do your job, and come home safe, Shalltear."

"My lord!" her dignified voice rang out.

"You can go, Shalltear. Once you've left my quarters, tell either Narberal or Entoma to have Demiurge come see me. Tell him I need to discuss with him something about our next move."

"Yes, Lord Ainz."

Chapter 1   Two Adventurers

Chapter 1 | Two Adventurers

1

Situated at a key location on the border between the Re-Estize Kingdom and its neighboring countries, the Baharuth Empire and the Slane Theocracy, E-Rantel looked the part of its title, the Fortress City, due to its three layers of walls. The townscapes within each layer had their own flavors.

The outermost area was where the royal army was stationed, so that's where the military facilities were. The innermost area was the city's administrative core. The storehouses for military provisions were there, and the whole zone was always under tight security. The space between those two zones was where the townspeople lived. It was the goings-on in this zone that usually sprang to mind when one heard the city's name.

In the center square, the area's largest, vendors at open-air stalls offered a wide range of goods, including everything from fresh vegetables to prepared foods. In the crowd of people, shopkeepers earnestly peppered passersby with lively sales pitches; elderly shoppers looking for the freshest produce haggled with merchants; lured by the grilling aromas, young men purchased kebabs dripping with meat juices.

Bursting with midday liveliness, it seemed as though the din in the square would continue on into the evening, but when a certain pair emerged from an adjacent five-story building, the commotion met its end. No one in the square could keep their eyes off them, and everyone froze.

One of the pair was a woman. She looked to be in her late teens or early twenties and had lovely almond eyes that flashed with an obsidian gleam. Her abundant hair, so black it looked wet, was pulled back in a ponytail. Her smooth, pale skin shone with the luster of a pearl in the sun. More captivating than anything else was her modest beauty, the air of exoticism that turned everyone's head. When worn by her, a completely ordinary brown robe seemed to transform into a luxurious gown.

Her companion's sex was unclear, which is to say there were no distinguishing features visible.

Someone in the square whispered, "The Dark Warrior…"

Yes, the figure was enveloped in dazzling full plate armor that gleamed raven black and had purple-and-gold accents. It was impossible to make out the face behind the slit in the close helmet. Appropriate for such a robust physique, two great swords laid across the individual's back, hilts jutting out from beneath a crimson cape.

The two of them looked out over the square, and the one in full plate armor set off walking first. Witnesses followed the departing figures with their eyes, murmuring rumors among themselves. It wasn't that they were frightened or put on guard by the weapons, but that they had seen a curious sight.

The reason they weren't more unnerved was because the building from which the pair had emerged was a place where people who specialized in monster extermination looked for work, the Adventurers Guild. It wasn't at all rare to see armed people coming and going from there. In fact, after those two, a number of other people carrying weapons went in and out. Those with sharp eyes had been able to spot the copper plate around each of the pair's necks. It was clear, then, that the only reason they were getting attention was the woman's beauty and the magnificence of the other's armor.

The pair walked silently down the not very wide street. Puddles in wagon wheel ruts reflected the sunlight. It wasn't a proper paved road but a mix of dirt and mud that made it hard to walk. One wrong step and there was nothing to do but trip, but perhaps due to their superior senses of balance, these two walked with the same gait they would have used on cobblestones.

Moving with a light step, the woman checked to make sure no one was around and then spoke to the one in full plate armor. "Lord Ai—"

"No. My name is Momon. And you're not Narberal Gamma of the Pleiades, but Nabe, Momon's adventurer friend." It was the armed figure—Ainz—who'd interrupted the woman—Narberal.

"Ah! Please excuse the error, Lord Momon!"

"Leave off the 'Lord.' We're just a couple of adventurers, and we're friends. It'll look suspicious if you call me Lord."

"B-but you're a Supreme Being!"

Ainz gestured for her to lower her voice and answered with hints of annoyance and resignation in his voice. "How many times do I have to explain this? In this land I am Momon the Dark... —I mean, Momon, and you're my partner. So don't call me Lord. That's an order."

There was a momentary pause, and then Narberal reluctantly acquiesced. "Understood, Mr. Momooon."

"Well, that's better, at least, but really, you don't even need the Mister. I'm your partner, so if you call me Mister, it makes it seem like there's kind of a gap between us."

"Is that...disrespectful or...?"

Narberal trailed off, and Ainz shrugged at her. "No one can find out who we really are. You understand that, right?"

"Of course, sir."

"You don't need the... Well, whatever. I'm just saying to be careful is all."

"Understood, Mr. Momooon! But are you sure I'm the right person for this? If you need a companion, wouldn't someone graceful and beautiful like Albedo be more suitable?"

"Albedo, huh...?" His voice contained a complex mixture of emotions. "I need her to manage Nazarick while I'm away."

"If I may be so bold, surely Cocytus could manage Nazarick. The guardians were all saying so, but…when it comes to your safety, my lord, wouldn't having Nazarick's best defender, Albedo, with you be most appropriate?"

Ainz reacted to her question with distress.

When he had announced he would go personally to E-Rantel, the guardian who had been most vehemently against it was Albedo, and her pushback started the moment she understood she wouldn't be accompanying him.

He still felt indebted to her for how, right after he had been transported to this world, she had covered for him when he'd been out walking on his own without telling anyone because he was loath to take an escort, so he didn't react too harshly. But this was different; it was a carefully planned trip, not a whim, so he wasn't going to back down.

She had probably suppressed her own desires and obeyed him because guardians were happy to submit when given an order, but Ainz didn't feel good about it. It bothered him to force things on the characters his guildmates had created.

Ainz had tried persuasion, but Albedo was firmly against him. Their opinions were running along parallel lines destined to never meet, and it seemed like the issue would never get resolved, but after Demiurge whispered something in her ear, Albedo had abruptly withdrawn her complaints and the decision was made. She even said, "I understand everything," and saw him off with a gentle smile.

He still didn't know what Demiurge had said to her; that paired with the dramatic change in her behavior made him a bit anxious.

"The reason I didn't bring Albedo is that there is no one I trust more than her. It's precisely because she's at Nazarick that I don't have to worry about being away."

"I see. That's what I thought! So you're closest to Albedo, then, huh?"

Saying *Uh, yeah, I guess* was impossible, so he just nodded. "And I know how dangerous this trip is." Ainz raised his gauntleted right hand and wiggled his ring finger. "But it has to be me doing this. If I were to just command from within Nazarick, I'd end up missing something because this world is an unknown. I need to get out and see what it's really like. …I'm sure there are many ways we could have gone about things, but when we're dealing with so many unknowns, I wanted to do something that didn't make me feel so uneasy."

Ainz watched Narberal through the slit in his helmet as she solemnly accepted his explanation, and then he asked with a hint of anxiety in his voice, "Just wondering, but do you consider humans lower life-forms?"

"Indeed I do. Humans are worthless trash."

Hearing this reply with no sign of hesitation that clearly came from the bottom of her heart, he muttered, "So you think so, too…," but it was too quiet to reach Narberal's ears. He continued, complaining, "That's why I can't just send you to a human city. I really should have made learning the personalities of my subordinates my highest priority."

One of the reasons he hadn't brought Albedo was because of how she had denounced humans as lower life-forms. He couldn't take her to a city where there were lots of people only to have her throw a mass murder party the moment he took his eyes off her. Plus, Albedo didn't have any disguise magic, so there was no way to hide her horns or wings.

And then there was the biggest reason—the one he couldn't tell anyone: Ainz, who had been a normal office worker, wasn't confident he could just sit at the top and manage everything with Nazarick's future in mind based solely on secondhand information. That's why he had decided to venture out, foisting operations onto Albedo, who had the skills to manage them. One should always delegate to a talented subordinate when possible. Nothing good came from a higher-up mucking around in an area outside his competence.

Also, where Ainz was concerned, Albedo was bound by two chains: loyalty and love. Under the circumstances, he felt safe leaving the Great Tomb of Nazarick in her hands.

Love… Whenever he saw Albedo, and whenever she said how much she admired him, he was reminded of his mistake in rewriting part of her backstory. Yes, right before the game's servers were supposed to go down, he'd edited her bio to say that she was "in love with Momonga"—in other words, with Ainz. Of course, he had no way of knowing they would all go flying off to some new, other world. He'd just meant it as a little joke on the last day.

Reflecting on it, though, Albedo herself didn't seem to mind, but what would Ainz's friend, her creator, Tabula Smaragdina, think if he found out? *What if it were me? If my friend had warped an NPC I made…* He also didn't like that he was taking advantage of her condition and assuming she wouldn't betray him.

He shook his head to banish those dark thoughts. His undead body suppressed major emotional waves, but little ripples like this still affected him like they had when he was human. *If I turn completely undead, will I stop feeling this guilt?* Thinking absentmindedly on these things, he turned his close helmeted head to face Narberal. "Nabe, I'm not saying you have to discard that sentiment, but at least suppress it. This is a human city, and we don't know how strong some of them might be, not to mention a lot of other things. Try not to do anything that could trigger hostility."

Narberal bowed deeply to signify her loyalty and submission, and he held her head down to make his final point. "One more thing. When we take a fight too seriously or think we'd like to kill someone, it…frightens the humans. I don't know if you really have bloodlust as such or not, but it comes off that way, so don't go all-out without my permission. Okay?"

"Yes, Mr. Momooon."

"Okay, the inn that lady told us about should be around here somewhere…" Ainz scanned the area.

There were some shops open and a few people going in and out. Looking to the side, he saw some artisans in aprons carrying goods, but there were only a handful. Ainz and Narberal looked for the inn based on the picture on the sign, since they couldn't read this country's writing.

Finally Ainz found the "picture" and began walking faster. Narberal noticed and matched his pace.

Scraping the mud off his sabbatons, Ainz went up the stoop, pushed open the swinging café doors, and stepped inside. The windows that would have let light in were mostly shuttered, so the room was dim. A human accustomed to the light outside might have felt it pitch-dark for a moment, but Ainz had the Darkvision ability, so there was plenty of light for him.

It was a fairly large space. The first floor was a pub with a bar in the back. Behind the bar were two built-in shelves lined with bottles. The door to the side of the bar probably led to the kitchen.

In the corner of the pub was a stairway that wrapped around on itself partway up. According to the lady at the guild, the second and third floors were an inn.

There was a handful of customers sitting at the few round tables, mostly men. The atmosphere suited the kind of people who constantly put themselves in dangerous situations.

Most eyes were on Ainz and Narberal, many aggressively appraising them. The only person not paying attention to them was a girl sitting at the edge of the room, staring at a bottle on her table.

Faced with this scene, Ainz furrowed his nonexistent brow under his close helmet. He'd prepared himself for this, but it was still dingier than he'd expected.

There were dirty and repulsive places in *Yggdrasil*, too. There were even some in the Great Tomb of Nazarick itself—places like the Prince of Fear's room and the Den of Poison. But this was a different kind of dirty.

Scraps of some kind of food had fallen to the floor, and there were puddles of some kind of liquid as well; the walls had strange stains on them, and in the corner something had coagulated and was growing mold…

Ainz sighed in his head and looked at the back of the room. There was a man standing there wearing a grimy apron. His sleeves were rolled up, revealing thick forearms; they bore several scars, but it was impossible to tell whether they'd been made by a sword or a beast. His features fell somewhere between intensely masculine and wild animal, and there were scars on his face, too. His head was shaved clean—not a single hair remained. This man with a mop in one hand, who seemed more like a hired guard than the innkeeper, had been openly observing Ainz.

"You need a room, eh? How many nights?" his gruff voice boomed.

"One, please."

"…A copper plate? It'll be five coppers for a shared room," the inn-keeper said brusquely. "Food is oatmeal—well, some days it's leftover bread instead of oatmeal—and vegetables. If you want meat, that's a copper extra."

"If possible I'd like a room for just the two of us."

Ainz heard a faint snort. "…There are three inns that serve adventurers in this city. The one at the bottom is mine. You were introduced by the guild, right? You know how I can tell?"

"No, I don't. Will you tell me?"

At Ainz's swift reply, the innkeeper's eyebrows tilted to a dangerous angle. "Think a bit! Or don't you have anything inside that fancy helmet of yours?"

Ainz wasn't fazed by the irritated voice projected from the pit of the innkeeper's stomach. Perhaps he could take the outburst the way he would take a tantrum thrown by a child, because of his experience in the battle the other day.

That battle, and forcibly extracting intelligence out of his prisoners afterward, had helped him get an idea of how powerful he was. He didn't need to get riled up about being shouted at.

The innkeeper noticed that attitude and emitted a faint *hmm* of admi-ration. "…Seems like you have some guts, eh? …The adventurers who stay here are generally copper or iron plates. If you're around the same ability level and start to recognize each other, you might decide to form a team and go adventuring together. My place is a perfect spot to look for team mem-bers…" The innkeeper's eyes widened into an intimidating stare. "I don't mind if you want to sleep in your own room, but if you don't meet people, you can't make friends. And if you can't organize a balanced team, you'll die fighting a monster. That's why greenhorns who don't have enough friends get themselves known by staying in a large room. So I'll ask you one more time: Do you want a shared room or a two-person room?"

"A two-person room. No need for meals."

"Tch, I'm just trying to be nice… Or are you saying that your full plate armor isn't just for show? Well, whatever. One night is seven coppers—up front, naturally." The innkeeper stuck out his hand.

Under the room's appraising eyes, Ainz, followed by Narberal, moved to go when suddenly a leg was thrust into his way. Ainz stopped and, moving only his eyes, looked at the man the leg belonged to.

He had a thin, nasty smile on his face. The others at his table were either smiling in the same way or staring at Ainz and Narberal.

Neither the innkeeper nor any of the customers went to intervene. At a glance it seemed like they either didn't care or were looking on in amusement as if something interesting had started, but there were a few people with sharp gazes mixed in, watching their every move.

Sheesh. Ainz breathed a faint sigh and shoved the leg away with his foot.

As if he'd been waiting for just that, the man stood up. Since he wasn't wearing armor, it was possible to see that he was well muscled under his clothes. A chain with a plate similar to the one Ainz was wearing—only iron—swung from his neck when he moved. "Hey, that hurt!" He implied a threat as he slowly sidled up. At some point he had grabbed his gauntlets and put them on. When he formed fists, the metal made a chilling squeak.

The two sized each other up from a distance that was a bit too close for throwing punches. They were about the same height. Ainz made the first move. "Oh, I didn't see your leg there. With this close helmet on, my field of vision isn't so great. Or maybe I didn't see it because it's so stubby… Anyhow, you'll forgive me, right?"

"…You bastard." A dangerous glint appeared in the man's eyes in response to Ainz's taunting. But when his gaze shifted behind Ainz to Narberal, something new got lodged where the anger had been.

"You really piss me off, but hey, I'm a nice guy. If you lend your lady to me for a night, I'll let you off the hook."

"Hah! Ha-ha-ha!" Ainz burst out laughing and put a hand out to stay Narberal, who had begun to move forward.

"…What?"

"No, it's just that what you said just now was such a textbook example of something a little punk would say that I couldn't help but laugh. Forgive me."

"Huh?" Now his indignation showed on his face, which had grown red in patches.

"Oh, before this comes to blows, can I ask you something? Are you stronger than Gazef Stronoff?"

"Huh? What are you talking about?!"

"I see. That reaction will do. I guess I won't even be able to use enough of my power to have any fun. Time to fly!"

Ainz whipped out his hands and grabbed the man's collar to lift him off the ground. Unable to resist, much less dodge, before being hoisted into the air, the man cried a startled, "Whoa!" and the men watching the commotion grew audibly excited. How strong would a person have to be to lift a grown man off the ground with one hand? There was no one in the room with so little imagination they couldn't guess.

The stir was followed by a collective held breath. Ainz shattered the tense air of astonishment by taking the frantically kicking man and lightly tossing him across the room—of course, "lightly" was from Ainz's perspective.

The man's body ascended with impressive velocity almost to the ceiling before describing the rest of its parabola and falling heavily onto a table.

The impact of the body, the shattering of the things that had been on the table, wood splitting, and the man's pained voice—all these sounds overlapped in a cacophony that resounded throughout the room. Then, as if the noise were dampened by the man's groan, silence descended. But a beat later—

"Nyaaargh!" A strange yell came out of the mouth of the woman who'd been sitting at the table—a scream from her soul that said something unthinkable had occurred. It was a natural way to react to a man falling down on one's table, but this was definitely about something else.

"So? Now what are you gonna do? It would be a pain to fight you each one-on-one, not to mention a ridiculous waste of time, so you can come at me all at once if you want." Ainz addressed the rest of the men sitting where the first one had been. Catching his implication, they all hurried to bow their heads.

"Ah? O-oh! How rude of our friend! Allow us to apologize!"

"...Sure, you're forgiven. This was no problem for me at all. Just make sure you pay the innkeeper for that table."

"Of course. We'll take care of that."

That's settled, then. Ainz had just started walking away when someone else called out to him. "Hey, hey, hey!" When he turned to look, the woman who'd screamed earlier was striding his way.

She was probably twenty or a little younger. Her red hair was cut to a practical length. No matter how generously one regarded it, the ends weren't remotely even—if anything, it looked more like a bird's nest. Her face wasn't bad, but there was no sign of any makeup on it, and she had bitterness in her eyes. Her skin was tanned to a healthy wheat color, and the muscles on her arms stood out, as did the sword calluses on her hands. The first impression she made was not *woman*, but *warrior*. The iron plate hanging around her neck swung with each step she took.

"Whaddaya think you're doin'?!"

"What do you mean 'what'?"

"Huh?! You don't even know what you did?!" She pointed to the broken table. "You threw that guy, and my potion, my precious potion, broke! What're you thinking, throwing around a huge fucking thing like that?!"

"Your point?"

"My 'point'?! Oh, man…" Her eyes grew sharper and her voice lower. "I demand compensation! For my potion!"

"It's just a potion…"

"I skipped meals and scrimped and saved, desperately economizing, all to buy that potion today—today!—and you went and broke it! I was trusting that potion to save my life on a dangerous adventure! This is your attitude after you crush my dreams?! I am seriously pissed!" She took another step toward Ainz. Her wide-open eyes were bloodshot; she had the look of an enraged bull.

Ainz suppressed a sigh. It *had* been careless of him to not look before throwing. But there was a specific reason he wouldn't agree to compensate her so easily.

"…So why don't you collect from that guy? If he hadn't been so desperate to stretch out his stubby little leg, this wouldn't have happened, right?" He glared at the man's friends through the slit in his helmet.

"O-ohh…"

"But—"

"Well, you can give me another potion or pay me the equivalent, either way…but it cost one gold piece and ten silvers." The men looked at their feet. Apparently they didn't have the money to pay her back. So the woman looked back at Ainz. "Figures. They're always here drinking themselves into a stupor, so why would they have any money? But you…you're wearing that fancy armor, so you must have at least a low-grade healing potion on you, right?"

I see, thought Ainz. *So that's why she started by asking me.* Things had gotten complicated; one wrong move could ruin everything. He thought a moment and then made up his mind. "I do, but…you're certain it was a healing potion?"

"Duh! I worked so har—"

"Yeah, I got that part. I'll give you a potion, so let's call it even." He took out a Minor Healing Potion and held it out to the woman.

She gave it a dubious look, and then made a sullen face and took it.

"…So there's no problem anymore?"

"…I guess it's fine." It sounded a little like there still might be an issue, but Ainz cleared the doubts from his mind. He had more important things to worry about, like whether Narberal was about to commit a fatal error or not. Even though he'd settled things, she was clearly still on edge. Seeming to sense this, several bystanders had anxious looks on their faces.

"Let's go," Ainz said, half as a check on Narberal, and stood before the innkeeper. Then he casually pulled a leather pouch from his pocket, took out a silver coin, and dropped it into the innkeeper's rough hand.

The innkeeper stuffed it into his pocket without a word, and when he brought his hand out again, it was clutching a few copper pieces. "Okay, then, six coppers is your change." He dropped the coins into Ainz's gauntleted hand and set a key on the counter with a *ka-ching.* "Up the stairs and first on your right. Put your luggage in the chests built into the beds. I don't think I have to tell you, but don't go near other people's rooms for no reason. If somebody thinks you're up to something, there'll be trouble. Although if you want people to know who you are, I guess that's one way to do it. Seems like you could handle almost any trouble that might arise. Just don't make any for me." The innkeeper's eyes flitted for a moment to the man still moaning on the floor.

"Got it. Also, please outfit me with the minimum provisions necessary for adventuring. I lost everything I had. When I asked at the guild, they said you'd be able to..."

The innkeeper looked at the things Ainz and Narberal were wearing and then eyed the leather pouch. "Yeah, sure thing. I'll have it all ready for you by dinnertime. Make sure you're ready to pay."

"Right. Okay, Nabe, let's go."

Narberal followed Ainz up the old staircase that shrieked its creaks, and they headed to their assigned room.

•

Once Ainz was gone, the comrades of the man who'd been thrown hurried to cast healing magic on him. As if that were the trigger, the silent inn suddenly began to stir.

"So that guy's actually as tough as he looks, huh?"

"Yeah, that strength is something else. I wonder how he trained!"

"He didn't have any other weapons besides those two great swords, but that must just show how confident he is."

"Argh, another guy who seems like he could knock us all flying at once?"

The conversations being had conveyed admiration, wonder, astonishment.

Actually, everyone had known from the start that Ainz wasn't a typical adventurer. The first tip-off was his impressive gear. Full plate armor did not come cheaply; it was only someone who had gone on adventure after adventure—someone with a lot of experience—who could afford to buy it. Factoring in only rewards, someone who'd earned a silver plate might have that kind of fortune. Of course, there were some who inherited gear or people who picked up things in ruins or on the battlefield; that's why they'd wanted to test how powerful he really was.

Everyone at this inn was friendly with one another but, of course, they were also rivals. If a new guy showed up, they would all want to know how strong he was, so incidents like the one that had just happened were common. Actually, they'd all taken their turn running this gauntlet; just no one could ask themselves if they had made it through so easily and say yes.

In other words, it was clear to everyone that whether they were friends or foes, the unfamiliar pair with the copper plates possessed genuine strength.

"How should we treat them now?"

"Guess I can't talk to that pretty lady ever again."

"If it's just the two of them, they can join my team!"

"You mean you'll beg them to join!"

"I wonder what his face looks like under that helmet."

"I'm gonna camp outside their room and listen in tonight!"

"He name-dropped Gazef Stronoff, the strongest warrior around!"

"Do you think he's his apprentice?"

"Could be."

"A job that important should be left up to me! I'm a thief with excellent hearing."

In the midst of all the chatter flying around about the unknown pair, the innkeeper walked up to one adventurer in particular—the woman who had received the potion from Ainz.

"Hey, Brita."

"Hmm? What?" The woman, Brita, moved only her eyes from the red potion she'd been staring at and looked at him with disinterest.

"What's up with that potion?"

"Dunno."

"C'mon now, whaddaya mean, 'dunno'? You only took it because you knew how much it was worth, right?"

"Yeah, right. Actually, I've never seen a potion like this before. You're over here looking at it because you haven't, either, right?"

It was just as she'd said. "You're okay with that? He really did break your potion, y'know? This one might be worth less than the one you had!"

"Mm, yeah. It's definitely a gamble, but I feel like I'll come out ahead this time. After all, that guy with his fancy armor offered this *after* hearing how much my potion was worth."

"Oh..."

"...Plus, I've never seen a healing potion this color before. That means there's a good chance it's a pretty rare find, right? If I'd hesitated, it would have been like going into a dragon's nest and bringing home nothing. Anyway, tomorrow I'll go get it appraised, and then I'll know how much it's worth."

"Oh yeah? Then let me cover the appraisal fees for you. And not only that, but I'll introduce you to a top-notch place."

"You'd do that?" Brita's eyebrows scrunched together. The innkeeper was a good man, but he wasn't a softy. He had to have an ulterior motive.

"Now, now, don't make that face. All you have to do is tell me what effects the potion has or whatever."

"That's the deal, huh?"

"Not a bad one, is it? And with my connections, I can introduce you to the best potion maker around—*the* Lizzy Baleare."

Brita's face showed her genuine surprise.

E-Rantel was a place where many mercenaries and adventurers gathered, so it was home to a flourishing market for buying and selling weapons and items aimed at them. The potion business was particularly brisk, and there were many more apothecaries there than in other cities.

Out of all of them, Lizzy Baleare was known as the best and could make the most complex potions of any of the city's apothecaries. Once the name of the best apothecary in E-Rantel had been brought up, the offer was no longer one Brita could refuse.

2

The wooden door gently clapped shut.

The only furnishings in the room were one small desk and two simple wooden beds with chests built in. Since the shutters were open, sunlight and air from outside came in directly.

Ainz looked around the room, slightly disappointed. He knew he was at an inn on the outskirts of town and couldn't expect the same facilities and cleanliness as at Nazarick, but this setup put him on his guard.

"That you should have to stay in such a place, Lord Momon, is so…"

"Oh, don't say that. Our goal is to gain a reputation in this city as adventurers. We have to aim for the top so everyone will know my name. Until then, adopting the lifestyle of the part can't hurt." Ainz comforted her, showing no sign of his inner feelings, as he closed the shutters. The light that came in through the gaps in the shutters was not enough to banish the room's darkness completely. Ainz and Narberal could use Darkvision, so it didn't affect them, but for anyone who couldn't do that, this room would probably be too dark to see much of anything. "…But, man, being an adventurer is more depressing than I thought."

Adventurer. The word had held some fascination for Ainz. They traveled the world in pursuit of the unknown. He'd been imagining it as an occupation that embodied the "correct way" to play *Yggdrasil*, but after talking to the receptionist at the guild, he realized it was more practical and boring.

In a nutshell, an adventurer was an anti-monster mercenary. They did resemble the adventurers Ainz had been dreaming of in some ways—e.g., there were opportunities to explore ruins, wreckage of the country destroyed by the evil spirits that appeared there two hundred years ago, and pursue the unknown in unexplored regions—but they were basically monster exterminators.

Monsters had various special abilities depending on their type, which is why tackling them required people with a larger variety of skills—countermeasures—than soldiers had.

Given that, one might think that they'd be in a position like the hero in a video game, with many people depending on them…

But that was not the case.

The ruling classes weren't too keen on having armed groups roaming around outside of their control. For that reason, even if adventurers were doing well enough from a monetary standpoint, their status was low. The reason they weren't brought in to work on a national level was that countries used the same logic that corporations do: Full-time employees cost money, so it was cheaper to just hire temp workers as necessary. And just as there are some companies that get by without hiring any temp workers, there were countries where the army could subdue the monsters; in those places, an adventurer's status was even lower.

The lady behind the desk at the guild had grumbled that there were no adventurers in the Slane Theocracy and that the standing of adventurers in the Baharuth Empire had been falling ever since the current emperor came to power.

Ainz cleared the faint disappointment from his mind. It wasn't so uncommon a thing for someone to take a job they'd always wanted only to discover it wasn't all it was cracked up to be.

He waved his hand loosely, and his raven-black armor and two great swords melted into thin air, revealing his skeletal figure wrapped in magic items. Every now and then, a red target sight appeared on his thin black-mirrored shades and then disappeared. The amethyst circlet around his head was like a rose vine—the outside had a number of thorns sticking out. On top, he wore a black long-sleeved shirt with a silky sheen and, on bottom, baggy pants. Around his waist was something closer to a black belt—as in the martial arts kind—than a simple belt. He took off his unsophisticated gauntlets, and all his fingers except his ring fingers had rings on them. His rugged, red-brown ankle boots were embroidered with gold thread. Around his neck was a necklace that featured a silver plate fashioned into a lion's face and then his crimson cape.

Normally, *Yggdrasil* items were augmented by inlaying them with data crystals. For this reason, it was extremely difficult to have matching gear. But there were enough people who hated looking like a jumble of east and west that the developers released an update that made it so a player who met certain conditions could keep their stats but align the style of their equipment.

The matching raven-black armor that had been covering Ainz's entire body up until moments before was created with Create Greater Item, which was one of the conditions.

The items Ainz had equipped included Direct Hit Glasses, a Crown of Psychic Defense, Black Widow Spider Clothes, a Black Belt, *Járngreipr*, a Nemean lion, Haste Boots, and—

In *Yggdrasil*, buying and selling was often done at the data-crystal level; however, there were times when players had created a more powerful item and would then sell what they had been equipping before. The problem was that if a player created an item, they could name it basically whatever they wanted (the admins would request a change if the name contained words prohibited on TV or insults against a particular individual).

There was an understandably strong tendency for items with strange names to be avoided on the market. The in-game purchase to change an item's name was rather inexpensive, but there were not a lot of people who would go so far as to use one in order to buy something. For that reason, most players racked their brains when it came time to name an item. Names from myths or English words were common solutions.

Of course, there were exceptions.

Naming rings Ring1, Ring2, Ring3, and so on was still on the charming side. Ainz had even seen Thumb, Pointer, Middle before. One of Ainz's friends, the Warrior Takemikazuchi, had two *ōdachi* that he used for different things. He named the eighth generation of one of them Takemikazuchi Style Eight.

Ainz's crimson cape also had one of these custom names: Necroplasmic Cape. The idea was borrowed from the dark hero of an American comic.

This was all relic gear. That was two tiers below his usual, but he could think of several good reasons to not bring overly powerful items to this place, so he had stopped himself there.

As Ainz rotated his shoulders and relished the freedom he felt after taking off his armor, Narberal asked him a question. "What should we do with that unpleasant lady from before?"

"Oh, you mean the one whose potion broke? We shouldn't have to worry about her. I mean, if something important to me got broken, I'd fly into a rage..." Remembering the changes in his psychology since he ended up in this body, he faltered for a moment and then continued, "...myself. Probably. I was careless, so of course she would blame me."

"But that only happened as a result of a stupid human committing so foolish an act as picking a fight with you, Supreme One. That man is surely the one to blame."

"That's true, but I was the one who threw him. In this case, we should practice tolerance and forgive. Plus, we're in this city to build reputations as Momon and Nabe, beings from this world. If word got out that we couldn't even afford a potion, we'd be off to a bad start."

Narberal didn't seem completely on board with his way of thinking, but she acquiesced with a low bow.

"Plus, she was more experienced than us. We should probably try to keep the more experienced adventurers from getting their pride hurt."

Momonga toyed with the other chain around his neck. *These are just metal plates, so I wonder if it's possible to counterfeit them… Well, I'll let the guild worry about that.* Hanging as it was, essentially, a dog tag.

Plates were the proof of an adventurer's ability level: copper, iron, silver, gold, platinum, mythril, orichalcum, adamantite. The latter metals indicated a better reputation, and higher ranks could not only select more difficult jobs but were also better compensated. The system was designed to avoid unnecessary adventurer deaths.

Ainz had just registered with the guild, so he had a copper plate, the lowest rank, while that woman was an iron plate. Showing a minimum level of respect for superiors is one of the ways to get ahead in any society.

"But Lord Ainz, adamantite is such a soft metal; you should be a prismatic ore like apoithakarah or scarletite. They must all be blind." Narberal was listing highly valuable metals from *Yggdrasil*.

Ainz narrowed his eyes and brought up something that had been bugging him. "Nabe, just in case, you should call me Momon while we're here."

"Understood, Lord Momon!"

"You really want to have this conversation again? It's just *Momon*."

"M-my apologies, Mr. Momoooon!"

"Mr. Momoooon sounds pretty dopey… Well, whatever. If Momon is too hard, then at least say Mr. Momon. Got it?"

"Yes, Mr. Momon!"

She bowed low again and Ainz put a couple fingers to his forehead. *She doesn't understand why I'm making her say Momon. I guess she's a little slow… Well, at least there's no one who can see us right now; I'll let it go for the moment.*

"For now, let's just discuss our plan of action."

"My lord!" She dropped to one knee and lowered her head—the posture of an attendant awaiting orders from her master.

What am I gonna do with her? They were fine now because he had locked the door the moment they had walked through it, but he had the feeling people would talk if they witnessed a scene like this. *And why doesn't she understand why I want her to call me Momon? I'm pretty sure I explained it on the way here…*

He began to speak, half resigned. "We're going to build reputations undercover as famed adventurers in this city. One reason for that is to obtain information that adventurers, i.e., powerful people, have. I want to put a special emphasis on rumors about other *Yggdrasil* players like me. Once we earn a higher ranking plate, we'll be offered jobs appropriate to that level, and the information we'll acquire will probably be more accurate and useful. So, for the time being, our top priority is to succeed as adventurers."

As Narberal acknowledged this, Ainz began to list the pending issues. "But we already have some problems." He took out his small leather pouch, loosened its mouth, and emptied it into his hand. There were coins, not very many, with not a glimmer of gold to be seen. "For starters, we have no money."

There were a few reasons he had handed over a potion in the dispute earlier, but one was that he wasn't confident he could settle things with cash. It would have been too pathetic to have to say he didn't have any money back there.

Narberal looked at him with a dubious expression, and Ainz added, "Well, I mean, we have money. But most of it is *Yggdrasil* gold. I want to only use that as a last resort."

"But why? Didn't you already confirm that *Yggdrasil* coins have monetary value here?"

"That's true. When I went to Carne, the gold coins… Yeah, they told me one was worth two of their gold coins used for exchanges. But if I use *Yggdrasil* gold in this city, there's no telling what might happen. If we're not careful, it could basically be the same as announcing that there's a *Yggdrasil* player here. I'd like to avoid that while we still don't know this world very well."

"Players…beings with the same rank as my lord, but recalcitrant rabble who once raided Nazarick."

Ainz furrowed his nonexistent brow at her use of "my lord," but he decided to say nothing for the same reason as earlier. "Yes. We need to be on our guard against them."

He, Ainz Ooal Gown, had reached the highest level in *Yggdrasil*, 100, but among players, that wasn't such a rare thing. Indeed, most players had done it. Among them, Ainz knew he was on the higher side of mid-ranking, power-wise. That was because instead of taking only classes suited for an undead caster, he had chosen some for the role-playing element, regardless of power. Taking into account his multiple god-tier items and how many cash shop items he had, he would probably land on the more powerful side of average, but there would always be someone stronger.

That was why he had to avoid being discovered by other players. If he rushed into the wrong battle, there would be any number of opponents he wouldn't be able to beat.

And players were originally humans, so many of them would probably side with humans. If players like that came up against someone like Albedo, who saw humans as lower life-forms, they might decide the Great Tomb of Nazarick and Ainz Ooal Gown in its entirety were enemies of mankind. That's why he'd decided it was dangerous to be out and about with her.

But I had no idea Narberal would be the same way… Ainz wasn't an enemy of mankind; however, he wouldn't hesitate to kill them if it was necessary to achieve his goals. Still, he wanted to avoid head-on confrontations with players.

"In that sense, it really was a waste."

"What was?"

"That we lost that Nigun fellow so fast. He probably had a lot of info, but we finished him off on such a simple question."

Of the members of the Sunlit Scripture he had captured in Carne, only ten were still alive. The others had died during their interrogations and become fodder for Ainz's undead summons. He recalled the info they'd forced their prisoners to cough up and laughed at himself.

"Most players would probably back the Slane Theocracy, huh?"

The Slane Theocracy was a religious nation that believed in the Six Gods who appeared six hundred years earlier. In the words of the Sunlit Scripture members, it was a country working toward a world where weak humans would prevail over the other more powerful races and prosper. If there were players who had retained their humanity, they might approve of the Slane Theocracy's teachings.

This world was not one where humans were top of the heap—here, humans were considered one of the inferior races. Yes, they had built grand cities like this one on the plains, but their living on the plains was simply a sign of their weakness.

In fact, the plains was a dangerous place to be. There was nowhere to hide, and it was easy to be spotted by enemies. The reason they had chosen to settle there was that, for a fragile race without eyes to see in the dark, stronger legs, or better stamina, there was nowhere else besides the plains where they could build a habitat for themselves.

There were races more physically able than humans, with superior civilizations, but they hadn't been able to conquer the continent because when the Eight Kings of Avarice tried to rule it five centuries earlier, the ensuing struggle resulted in diminished racial power. If that hadn't happened, humans probably would have been wiped out.

Arriving in such a world, one would probably want to side with the humans. That's precisely why Ainz was keeping his distance from the Slane Theocracy—he was wary of other players.

"Anyhow, as far as money goes, I had you bring those swords the fake knights from the Slane Theocracy had because I figured we could sell them in a pinch, but…I'd like to find some work before it comes to that."

"Understood. So you're saying we'll go to the guild again tomorrow, then?"

"Yes. Really, I'd like to tour the city and gain some knowledge, but that will have to wait until we earn some money."

"Very good, my lord. I, as a combat maid, shall provide my full support."

"Great. Thanks, Narberal."

Satisfied with Narberal's deep bow, Ainz cast some magic and clad himself in illusion and armor. "I'm going to go have a look at our surroundings. You stand by here."

"I should go with—"

"No thanks. It'll just be a quick peek. I heard there is a huge graveyard; I'd like to see that, if possible… And the reason I'm leaving you here is in case any intruders show up. Make sure not to let your guard down for a second. So far, I don't think we've made any slipups, but it's not an exaggeration to say we're in enemy territory. Stay alert."

"Yes, my lord."

"And take care of our periodic check-in."

Ainz left the room and Narberal heaved a sigh. She then massaged her temples up and down. Her eyes had been sharp, but now they drooped as all the tension went out of her expression. Even her ponytail sagged as though it, too, were out of energy.

But she hadn't forgotten her supreme master's orders.

She focused her senses to see if she could perceive what was happening outside the room, but as a caster, it was difficult to mimic a thief's abilities. She compensated by using a trick of hers.

"Rabbit Ears!" When she cast the spell, a pair of cute rabbit ears sprouted from the top of her head. They began to twitch and pick up sounds in the area.

Rabbit Ears was one of three spells *Yggdrasil* players called "bunny magic." The other two were Rabbit's Foot, which upped the caster's luck, and Bunny Tail, which slightly reduced the amount of enmity they generated. These spells were ridiculously popular because when a female character cast all three, her outfit would change. Narberal didn't need the other two at the moment, so she didn't bother.

This was one of the few spells she had learned that wasn't for combat.

After listening enough to determine the coast was clear, she cast Message.

As if she'd been waiting for the call, a woman's pretty voice echoed in Narberal's head almost instantly. "Narberal Gamma. Is something wrong?"

"No, just checking in."

Narberal was speaking with Albedo, captain of the Great Tomb of Nazarick's floor guardians. After touching on every detail of their current situation, she said what she knew Albedo would want to hear. "Lord Ainz said there is no one he trusts more than you."

"Tee-hee!" A strangely excited squeal echoed in Narberal's head. "Great, great. Good girl, Narberal! Keep on talking me up! That's an order from the captain of the floor guardians!"

Narberal wondered if that was worth giving an order over, but she realized Albedo was fighting a battle with Shalltear to decide which woman would serve by their lord's side. When she thought of it that way, an order made perfect sense.

All the while Narberal was coming to understand this, Albedo's voice kept ringing in her head. "While Shalltear is out, I'll be gently closing the gap between Lord Ainz and me. He may be an impregnable fortress, but if I strike with wave attacks and establish a bridgehead, he must one day fall! And on that glorious day, Shalltear will cry oh so bitterly!"

Narberal's brow creased slightly in response to Albedo's delighted screams. As might be expected, the captain was a bit of a hassle when she got this worked up.

Sounding so cheerful it seemed like she might start skipping, Albedo plotted quietly how she'd have to do this and that, but all at once her voice grew serious. "But why are you helping me? What's the reason you chose to support me and not Shalltear? Are you trying to get something?"

"It's simple. If I were asked who was worthy to sit at Lord Ainz's side, you or Mistress Shalltear, I would answer that you are."

"Tee-hee! Wonderful! Now, here's a girl who can see Nazarick's future—the big picture. Impressive!"

"On top of that, Yuri isn't very fond of Mistress Shalltear."

"Ah, Yuri Alpha. I see, interesting. So is it safe to consider the others my allies as well, do you think?"

Narberal pictured deputy leader Yuri Alpha and her other teammates one by one as she answered. "Hmm, I'm not so sure. Lupusregina is more on your side, but Solution probably leans more toward Mistress Shalltear. I don't know about Entoma or Shizu; they don't seem particularly attached to either side at the moment."

"Do you think there's a way to win Solution over?"

"I imagine it would be difficult. She and Shalltear have some things in common…"

"Oh, right. Their bad taste, huh?" Narberal confirmed, cocking her head in her inability to understand Solution Epsilon's twisted hobby. Narberal, too, considered all humans save one lower life-forms, but that didn't mean she wanted to torment them. If they got in her way, she would kill them, and if they made trouble, she would kill them, but that didn't mean she'd want to go out of her way and take all kinds of time to do it.

"Well, we can't do anything about that. Very well. Let's try to get the other girls in my camp, starting with Entoma and Shizu."

"That sounds good. Solution and Entoma both enjoy eating humans, so it's possible that if we can get Entoma to ally with you, Solution might follow."

"Hmm… Got it. Then, to change the subject…will you give me more details about how Lord Ainz, my beloved, is doing?"

"Yes, mistress."

And so the check-in with Albedo livened up, although there were some brief tiffs such as when Albedo raised a bizarre war cry when she heard that Narberal and Ainz would be sleeping in the same room. Narberal had to cast the same spell four times and Ainz was somewhat disgusted when he returned, but that's another story.

3

Feeling the air had taken on a color, Brita sniffed several times like a dog. The faint green component of the smell was probably not her imagination. It was some chemical or mashed plant. That told her she was nearing the block she was aiming for.

Brita followed the road and reached the block where the smell was even stronger. Looking both ways, she stopped before the largest house on it. The other houses in the area were constructed with a store in the front and a workshop in back, while this one was more like workshop, workshop, workshop. Reading the letters on the wooden plate hanging from the door and the sign out front confirmed she was in the right place.

She pushed open the door. The bell attached to the top of it jangled so loudly she jumped. Inside seemed like a sitting room where discussions with customers could take place. Two sofas faced each other in the center of the room, and along the walls were shelves lined with things that appeared to be documents. There was a houseplant in the corner.

The moment Brita stepped inside, a voice called out to her. "Hello there!" A man's voice. No, it was too young sounding.

When she looked over, there was a boy standing in the back of the room wearing a beat-up work apron, which seemed likely to give off a pungent odor, judging from all the mashed plant material sticking to it. His long blond hair hid half of his face, so she couldn't tell how old he was, but judging from his height and voice, he was probably in the middle of a growth spurt.

Brita had an idea who he might be. Yes, his grandmother was renowned, but this boy could also be counted among E-Rantel's celebrities due to his talent.

"…Nfirea Baleare?"

"Yes, that's me." He nodded and then asked, "What can I do for you today?"

"Oh, uh, just a moment."

Brita took out of her pocket the folded paper the innkeeper had given her and handed it to the boy, who had come closer. He opened it and began reading carefully.

"So this is… I see. Then, could you show me the potion?"

Nfirea took the potion she'd taken out and raised it up to the level his eyes must have been under his hair.

Something in the atmosphere changed.

Nfirea parted his bangs, exposing regular features that made it seem certain girls would fuss over him in the future. He still looked so young, but now, a sharpness appeared in his expression. His gaze was incredibly keen for the casual tone he had taken earlier. He blinked several times, and his excitement was visible in his eyes. Then, he rocked the bottle a few times and nodded once. "Excuse me. There's not much I can say about it at this point, so would you come this way?"

Assenting, Brita followed Nfirea to a messy room. No—it only seemed messy because she didn't have the knowledge to understand it.

On a table were round-bottom flasks, test tubes, a still, mortars, funnels, beakers, burners, a balance, strange jars, and other various pieces of equipment. The walls had shelves full of countless medicinal herbs and ores. The whole room assaulted her nose with a singular reek that seemed like it might be harmful to her health.

The occupant of the room turned to glare at the two intruders. It was an extremely old woman. Wrinkled face, wrinkled hands. Her hair, cropped to shoulder length, was pure white. Her work clothes had even more green splotches than Nfirea's and smelled strongly of herbs.

Entering the room, Nfirea called out to her, "Grandma!"

"What is it? What is it? I can hear you without all the shouting. My ears are doing just fine."

Nfirea only had one grandmother. This was the woman said to be the best apothecary in the city, Lizzy Baleare.

"Look at this!"

Lizzy took the bottle as he thrust it into her hands, and her perceptive gaze was so sharp that Brita was almost compelled to brace herself. She sensed that she was in the presence of a powerful veteran.

And it wasn't just her imagination. Apothecaries needed to use magic in the course of making medicines, so the better the reputation of the apothecary, the higher tiers of magic it indicated they could use. That meant that as the best apothecary in E-Rantel, Lizzy's individual combat ability surpassed Brita's.

"This… She brought it? The legendary…? It can't be… Gods' Blood? Hey, what is this thing?"

"Huh?" Brita blinked. That was *her* question.

"This potion…it shouldn't exist. Where did you get it? Is it from the ruins?"

"Huh? Uh, no, I mean…"

"You're not very good at making yourself understood, child. Just spit out what's asked of you! Where did you get it? It's not like you stole it, right? Hmm?"

Brita's shoulders jumped. She felt like she was being scolded even though she hadn't done anything wrong.

"Grandma! Don't frighten her!"

"Whaddaya mean, Nfirea? I'm not frightening her one bit. …Right?"

Nope, definitely scared, Brita wanted to say, but of course, she couldn't, so she swallowed hard and quit beating around the bush about how she acquired the potion. "Someone, uh, gave it to me."

"Huh?" Lizzy's gaze became more damning. "You think—"

"Grandma, just wait a minute. Um, Brita, who gave it to you and for what reason?"

Reaching out for the lifeline Nfirea offered, she gave a simple explanation of how she'd received it from a mysterious person in full plate armor. Lizzy's wrinkled face grew even more wrinkly.

"…Did you know that there are three types of potions?" Despite asking the question, she didn't wait for Brita's response before continuing. "There are potions made just with herbs. These don't have instantaneous effects, but basically work by enhancing humans' natural healing processes. They aren't terribly effective, but they're extremely cheap.

"Next are potions made with herbs and magic. These take effect more quickly than the ones I just mentioned, but they still take some time. These are the ones you often see adventurers drinking after a battle or something when they have more time.

"Lastly, there are potions that use only magic. They're made by infusing alchemical solutions with spells. They take effect immediately and can work just as well as spells would. Of course, you pay for it.

"This one you brought me doesn't have any herbal sediment, so we can assume it was created entirely with magic, but..." Lizzy picked up a potion bottle full of blue liquid and thrust it at Brita. "This is your typical healing medicine. Notice the color difference? No matter what we do, they end up turning blue during the production process. But yours is red. In other words, your potion was made with some completely different process. That means that you have something incredibly rare—it may have the potential to change potion-making technology! Though I'm not sure if that makes any sense to you..."

After saying that much, Lizzy cast two spells on the potions. "Appraise Magic Item! Detect Enchantment!" Astonishment and fury registered in her expression. "Heh-heh... Waa-ha-ha-ha!"

Suddenly an almost cracked sort of laughter echoed throughout the cramped room. Lizzy looked up slowly. She had the crooked smile of a crazy person. Brita was so taken aback by the sudden change that had come over the old woman that she couldn't move a muscle, much less speak.

"Heh-heh-heh. I knew it! Take a good look at this, Nfirea! This, this is potion perfection! This is what has eluded us—apothecaries and alchemists, anyone involved in potion making—even after all our research over the years: the ideal potion!" Lizzy's face was flushed with excitement, and she breathed in quick gasps. She held the potion bottle out toward Nfirea, her hand clamped around it as if to say she would never let it go. "Potions degrade, right?"

"Yes, everyone knows that." Nfirea spoke in even tones, quite a contrast from Lizzy's state, but Brita could see a hint of excitement on his face.

She just couldn't understand *why* they were so excited. But she could sense quite acutely that she was involved in something big. It had to be huge if the greatest apothecary in the city was getting this fired up over it.

"Potions made entirely with magic use an alchemical solution. Those are made by using alchemy on minerals, so it stands to reason that they would degrade over time! That's why we have to cast Preservation!" She paused for a beat for effect. "Or rather, 'had to'!"

Brita vaguely understood what Lizzy was saying and eyed the red liquid in surprise.

"This! This potion—this potion! It won't degrade! In other words, it's a perfect potion! No one has ever been able to produce one! According to legend, a true healing potion signifies blood of the gods. This story has been told for ages!" The potion shook in her hand and the crimson liquid sloshed. "Of course, it's only a legend, and apothecaries even joke with one another that the gods themselves must have blue blood, but…" She paused for a moment to stare at the bottle clasped tightly in her trembling hands. "This potion must be true Gods' Blood!"

Lizzy wheezed, out of breath. Nfirea rubbed her back. Brita was speechless. The silence the three of them created was broken by Lizzy. "… And I think you're here to inquire what the effects of this potion are. This is equivalent to a tier-two healing spell. Without adding value for rarity or anything, it would fetch eight gold pieces. Factoring in added value, the price goes so high that it's possible people might try to kill you for it."

Brita's whole body shivered. Even just the value of its effects was worth quite a lot to an iron-plate adventurer like her. That added value, though, was a problem. She even felt like Lizzy, with her perceptive eyes, was waiting for a chance to jump her.

But she still didn't understand everything. How could that mysterious man in the full plate armor give a potion like this to her as if it were nothing? What in the world did his face look like under that helmet?

Countless questions assailed Brita, and Lizzy added one more. "You wouldn't be interested in selling that to me, would you? I'll make it worth your while. How does thirty-two gold pieces sound?"

Brita's eyes widened even more.

To Brita, it was an incredible fortune. A family of three could probably live modestly on that for three years.

She couldn't make up her mind. She knew the potion was ridiculously valuable. So was selling it here for thirty-two gold pieces the right move? The chances she would acquire another one were extremely low.

But if I turn her down, will I make it home in one piece?

Picking up on Brita's indecision, Lizzy shook her head—it couldn't be helped. Then she made an alternative suggestion...

4

The next morning, Momon/Ainz pushed open the door to the guild once more. When he entered, he saw the desk at the back. Behind it were three smiling receptionists assisting adventurers. There was a knight in full plate armor, an agile-looking guy in light armor carrying a bow and arrows, someone wearing priestly garb with the sigil of a god, a magical magic caster in a robe holding a staff—there were all sorts of adventurers.

On his left was a big door and, on his right, the board. There were several sheets of parchment posted that hadn't been there yesterday. Naturally, there were adventurers clustered around them as well. A team was conferring with one another in front of one of the parchments. With a bad feeling about that scene and the posting, he headed toward the reception desk.

Ainz felt the room's eyes gather on the plate around his neck and then lap up and down his body, taking in his appearance. It was the same vibe he'd gotten at the inn the previous day.

He observed the other adventurers back from the corners of his eyes. Their plates were silver and gold. Not a single copper. Feeling a bit like he was playing an away game, he stepped up to the counter.

It seemed as though a team had just finished, so there was a receptionist open. He stepped in front of her and said, "'Scuse me. I'm looking for work..."

"Oh! Then please select a sheet of parchment from the board and bring it over."

As Ainz acknowledged her, he was assailed by the feeling that the sweat glands he'd lost had now returned. He arrived in front of the parchments and swept his eyes over them. Then, he nodded firmly.

Yup. I can't read.

One of this world's laws was that foreign languages would be translated, but that didn't extend to the written word.

Last time, the receptionist lady had done everything for him, so he assumed it would work the same way this time. *That was naive.*

Aah! He wanted to scream and roll around on the floor, but then his mind settled down. Feeling grateful for the changes in him since taking on his new body, he racked his brains.

The literacy rate didn't seem terribly high, but it would still be embarrassing to not be able to read in a place like this, and it could only end with him in the disadvantageous position of being looked down on. He'd given all his items for reading foreign characters to Sebas and had sneered at the idea of acquiring spells for that back in his *Yggdrasil* days—"I have scrolls, so that magic is pointless."

He felt like a fool. He'd known he couldn't read the writing in this world, so why had he neglected to come up with a plan? But there was no use crying over spilled milk; what's done was done. Narberal couldn't read the characters, either. *Checkmate, the end.*

Those were the thoughts going around in his head, but the ruler of Nazarick couldn't knowingly embarrass himself. He made up his mind, took down a piece of parchment, and strode back toward the desk.

"I'd like to take this job."

The receptionist looked over the sheet that he'd thrust at her rather too firmly and her expression became awkward. Then with an embarrassed smile, she said, "I'm sorry. This is a request for mythril-plate adventurers."

"I know. That's why I brought it over."

Hearing the quiet dignity of his voice, something doubtful appeared in the receptionist's eyes. "Uh, um…"

"I'd like to take that job."

"Huh? Uh, I mean, I see what you mean, but it's a rule—"

"It's a stupid rule. I can't believe I have to keep grinding out these crummy, easy jobs until the promotion exam."

"But your failure could result in the loss of many lives." *Not to mention the reputation of the guild that so many adventurers worked so hard to cultivate,* her hard voice implied.

"Hmph." The expressions of the adventurers in the vicinity grew hostile to match the receptionist's. Here was a newbie mocking the rules they'd all diligently followed. *It's only natural for them to be upset,* he thought. It didn't particularly bother the undead Ainz, but the vestige of office worker Satoru Suzuki inside him was bowing apologies with all his might.

What Satoru Suzuki hated were people who turned down proposals without listening to explanation—and without even bothering to suggest an alternative—and whiners with no common sense. Ainz was currently a textbook example of the latter—those eminently punchable jerks.

But he wasn't going to back down so easily. Really, he'd meant to, but he needed to push things to a certain point first, so he played his trump card.

"The woman behind me, Nabe, is with me. She can use tier-three magic."

The air buzzed, and all at once Narberal became the target for amazed stares. In this world, tier three was the level of an accomplished caster. Was it true or false? Everyone was wavering between the two answers and looking back at Ainz's full plate armor. Adventurers acquired better gear as they ranked up. Nothing was more convincing than the fact that this guy who was probably Nabe's friend had such fancy armor.

Seeing the change in everyone's eyes, he gave himself a round of applause in his mind and played another card. "And of course I'm a warrior just as strong as she is. That job will be no problem for us, I assure you."

Everyone's reaction was a bit subdued compared to his first revelation, but he could see that they saw him in a different light now.

"I didn't become an adventurer to do odd jobs for a handful of coppers. We want to take on higher-level assignments. If you want to see what we can do, we'd be happy to demonstrate, so can't we take that job?"

The hostility from earlier was rapidly dissipating. The atmosphere was one of *Ah yeah* or *I know the feeling.* For this rough bunch who valued an adventurer's strength above all, what he was saying made sense.

But the receptionist was not so understanding. "…I'm sorry, but rules are rules."

Ainz did a mental victory pose in response to her apologetic bow. "I see—there's nothing I can do, then. Sorry to have been so presumptuous." He bobbed his head. "In that case, please give me the most difficult thing you have for a copper plate. Maybe something not posted to the board yet?"

"Uh…yes, sir."

Just as the receptionist stood up and Ainz was about to cry mental tears of joy at his victory, a man's voice called out, "If it's a challenge you're after, how about helping us out on our job?"

"Huh?" Ainz let some intimidating irritation slip into his voice. He looked up to try to gloss that over and saw four adventurers, silver plates gleaming in the light. *But I finally had things going my way,* he grumbled in his head as he turned to face them.

"Is the job…worthwhile?"

"Well, hmm, I think it'll be what you make of it," a man who seemed like the leader of the group replied. He was a warrior type wearing banded mail, a type of armor where thin bands of metal covered layers of chain mail and leather.

Should I go with this guy on his job? Of course, I can decide after I hear what it is, but I'm not sure if the receptionist will pick a job for me next time. But if I take this job, I can network a bit and maybe even get some info.

His indecision lasted several seconds.

Then he slowly nodded. "That's exactly the kind of job I'm looking for. Allow me to join you. But do you mind telling me what kind of job it is?"

At this reply, the men had the receptionist prepare them a room.

It was basically a conference room. There was a table in the center with chairs placed around it. The four men seated themselves on the far side.

"Okay, have a seat right there, please."

Ainz did as he was told and sat in one of the chairs. Narberal sat noiselessly beside him.

The men were young—none of them seemed more than twenty—but

they didn't look green. They seemed more composed than one would expect of people their age. They were relaxed, but they had sat down with space between them so they could take up arms at a moment's notice. They'd done so unconsciously, so it must have been a habit that stuck with them from many life-or-death battles.

"Okay, before we talk business, let's introduce ourselves." The warrior-type man from before spoke up as their representative. He had the typical blond-haired, blue-eyed look of kingdom people, and although there was nothing about his features that made him stand out, he was still handsome. "Nice to meet you. I'm the leader of the Swords of Darkness, Peter Mauk. Over there is the eyes and ears of our team, ranger Lukrut Volve."

A blond man in leather armor bobbed his head. There was a jokey tenderness in his brown eyes. Overall he was slim with especially long arms and legs, almost bringing to mind a spider. It was clear, however, that his thin frame was the result of trimming away any excess.

"And this is the brains of our team, a caster, Ninya the Spell Master."

"Looking forward to working with you."

He was probably the youngest of the group. He had blue eyes and brown hair, and a smile too youthful to belong to an adult spread across his face as he bowed. Compared to the other members of the group, who were rather suntanned, he had pale skin. He was also the most attractive of the bunch. It wasn't so much a masculine beauty as androgynous. His voice was also a bit high for a man's.

Although his smile didn't seem insincere, there was something about it that made it seem pasted on like a mask.

And though the other members all wore armor, he was just wearing some leather clothes. Instead, a number of curious objects could be seen hanging from his belt in the shadow of the table—strangely shaped vials, odd bits of woodwork. If he was called the Spell Master, he was probably a magical-type magic user, like Ainz.

"Peter, can you stop calling me that? It's embarrassing."

"Why? What's wrong with it?"

"He has a nickname, huh?"

Lukrut hopped in to provide an explanation, since Ainz didn't seem to know what it really referred to. "He has a talent, you see! This kid's a famous casting genius!"

"Oh?" Ainz reacted. They'd gone through three of their Sunlit Scripture captives to get information about talents—powers people were born with. He was delighted to have an example of one in front of him.

Narberal, on the other hand, snorted a scoff; Ainz was relieved no one else seemed to hear it. Feeling like a manager whose report had done something strange on a client visit, he got angry for just a second before regaining his composure, since it wouldn't help things if they made a scene.

"It's not such a big deal. It's just that the talent I was born with happened to be that type."

"Oh-ho." Ainz was even more interested and leaned in with ears pricked up.

Talents, like martial arts, did not exist in *Yggdrasil*—they were specific to this world. About one in every two hundred people was born with one, so having a power itself was not so rare, but there was an infinite variety of them, spanning the continuum from weak to strong. They ranged from things like predicting the next day's weather with 70 percent accuracy to being able to speed up the harvest times of Poaceae family grains by a couple days to summoning stronger monsters or being able to use the magic of the dragons who once ruled the world.

However, the type of power was fixed upon birth; it was not possible to change or select powers later in life. That meant there were lots of times talents didn't match the natures of their holders. For example, if someone were born with the talent to boost the destructive power of spells but didn't have the knack or physical strength to become a caster, the talent would go to waste.

If a talent did match a person's nature, they just considered themselves lucky—with the exception of some truly major powers, having a talent didn't generally determine the entire course of one's life. The fact that a warrior like Gazeff Stronoff wasn't a talent holder illustrated that well enough.

Even so, there was a tendency for people with talents useful in combat to slide easily into the adventuring occupation, so there were many adventurers with talents. Among them, Ninya was a fine specimen of the fortunate variety where the talent matched the holder very well.

"Didn't it take you like four years with your magic aptitude or whatever to master what took others eight years? I mean, I'm not a caster, so I don't have much of a sense of how awesome that really is, but…"

As a magic user, Ainz was curious, but he was also motivated by the *Gimme that* greed of a collector. If he could acquire a power no one in the Great Tomb of Nazarick had, it would surely make their organization stronger. If there was a way to steal the ability, it might be worth the risk of making enemies to do it.

Assuming there was a way, it would probably be the super-tier spell Wish Upon a Star.

Ninya didn't realize that Ainz was thinking such things under his helmet and looking at him as if he were sizing up his prey, and the two continued their conversation.

"It was really lucky that I was born with this power. It helped me take the first step toward making my dreams come true. If I didn't have my power, I'd have ended up some crummy villager." His mumbling voice was gloomy.

Attempting to brighten things up, Peter spoke in a tone that was, of course, the exact opposite. "Anyhow, he's a famous talent holder in the city."

"Still, there's someone way more famous than me."

"The leader of the Blue Roses?"

"The leader of the Blue Roses is famous, too, but I mean someone in this city."

The last member of the team, whose name Ainz hadn't heard yet, mentioned someone in a loud voice. "He means Mr. Baleare!"

His curiosity piqued, Ainz asked, "What kind of talent does he have?"

Everyone looked surprised. Apparently this was something anyone would know. Ainz had been so eager for info and so focused on improving Nazarick's position that he'd let his guard down. It was unfortunate, but he was confident he could bounce back from this minor of a mistake. But before he could even make an excuse, they seemed to have reached their own conclusion.

"I see! So the fact that we hadn't ever heard of you despite your magnificent armor and that companion so beautiful she'd be the talk of the town means you're not from around here?"

Ainz took the timely cue. "That's exactly right. We just arrived yesterday."

"Ah, then you wouldn't know, huh? He's quite famous here, but I guess word of him hasn't spread to other cities."

"No, it doesn't seem like it; I've never heard of him. Do you mind telling me?"

"His name is Nfirea Baleare. He's the grandson of a well-known apothecary, and his talent is the power to use any and every magic item. He can use scrolls from different magic types, which you usually can't do, and he can even use items that only nonhumans are supposed to be able to use. I'll bet he can even use items that require the user to have royal blood."

"…Hmm…" Ainz took pains to not let his wariness show in his voice.

How far does this talent go? Could he use items that with few exceptions only guild masters can use, like the Staff of Ainz Ooal Gown? World Items, too? Or is there some limit?

That was someone to keep an eye on. Of course, he might also make a valuable pawn.

Narberal must have had the same take. She brought her mouth near where she seemed to have decided Ainz's ears were under his helmet and whispered, "This guy could be dangerous," her voice wary.

"…I know. Coming to this city was the right move."

"Momon, is something wrong?"

"Oh, no. It's nothing. More importantly, could I ask you to introduce the last member of your team?"

"Sure. This is Dyne Woodwonder, a druid. He uses healing magic and magic that manipulates nature, and he also has a wealth of knowledge about medicinal herbs, so if you ever need anything, don't hesitate to ask. He even has medicines for stomachaches and that kind of stuff."

"Looking forward to working with you!" The man whose messy beard and solid build combined to create a somewhat barbaric impression spoke in a dignified voice. That said, he was still younger than Ainz appeared to be. A faint grassy smell came from a pouch at his hip.

"Okay, now it's our turn, huh? This is Nabe and I'm Momon. Looking forward to working with you."

"Likewise."

"Yes, we should make a good team. Momon, feel free to call us by our first names. Now, I don't mean to hurry us along, but I'd like to get down to business. Not that it's a real job per se…"

"Uh…"

In response to Ainz's dubious interjection, Peter held up a hand entreating him to wait. "Our aim is to hunt the monsters that pop up near town."

"Subduing monsters…?" Ainz thought that fell pretty squarely under the work umbrella. *Or is there some reasons adventurers don't consider it work?* he almost wanted to ask, but if it turned out to be basic common sense, it would seem like he didn't know anything, and that would be bad. Instead, he chose a more benign subject to ask about. "What are the monsters called?"

"Oh no, not like that—I wonder what they call it in your country— where you hunt monsters and get rewarded by the city via the guild based on how strong the monsters you got were. That thing."

Aha. Ainz understood now. Putting Peter's work that wasn't work into *Yggdrasil* and similar game terms, they would grind monsters for drops.

"If you want to make a living, it has to be done," the druid, Dyne, solemnly noted.

Then Lukrut chimed in, "We get to eat. Things are less dangerous for other people. Merchants can travel safely. The country can collect their taxes. Nobody loses!"

"Nowadays, any country with guilds has this system, but it's surprising because even just five years ago it wasn't like that," Ninya said, and everyone nodded nostalgically. They practically forgot about Ainz and started going off on various tangents. He couldn't participate in the conversation at all. It would be too suspicious if he knew nothing about the country he was in, so he decided to just listen silently.

"Long live the Golden Princess, right?"

"The proposal ran into some setbacks, but I heard she was motioning to get rid of the foot tax for adventurers, too."

"Whoa. It's amazing that she thought so highly of us."

"Right? She did all that even though we're armed groups that haven't proven our loyalty to the kingdom. Depending on the team, some might even be enemies! Not even the empire is that tolerant."

"That princess really does have some wonderful ideas...even though they mostly get shot down."

"I hope I get to marry a lady that gorgeous!"

"You got a lotta work to do if you're hoping to join the ranks of the nobles!"

"No—no way, no way. That stiff, formal life ain't for me."

"Oh, c'mon, it'd be great to be a noble! It's established by the country that you get to screw over the people and do whatever you want!"

The true feelings behind Ninya's smile were beginning to show. Ainz knit his nonexistent brow under his helmet, but Narberal was unfazed.

Lukrut called out in a purposely lighthearted voice, "Yikes! Always with the harsh words! You hate the nobles as usual, huh?"

"I know that some of them are honest people, but...as someone whose older sister was abducted by those pigs, I just can't..."

"Well, this conversation has taken an unexpected turn! We probably don't need to discuss this sort of thing in front of Momon and Nabe!"

On board with Dyne's course correction, Peter cleared his throat rather deliberately and continued his explanation, "Well, so that's about it. We'll be on the lookout for monsters in this area. This close to civilization there probably won't be anything too strong... I hope that doesn't bother you, Momon?"

Peter took out a sheet of parchment and opened it across the middle of the table. It seemed to be a rough map of the area, with groves and forests, rivers, and other features indicated.

"Our basic plan is to head south and hunt around here." He started from the middle of the parchment and traced down with his finger to an area near a forest in the south. "We'll mainly be fighting monsters that come out of the forest on the Slane Theocracy border. The only monsters that are likely to use weapons or launch an attack on someone with an escort are goblins at the nastiest."

"Yeah, they're weak, though, so even if we take 'em out the pay is peanuts."

Ainz wondered a bit about their relaxed attitude. The goblins he'd known in *Yggdrasil* all had various names and had been anywhere from level 1 to 50—it wasn't possible to lump them all together like that. If they weren't careful, they could find themselves in trouble.

Are they so laid-back because they're sure high-level goblins won't show up around here? Or is it because in this world goblins just aren't so tough?

"…There aren't any strong goblins?"

"Yes, there are. But they don't hide out in the forest we're headed to. The strong goblins are the ones who lead tribes. I can't imagine they'd have their whole tribe attack."

"Goblins are also aware how far the humans' sphere of influence extends. They know how much of a pain a huge invasion would be, especially the stronger, more clever, elite types.

"Plus, if Nabe can use tier-three magic, then even the more elite types will be a piece of cake."

"I see. I just want you to be aware, though, that there are some goblins who can use tier-three magic, too. Just for reference, would you mind telling me the names of the monsters we are likely to encounter?"

All the Swords of Darkness members looked immediately at Ninya, who assumed a professorial expression and began his explanation. "The monsters we often encounter are goblins and their pet wolves. I have no records of encountering any other wild beasts that put up much of a fight in this area. On the plain, the most dangerous thing we could encounter would probably be an ogre."

"So we won't be going into the forest?"

"No, the forest is quite dangerous. We could probably handle jumping leeches, giant beetles, and the like, but the hanging spiders that dangle down from the trees and the forest worms that come out of the ground to swallow you whole are a bit tough."

I see. Ainz nodded. *So we'll fight the monsters that spill out of the forest onto the grass.*

"So that's the job, Momon. How about it? Will you help us out?"

"Uh…I suppose…but actually, before that, could you tell me what kind of reward we'll get?"

"Oh yeah. That's important, isn't it? Since there are two teams, yours and mine, we'll split it in half."

"Considering the number of members in each team, that's awfully nice and generous of you."

"But if some monsters appear, we'll have you guys take half of them, and we can only use up to tier-two magic. I think it balances out if you take those things into account."

Ainz pretended to think for a moment and then nodded. "That's fine by me. It's a deal. And since we're going to be working together for a while, I'll go ahead and show you my face."

Ainz removed his helmet. Mild surprise registered on the faces of the four adventurers.

"…Black hair and black eyes, like Nabe. You're definitely not from around here. I heard that down south there's a country where people look like you… Are you from that area?"

"Yeah. I traveled a pretty long ways."

"He's older than I thought…kind of an old dude."

"Don't be rude! A warrior on a level equal to a tier-three magic user would be about that age!"

"Miss Nabe must have learned so fast!"

Ainz had sharp enough hearing that he could pick up the other three's whispers. He felt a little young to be called an "old dude," but compared to these kids, he probably *was* old. Considering people came of age here at sixteen, he was pretty ripe.

"Well, now that you've seen my face, I'll cover it up again," he said, replacing his helmet. "If it got around that we're both foreigners, there might be trouble."

He smiled under his helmet. He'd used a low-tier illusion that would break if it were touched, but he was glad he'd thought of it.

"Okay, if we're going to go hunting together, we should get any questions out of the way ahead of time. Do you have anything you'd like to ask?"

"Yes!"

In response to Ainz's question, a hand flew into the air. It was Lukrut. When he saw no one else had anything to ask, he threw a question loudly at Narberal. "What exactly is the relationship between you two?"

Silence.

Ainz couldn't fathom why he would ask such a thing.

Peter and the rest could, though, and keenly.

"…We're friends."

Lukrut's reaction to Ainz's answer completely disrupted the mood of the meeting. "I'm in love! It's love at first sight! Will you go out with me?"

Everyone stared at him. When they realized he hadn't said it as a well-intentioned joke, their eyes moved to Narberal. Under everyone's gaze, she sighed before replying, "Shut up, you slug. Don't speak to me again until you know your place, or I'll rip out your tongue."

A silence descended, incomparably more still than the previous one.

"Uh, er…" Before Ainz could get a word out, Lukrut was talking.

"Thank you very much for that intense rejection! Let's start as friends!"

"Drop dead, maggot. As if I'd be your friend! Do you want me to gouge out your eyes with a spoon?"

Peter and Ainz looked away from the back-and-forth and bowed to each other.

"…I'm sorry my friend is causing trouble."

"…Not at all, I'm the one who should be apologizing."

"Okay, can we say that no one has any questions?" Peter addressed the group once more, leaving out Lukrut with his goofy grin and icy Narberal. "Then let's head out once you're ready. Our preparations have already been made."

At the word *preparations*, Ainz remembered something. He'd purchased the minimum necessary provisions from the innkeeper, but neither he nor Narberal required the bulky food and drink. Of course, it would be suspicious if they ate nothing, so he supposed it was necessary to some extent.

"Okay. We'll be ready to leave once we replenish our food supply."

"Just food? If you don't need to buy from a particular store, the desk has nonperishables. They can get you ready in no time."

"Oh, that sounds good. And then we can leave right away."

"Shall we go, then?"

They all stood up and left the meeting room.

When they got back to reception, there were more adventurers around than before, and several groups had gathered around where the parchments were posted, but almost everyone was focused on one boy.

The blond youth was talking with one of the receptionists, but the other two were listening in. The atmosphere had done a complete one-eighty from the earlier bustle.

Just then, the receptionist's mouth made a perfect O—of surprise. And her line of sight led to Ainz.

What the heck? As Ainz wondered what was going on, the receptionist stood up and came over.

"You have been requested by name."

At her words, the vibe in the room changed dramatically. Ainz felt the unreserved stares of numerous curious eyes. The members of the Swords of Darkness also seemed surprised.

Narberal made a slight move in response to the mysterious change in atmosphere. She was shifting just in case she had to deal with a situation, preparing for combat.

Ugh. Narberal's movements were bad, no matter what her reason. She may very well have been acting to protect him after detecting something off about the vibe, but it wasn't appropriate here. Or rather, someone with common sense wouldn't do what she was doing. Even if she was prioritizing Ainz's safety above all else, she was being too thoughtless.

That idiot. She's as bad as Albedo, but gah, what is she thinking? Actually, she's probably not thinking. She looks down on humans, so to her it would be like stepping on some noisy bugs. I guess it makes sense to have that attitude, since Ainz Ooal Gown is a guild made up entirely of grotesques, but there's still a time and a place for it.

Ainz put his head in his hands. He wanted to ask his old guildmates why all their NPCs were like this. *I don't care what kind of backstory you assign them—at least give them minimum interpersonal skills, like being able to read a room and understanding the context of their actions.*

He didn't have time to reprimand her now. But he didn't know what would happen if people picked up on the fact that she was going into combat mode. He quickly karate-chopped her on the head—not with full strength, of course, but the pain he inflicted with his gauntleted hand had apparently been pretty serious; Narberal looked up at him, her tearful eyes taken over by surprise and confusion.

Completely ignoring her, Ainz asked the receptionist, "By who?"

The minute he'd said it he felt stupid. It had to have been that boy.

"Nfirea Baleare."

Ainz realized it was the name he'd heard earlier, and the boy was already approaching.

"Nice to meet you. I'm the one who made the request." He tilted his head, and Ainz reciprocated. "So about the reque—" He started to speak, but Ainz held up a hand to stop him.

"I'm terribly sorry, but I'm already contracted for another job. I can't take on your request right away."

A commotion went through the room. The Swords of Darkness members were especially startled.

"But Momon, he's requesting *you!*"

Seeing Peter's reaction, Ainz wondered if a request by name was really worth getting so excited about, but…

"That may be, but it's only right to prioritize the previous engagement, don't you think?" It seemed Ainz's conclusion was not mistaken. Some of the onlooking adventurers nodded; he'd made a favorable impression.

"But…our request can't even properly be called a request, and we can't even pay you if we don't encounter any monsters…," Peter mumbled.

The difference in value of the work between a request from this boy (who is not only famous himself but also has a famous grandmother) and roaming around hunting monsters is enormous. That must be why Peter is trying to give me some space. Guessing that was the case, Ainz replied with kindness in his voice. "Then how about this, Peter? I haven't heard anything about the job or the compensation, so I'll listen to what Mr. Baleare has to say and then we can decide."

"That's fine with me. We'd like to go sooner rather than later, but we weren't even planning on today or tomorrow anyhow."

"Then let's have the Swords of Darkness come while we talk it over. If we can come to an agreement…or rather, if we can't, I suppose, I'll go ahead and prioritize my previous engagement."

"What? You want us in your meeting?"

"Yes. As a concerned party, your input is important to me."

Once the Swords of Darkness agreed to the plan, they all returned to the meeting room they had just come from.

Well, this is a bit hectic. Ainz smiled wryly and sat in the same seat as before. Narberal sat next to him again, and Nfirea sat one seat down from her. The Swords of Darkness members, like Ainz, all took the same seats as before.

The first to speak was, naturally, Nfirea. "The woman at reception mentioned my name before, but allow me to introduce myself. My name is Nfirea Baleare. I'm an apothecary in this city. As for my request, I'm planning to go to a nearby forest, but as you know, the forest is a dangerous place. So I'd like you to escort me but also, if possible, help me collect medicinal herbs."

"An escort job? I see." Ainz nodded confidently, but privately he thought it sounded like kind of a pain.

Ainz knew that he was strong himself, and if he teamed up with Narberal, annihilating any monster that came at them would probably be a piece of cake. The problem was that when it came to escort duty, he wasn't so certain he could pull it off. As casters, neither he nor Narberal had the tanking skills that would be useful to guard someone.

"Compensation would be a fixed amo—"

"One moment. How convenient that it's an escort job. Hey, Peter, what would you say to *me* hiring *you* instead?"

"Huh?"

"For an escort job in the woods collecting herbs, wouldn't it be better to have a ranger and a druid along?"

"Indeed! That is very perceptive of you, Momon. Druids are really in their element in the forest. I'd probably be even more useful than Lukrut!" Some pride slipped into Dyne's dignified tone.

Lukrut didn't seem so amused. "Keep talkin', Dyney."

"With my druid powers, it's a given that I'd be more useful. And don't forget that I dabble in the medicinal arts."

"Hmm. I'm game, Peter. Seems like I need to show Mr. Druid here who has the superior gathering skills."

"Then that seems fine. And if any monsters show up along the way, we can slay them and get the reward from the city, too. Mr. Baleare's compensation can be split by head count, right, Peter?"

"I have no objection if it's all right with you, Momon."

"Sorry to keep you waiting, Mr. Baleare. If you don't mind, we'd all like to take on your request."

"Oh? That's fine with me. Then, I'm looking forward to working with all of you. Oh, and you can call me Nfirea."

Then, they all introduced themselves to Nfirea, and although Narberal whipped her sharp tongue at Lukrut a couple times, there was no real trouble.

"So, our plan will be my normal pattern of proceeding to the village of Carne, getting a place to stay, and then heading to the forest. The time we spend gathering herbs will depend on how much we can get, but it'll be three days at most. The average has been two."

"How will we get there?"

"I have one single-horse cart, but that's where the bottles for the herbs will go, so there won't be room to carry everyone."

"Can we restock provisions in Carne?"

"Water is no problem, but food might be difficult. It's not a very big village."

The Swords of Darkness discussed preparations among themselves and peppered Nfirea with questions. Then Ainz spoke up. "Do you mind if I ask some questions?" Nfirea smiled and said to go ahead, so Ainz asked his first question. "Why did you specifically want me? It was only just recently that I boarded a carriage and arrived here, so I have no friends in this city, nobody knows me, and yet you requested me? And you mentioned you have a 'pattern,' so doesn't that mean you've been hiring a different adventurer up till now? What happened to that person?"

Ainz's eyes were sharp under his helmet. He didn't recall ever being introduced to this boy. If his true identity had been discovered, he would need to take a different approach with his disguise. He tried to discover the boy's real motives, but he couldn't detect changes in his eyes because of the long hair that covered half of his face. As Ainz was wondering if he was overthinking things, Nfirea spoke.

"The person I used to hire left E-Rantel to go to a different city. That's why I was looking for someone new. And then…actually, I heard about the incident at the inn from someone who came to my shop."

"The incident at the inn?"

"Yes, how you beat up an adventurer a rank above you in the blink of an eye."

"I see."

He had shown off his strength there to try to spread his name, and it seemed like it had worked. Ainz was about convinced when Nfirea joked, "Plus, copper-plate adventurers cost less, right? I'd like it if we could work together for some time."

"Ha-ha, that's right." Ainz could certainly understand the concept of getting in on the ground floor. He felt his caution being dispelled. But there was one thing he feared. If that were the case…

As Ainz was thinking it over, some other questions were asked and Nfirea answered them. When it seemed like the questions had petered out, Nfirea raised his voice. "Then, let's get ready and be off!"

5

In the dead of night, a hooded shadow slipped into E-Rantel's huge graveyard. The jet-black hooded cape combined with the shadow's singular way of moving, keeping its shoulders and hips from bouncing, made it look like a ghost. It nimbly avoided all the magical light sources that had been placed around the graveyard, going in deeper and deeper.

Before long, it came upon a mausoleum. The shadow slowly removed its hood. It was a young human woman. Age-wise she was somewhere around a fresh twenty or so. Her face was attractive but in a vaguely feline way. She had ample charm, but there was also something dangerous about her—like she might reveal her true nature as a carnivorous beast at any moment.

"This is the place!" she said playfully, smoothing back her short blond hair before pushing open the stone door. From beneath her cape came a sound like the soft rubbing of metal on metal, almost exactly like the sound chain mail makes.

When she entered the mausoleum, there were no bodies on the stone platforms for laying out corpses, and the ornaments put up when praying for the departures of deceased souls had already been taken down. Still, a cloying smell tingled her nose, as if the rocks had absorbed all the tons of incense.

With a slight wrinkle in her brow, she approached a large platform in the back. "Hmm-hmm-hmm! Let's seeee..." Humming, she pressed one of the surprisingly detailed carvings near its base.

Something went *ker-chk* as if catching, and a beat later the platform rumbled to the side to reveal a staircase leading underground.

"I'm coming iiin!" she shouted down the stairs, stretching the final vowel in a carefree way, and began her descent. There was one turn along the way, and at the bottom yawned a huge cavern.

The walls and floor were dirt, but since it was partially man-made, it didn't seem like it would collapse anytime soon. The air wasn't stale, either; it wasn't clear where it was coming in from, but it was fresh.

This place was not part of the graveyard. No, it was something far more sinister.

Strange tapestries hung from the walls and below them burned a number of bright red candles with blood mixed into the wax, sending up the stench of scorched gore as they gave off their dim glow. Among the countless shadows cast by the dancing light were several holes, big enough for humans to pass through, that reeked in the putrid way only lower-tier undead do.

The woman swept her eyes across the room before focusing on one point. "Oh! Hey, you hiding over there! You have a guest!"

The shoulders of a man watching from the shadows of a passage flinched.

"H'lo! I'm here to see Khaj! Is he here?"

The man wasn't sure what to do, and his shoulders flinched again at the sound of more footsteps.

"It's fine. Leave us." The newly arrived man dispatched the hesitant one with just that and showed himself.

He was very thin. His eyes were sunken, and he had so little color in his face it was questionable whether he was even alive—*ashen* was the perfect word to describe it. Not a single hair could be spotted on his head. In fact, he had neither eyebrows nor lashes and there was so little evidence of anything hairlike on his body that one began to wonder if he had any at all. With those looks, it was impossible to guess his age, but since his skin didn't have wrinkles, he must not have been too terribly old. He wore a deep, bloody-red robe and a necklace that was a string of small animal skulls. His skin-and-bones arms ended in hands with yellowed nails that gripped a black staff. He looked more like an undead monster than a human.

"H'lo, Khaj."

The man frowned at the woman's lighthearted salute. "Stop using that bastardized greeting! It's an insult to the proud name of Zurrernorn."

Zurrernorn—an evil secret society made up of casters who always had their powerful leader in mind and kept death close. They had caused more than a few tragedies and were considered an enemy by the countries in the area.

"Hmm!" Her response containing no sign that she would change caused the creases in the man's face to deepen.

"And? What reason could you possibly have for being here? You know I'm pouring energy into the Jewel of Death in this place. If you came to make trouble, I'll take the liberty of dealing with you as I see fit." The man squinted and power began to build up in his staff.

"Aw, Khaj, don't be that way. I even brought you a present!" The woman grinned and dug around under her cape. There was some jangling, but eventually she found what she was looking for and gleefully pulled it out.

It was a circlet. Innumerable tiny gems were delicately attached to metal thread as thin as spider silk, making it look like a spiderweb covered in water droplets. A large black crystal was set in its center, about where the wearer's forehead would be.

"That's—" The man's eyes opened wide. He'd seen one once from a distance, so there was no way he would mistake it. "—the sign of a shrine princess, a Crown of Wisdom—one of the Slane Theocracy's greatest treasures!"

"Yup! A cute little girl was wearing this, but it wasn't her style, so I did her a favor and stole it. And then—what a surprise! She went crazy! Pooping and peeing all over the place!" The woman cackled.

She was formerly with the Black Scripture, so there was no way she didn't know what would happen when she removed the Crown of Wisdom from its wearer—one of the shrine princesses, who play key roles in the magic ceremonies the Slane Theocracy performs. When it was time for a new princess to be crowned, sending the one driven insane by the removal of her crown to be with the gods was the Black Scripture's job.

"I mean, there was nothing I could do. There's no other way to take it! It's the guy who made 'em's fault! Can't believe he got away with that."

There was no way to safely remove a Crown of Wisdom; the only option was to destroy it. But a Crown of Wisdom transformed a human being into nothing but a font of super-high-tier magic by sealing off their sense of self; it would be a waste to destroy a sacred treasure like that.

And so, crazy people.

"Hmph. I can't believe you betrayed the Black Scripture to steal such a piece of junk. If you were gonna do that, you could have at least stolen one of the sacred treasures left by the Six Gods!"

"'Junk'? That's a bit harsh!" She puffed up her cheeks to pout in a contrived way, and the man sneered at her.

"Oh, I'm pretty sure it's junk. The girls who can use that thing are one in a million. You can't even begin to look for someone to use it unless you're a nation, like the Slane Theocracy."

The Slane Theocracy was the only country in the area that had a registry of inhabitants. That's how they were able to find the ones who could use the crowns—the sacrifices. Without that kind of system, it would be incredibly difficult to search for them, even with the power of Zurrernorn.

"Plus, how am I supposed to steal a sacred treasure? The Black Scripture's strongest monster, with beyond otherworldly powers—the atavistic son of a bitch said to have blood of the gods in him—is guarding them!"

"That demigod…? Are they really that strong? I've only ever heard of them from you."

"Oh, man, they're on a whole 'nother level! But I guess you wouldn't know because the info is so locked down. Being brainwashed into spilling the beans would mean big trouble, too. I wish there were more info, but they say if word got out, the whole theocracy would get swept up in a war with the remaining true dragonlords and get wiped off the map."

"…I highly doubt that."

The woman's tone suddenly changed. "Yeah, I guess you would if you hadn't seen his power… Anyhow, to get back to my point, Khajit Dale Badantel… We're both one of the twelve leaders. Let's work together."

"Oh? Is this a peek at the true you? One of the Quintias? But leave out the Dale. I don't use that name anymore."

"Only if you cut out the 'one of the Quintias' stuff. Just call me Clementine!"

"…Clementine, then. What's this about working together?"

"There's someone in this city with a wonderful talent, right? I bet he could use this item."

"…Ah. I've heard the rumors. But surely you can kidnap a single person on your own?"

"Well, yeah! But while I'm at it, I want to cause a big commotion."

"To escape during the confusion? I see…"

"So, I thought, what if I said I'd help out with your ritual? Not a bad offer, right?"

Khajit's eyes narrowed and a superbly evil smile spread across his face. "Splendid, Clementine. In that case, we can perform the Ritual of Death sooner than planned. I'll do it. You have my full cooperation."

Chapter 2 **Journey**

Chapter 2 | Journey

1

There were two main routes carriages could take heading from E-Rantel toward the village of Carne to the northeast. They could go north and then follow the forest to the east, or they could start off going east and change course to head north. This time, the group chose the former.

Going along the forest made the monster-encounter rate slightly higher, so it was technically the wrong choice for an escort job. But the reason they did it was the monster-hunting work Ainz originally agreed to take on with Peter and his crew. There was the risk of chasing two hares and catching neither, but everyone felt secure in knowing that the powerful Momon and Nabe were there, so they chose that route. The Lightning Ainz had had Narberal cast once they were outside the city as proof she could use tier-three magic had surely helped put them at ease.

In any case, they weren't going deep into the forest, just out to the plains, so they wouldn't run into any terribly powerful monsters. Since they would be more than able to deal with them, they decided it would be a good chance to verify each team's abilities in actual combat.

They left E-Rantel when the sun was a bit past its peak. Far in the distance they could see a virgin forest so dense it looked like a dark green lump. The thick trees stood straight up, and because their magnificent branches spread out and blocked the sun, visibility inside the forest was poor, and it almost felt as though one were being swallowed up by the darkness. The gaps between trees inspired terrible uneasiness—they seemed almost like gaping maws waiting for prey to jump in.

The party was arranged with the cart in the center. The driver was Nfirea, naturally, and the others proceeded in a formation where Lukrut the ranger was out front, Peter the warrior was on the left flank, druid Dyne and caster Ninya took the right, and Ainz and Narberal brought up the rear.

They hadn't been terribly cautious, partly because visibility was good, but now for the first time Peter spoke in a slightly harder tone. "Momon, we're entering a bit of a dangerous area. I don't think there will be any monsters we can't handle, but be on your guard, just in case."

"Understood." As he nodded, Ainz suddenly thought of something.

In a game, the monsters a player could encounter in a specific area were set, but there was no way that would hold in real life. *God only knows what kind of tricky enemies we'll be up against.*

Ainz was confident in his own strength after the battle at Carne and based on the info they were able to get out of the Sunlit Scripture members they'd caught. But that was confidence as a caster. At the present moment, Ainz could hardly cast any spells because he was wearing a suit of armor. With his specialty removed from the picture, would he be able to perform as the vanguard everyone was counting on him to be? Also, since this was an escort job, it wasn't simply a matter of defeating monsters—he had to add keeping Nfirea alive to the victory conditions. Thinking about all of that made him a little anxious.

If push came to shove, he would ditch the armor and handle the situation with magic, but then he would either have to kill his party or use memory manipulation on them, so he didn't want that to happen. *It'd be a pain.*

Ainz moved his head to look over at Narberal. She noticed him and nodded once. They'd planned so that she would cast spells higher than tier three—up to tier five—if it became necessary. Hopefully that would take care of things. If it didn't, then Ainz would take off his armor and get just a little bit serious.

Lukrut seemed to have misunderstood something about the pair's eye contact (even though Ainz was still wearing his close helmet), and he called out to them in his jokey way, "We're fiiine. You don't need to worry so much. As long as we don't get ambushed, nothing bad'll happen, and as long as I'm our eyes and ears, that's no problemo. Right, Nabe? Aren't I amazing?"

He pulled a gallant face, and Narberal laughed derisively. "May I have permission to beat that mosquito to a pulp, Mr. Momon?"

"That's cold, but I'll take it!" Everyone looked annoyed as he stuck his thumb up, but no one seemed to think anything of Nabe speaking so severely. Luckily they seemed to have interpreted it as her looking down on Lukrut, not calling the entire human race lower life-forms.

Ainz dismissed her entreaty and felt like he had an ache in his nonexistent stomach. *You're traveling with humans! Be a tiny bit more discreet!*

Nfirea must have understood his body language differently. He jumped in to say, "We're all right. Actually, from here to around Carne is the territory of the mighty magical beast known as the Wise King of the Forest, so it's very rare for other monsters to show up."

"The Wise King of the Forest?" Ainz recalled what he'd found out in Carne. The Wise King of the Forest was supposedly a magical beast who possessed a terrible amount of power and could even cast spells. He lived so deep in the forest that there were next to no eyewitness accounts, but tales of his existence had been passed down since long, long ago. One account said he was a silver, four-legged beast with the tail of a snake who had lived for hundreds of years.

I'd like to meet this guy. That story's hard to swallow, but if he's really that old, he might have a crazy amount of wisdom. I mean, he's called the Wise King of the Forest! Capturing him…should help strengthen Nazarick's position. Ainz vaguely remembered what the magical beast looked like. *The Wise King of the Forest…I'm pretty sure there was an extinct animal called something like that… It looked kinda like a monkey… Oh, right, an orangutan. A person…er, a wise man, who lived in the woods…? With a tail like a snake…? I think there was a monster like that.* Ainz thought there had been something like that in *Yggdrasil*, and then he realized what it was. *A chimera! Pretty sure that had the face of a monkey, the body of a badger, the limbs of a tiger, and the tail of a snake… I don't know for sure that this'll be the* Yggdrasil *monster, but if this is anything like those angel summons, there's a good chance.*

As Ainz was recalling everything he knew about *Yggdrasil*'s chimera, Lukrut was casually talking to Narberal again. "Mm, okay, I gotta do a flawless job so that lovely Nabe will like me more."

Narberal's response was a click of her tongue that seemed to contain all the hatred from the bottom of her heart.

Lukrut appeared shocked, but no one moved to console him. It seemed they had started considering the pair's back-and-forth a comedy act.

Chatting like that now and then, the party continued on, the scorching sun at their backs. As they tramped through the grass, some of the juices from the crushed plants stuck to their leather boots, giving off a green smell.

Watching everyone mop their sweat, Ainz was thankful for his undead body, which had no trouble at all with the sun beating down and didn't tire out even though he was wearing heavy armor.

Lukrut continued to be the one to break the silence with his perky remarks. "You guys don't have to be on the lookout so much. I got my eyes open! I mean, check out Nabe—she's totally relaxed because she believes in me."

"Not you. It's because of Mr. Momon." Creases appeared in her brow. Sensing that in another second or two she'd explode and do something outrageous, Ainz laid a hand on her shoulder and her expression softened immediately.

Seeing that, Lukrut had a question for them. "Heyyy, are you sure you two aren't actually lovers?"

"L-lovers?! What are you talking about?! He has Mistress Albedo!"

"You—" Ainz blurted. "Watch your mouth, Nabe!"

"Ah!" Narberal's eyes popped wide open, and she slapped her hands over her mouth.

Ainz cleared his throat and spoke in a cold voice. "…Lukrut. Could I ask you to please not inquire any further?"

"…Oh. Sorry about that. I was just joking. Hmm, so you're with someone already, huh?" Lukrut didn't seem very sorry as he bobbed his head, but Ainz wasn't so mad at him. This time Narberal had been too careless.

He wondered if he'd brought the wrong person, but he was going nuts in his head because there wasn't anyone else for him to mobilize. In Ainz Ooal Gown, all the members were grotesques, and almost all the NPCs they'd created were also grotesques, so there was almost no one who could infiltrate a human city. Narberal was one of the few who had a human appearance, even though it was fake…but Ainz hadn't taken her personality into consideration when he'd picked her. Looking back, Lupusregina Beta, also a member of the Pleiades, might have been more suitable, but it was too late now.

Narberal was looking pale in the face following her error, so Ainz patted her back a few times to make her feel better. A great boss forgave his subordinates their first mistake. He would just let her have it if it happened again. Having her get all depressed and listless about it could impinge on her performance going forward and that would only make things worse.

And after all, she had only said Albedo's name. It probably wasn't even necessary to manipulate anyone's memories.

"Lukrut, cut the chatter and focus on keeping watch."

"Yes, sir."

"Momon, I apologize for my friend's behavior. He knows he shouldn't be asking personal questions."

"It's okay. As long as it doesn't happen again, I'm fine overlooking it this time."

Both of them looked simultaneously at Lukrut's back, only to be discouraged by hearing him say, "Ahh, now Nabe hates me. Her affection for me is negative!"

"That idiot… I'll give him a good talking-to later. And we'll pretend we never heard that earlier detail."

"Ah well, okay. Thanks. And then if Lukrut's on watch, I'd like to leave it to him and take the opportunity to talk a bit."

"Sure, go ahead. We'll make him work to offset the trouble he caused."

Peter smiled and Ainz moved to walk alongside Ninya and Dyne. In exchange, Dyne dropped back to line up with Narberal.

"I'd like to ask you a few things about magic..." Ninya said that was fine, so Ainz asked a question. Nfirea looked on, seeming to have taken an interest in their conversation. "People being manipulated with charm or dominate spells end up giving up all the intelligence they have, but is there a spell that, as a counter to that, would cause someone to die if they were asked the same question multiple times under certain circumstances?"

"I've never heard of a spell like that."

Ainz moved his head to look at Nfirea through his helmet.

"Me neither. You might be able to do a delayed cast using magic modification buffs."

"I see..." That wasn't the answer he'd been hoping for. He was no closer to solving the issue of how to use the remaining Sunlit Scripture prisoners.

There weren't very many survivors left, and using them up for nothing would be a pity. In order to see if they had some magic medical device that would make them disappear when they died, Ainz had had a few of them dissected live, but it had been a pretty big waste. If things were going to end up like that, then he should have tried to get info out of them once he realized they would die. He missed three chances per captive to get information out of them.

But Nigun was the biggest waste. Using him first had been a mistake. He was the man with the most intelligence among them, and he'd been finished off on such a simple question.

Well, it hadn't been *all* for nothing. That failure led to the understanding that he wouldn't be able to deal with everything in this world using the knowledge he'd cultivated in *Yggdrasil*. It was better to consider things optimistically—he had learned a lot.

While Ainz was thinking absentmindedly on those things, Ninya continued his answer. "Still, I only know a fraction of all the spells that exist. In countries that cultivate casters on a national level, it's possible they've created that sort of spell. In the Slane Theocracy, for instance, they train priests—casters who use faith magic—and in the Baharuth Empire they have an academy for arcaners, sorcerers, wizards, and other magical-magic classes. I wouldn't be surprised if the Argland Council State had some kind of magic using the dragons' wisdom."

"I see. So you wouldn't be surprised if it existed."

The Argland Council State, according to the information he'd gathered so far, was a subhuman nation governed by a group of councilors. Given the Slane Theocracy's principle of human superiority, the two nations were a conflict waiting to happen. The council state was especially known for its five dragon councilors, who were said to possess great power.

Ainz was interested in that country, but since he was still not all the way on his feet, he couldn't quite get there at the moment, especially given the sharp drop in Nazarick's war potential.

"Okay, then, there's something else I'd like to ask." Asking Ninya his other questions, Ainz felt very satisfied.

The other members of the Swords of Darkness only looked at him to note that Ainz was at it again. He'd gotten Ninya, Peter, and the others to tell him so much that it had become a routine. He learned about a myriad of topics such as magic, martial arts, adventurers, nearby countries, and so on. He had to be careful about what he asked, but everything he heard was extremely useful, and he was confident that his knowledge about the world had increased a great deal.

But it still wasn't enough. Every time he learned something, the things he needed to know multiplied. That was especially the case with magic. He was surprised by how different things were in a world based on magic.

One thing that was especially affected was the level of civilization. It appeared to be something like the Middle Ages, when in fact it was probably closer to premodern or in some cases nearly modern. Supporting this level of technology was magic.

Once Ainz realized that, he gave up thinking too hard about the progress of technology. For someone who had lived in a world with scientific technology, it was impossible to think too deeply about this world with its entirely different system. They even had magic to produce spices like salt and sugar, as well as magic to return nutritive value to the soil to avoid damaging it by replanting the same crops over and over.

On top of that, he wasn't sure if it was true or false, but he'd heard that the ocean wasn't salty—that was how far this world departed from Ainz's common sense.

How long had he been cautiously satisfying his curiosity when—?

"Something moved," Lukrut announced abruptly with palpable tension in his voice. None of the silliness from the tone he used when talking to Narberal was present; this was the voice of an experienced pro adventurer. Everyone immediately readied their weapons in the direction Lukrut was looking.

"Where is it?"

"There. Right there." Lukrut pointed in response to Peter's question to a part of the giant forest. Since it was shaded by trees, it was difficult to see inside, and there was no sign of anything there. Even so, no one doubted him.

"It'd be pushing it to just rush in there, so unless it comes out of the woods, let's ignore it."

"Well, it's probably smart to follow our plan and have Nfirea move back."

While they were talking, the forest stirred and the monsters slowly came into view. There were fifteen small creatures about as tall as children. Surrounding them were six large ones.

The smaller ones were subhumans called goblins. They had flattened noses, and two little fangs stuck up out of their mouths, which seemed almost like big rips in their squashed faces. Their skin was light brown. Their messy, oily clumps of grimy hair were black. It was hard to tell if their raggedy dark brown clothing was dyed or just dirty. Over it, they wore animal hides in place of armor. Each carried a wooden club in one hand and a small shield in the other. They were like a cross between a human and a monkey, with a handful of viciousness on top.

Each of the fewer, larger monsters stood between around seven and a half to almost ten feet tall. With their jaws jutting way forward, their faces were imbecility incarnate. Their arms bulging with muscles brought to mind large trees, and their hands nearly reached the ground, although their stooped backs helped. They carried clubs that looked like they had ripped them straight off a tree and wore untanned animal skins around their waists. Their horrid stench seemed to waft all the way to where the adventurers were. Their warty skin was darkish brown and their pecs and abs were built. From the look of them, they seemed quite strong, and the overall impression they made was of big, hairless chimpanzees with a warped twist. These monsters were of the subhuman race known as ogres.

Almost all of them were carrying bags that looked to be made of rags. They must have been migrating some distance.

The monsters looked over the party of adventurers and then began stepping out onto the grass. They were still some distance away, but the hostile looks on their ugly faces could be read easily enough.

"…There are quite a lot of them, huh? We're not going to be able to avoid a fight at this rate."

"Yeah, goblins and ogres tend to go on the attack when they see they outnumber their opponents. Or rather, they're too stupid to evaluate their opponent's strength on anything besides numbers—what a pain."

Ainz understood his situation, and things had definitely sunk in, but he still cocked his head slightly at how different from a game it felt. The goblins and ogres all had individualized features, whether it be their height or the darkness of their skin. In other words, they weren't all identical. That made him feel like he was facing twenty-one unfamiliar monsters.

"Reality is no game," he lamented in a voice the others couldn't hear. He was seized by the feeling he used to get when hurtling into a new area without reading a strategy guide and clashing with monsters he'd never heard of; it reminded him of the things he'd realized during the battle of Carne.

"So, Momon."

"…Oh, what is it?"

"We said we'd have you take half of them, so how would you like to divide them up?"

"We can't just split into our two teams and kill them as they come?"

"That'll get complicated if they all bunch up on one team. Nabe, is it possible for you to take out all the goblins at once with an area-of-effect spell like Fireball?"

"I can't use Fireball. The spell I have with the most firepower is probably Lightning."

So it's that kind of setup, Ainz murmured in his head.

"Lightning pierces in a straight line, right?"

"In that case, if we managed to get them all lined up, could you shoot through them from the side?"

"We'd have to have someone preventing them from charging…"

"Oh, I'll take care of that. But most importantly, Nfirea's in the cart—can everyone else protect him?"

"Momon…?"

"I'd be all talk if I had trouble with a couple ogres. I'll show you how easy it is to butcher these guys."

The Swords of Darkness members understood what Ainz, in a voice brimming with confidence, was saying and were relieved that they felt they could trust him.

"Got it. That said, we shouldn't be allowing the enemy to charge, either. We'll back you up as much as we can."

"Um, do you need any support magic?"

"Oh, we're fine. You should support your teammates."

"Okay, I'll do that. Everyone, if we engage here, we're close to the forest, so there's a chance they'll run away."

"Then let's do what we always do! We'll draw them out just like yankin' a turtle's head out of its shell!"

"Oh, that's a fine plan. So Momon is blocking the charge, but how should we deal with the ones who get by, Peter?"

"I'll trap the ogres with the martial art Fortress. Dyne, you deal with any goblins that slip through. Ninya, cast defensive magic on me. After that, although it might not be necessary, pay attention to how Nabe is faring while you focus on using attack magic. Lukrut, pick off any goblins you can. If any ogres get by, get in their way. In that case, Ninya, prioritize cleaning up the goblins." Everyone took Peter's orders simply by exchanging firm nods. The battle plan was coming together quite smoothly. They were really on the same wavelength.

Impressed, Ainz couldn't help but sigh. He remembered his days in *Ygg-drasil*. He and his guildmates had also been on the same wavelength when they went out grinding together. Decoy, pull, block, select targets—the kind of team play that can only be done when all the members know one another's abilities inside out.

Maybe Ainz was biased, but he didn't think chemistry like that was so easy to create; that said, he caught a glimpse of it in the Swords of Darkness, even if they weren't as in sync as his old friends.

"Momon, do you need any backup from us besides magic?"

"No, that won't be necessary. We're fine as the two of us."

"You're…really confident, huh?"

Ainz could sense some worry in Peter's tone—*Are you really going to be all right?* If the block were easily broken, they were in danger of being wiped out one by one. He was uneasy about that.

They weren't playing a game—lives would be taken.

"You'll understand once we get started." With that as his only response, Ainz cut the conversation short. "If your team is ready to go, we can start the fight."

Lukrut drew his composite longbow. The creaking of the bowstring stopped, and then came the *bing* of it slicing through the air. The loosed arrow flew straight across the grass and landed about ten yards from the goblins, who were on the move. They had put their shields up and were slowly closing the distance, but in response to Lukrut's sudden attack, they jeered. They were laughing at him because he missed. Of course, they couldn't hit a target more than 140 yards away, either, but they had conveniently forgotten that.

Then, the fact that they had been attacked and the overwhelming imbalance in respective numbers incited their inherent violence—so they all screamed and ran full speed, unthinking, toward Lukrut. The ogres also charged, after a short delay.

Having lost themselves in their thirst for blood, they had no formation and didn't even take the defensive measure of keeping their shields up. There was nothing left inside their heads.

Noticing as much, Lukrut cracked a smile. "Heh."

The distance separating them was about one hundred yards when he took his next shot. This one didn't miss, but went through a goblin's head. It was the one farthest to the rear; it tottered a few more steps forward before crumpling to the ground, dead.

The distance was closing before Lukrut's eyes, but his hand nocking the next arrow showed no sign of nervousness; even if they got right on top of him, he knew he had a friend nearby who would protect him.

"Reinforce Armor!" With the sound of Ninya casting a defensive spell behind him, Lukrut loosed another arrow.

Another shot at sixty yards. Another pierced head, another goblin tumbling to the ground. Then Peter and Dyne started to move.

The goblins were nimble, but the ogres took larger steps, so there wasn't much of a pace gap between the two groups. That said, they were running over about 110 yards of grass, so the ogres with their more powerful legs were out front and the goblins followed. Each group was spread out to some extent, making it difficult to capture very many of them in an area-of-effect spell.

But that was fine. Dyne's first job was to trap an ogre.

"Twine Plant!" When he cast the spell, the grass under one ogre's feet began to flail like a whip and twist around them. Restrained by plants tough as chains, the ogre began to get frustrated, and its roar resounded across the plain.

Into this scene at a leisurely pace walked Ainz, followed by Narberal. No one, looking at his gait, would imagine he was headed into a fight against charging monsters. It looked more like he was taking a stroll through the meadow than navigating a combat zone.

As the nearest ogre was getting closer, Ainz crossed his hands over opposite shoulders to clutch the hilts of his swords. Narberal put her hands under his cape to pull the sheaths off. Then the blades slowly appeared in two great, huge arcs.

Every one of the Swords of Darkness gasped at the dazzling spectacle.

The nearly five-foot swords Ainz gripped were so splendid they seemed like they might have more value as works of art than as weapons. The keen blades coldly gleamed, their tips spreading into fan shapes and their grooves engraved with a pattern resembling two intertwining snakes.

They were weapons a hero would wield, and Ainz had one in each hand. Seeing him like that caused all the Swords of Darkness to gasp again. If the previous gasp had been in admiration, this time they were knocked completely speechless.

Swords get heavier the longer they are—it was only natural. No matter what kind of spell was cast to lighten the load, swinging these around would have been no easy feat. After traveling with Ainz for a short time, they understood he was exceptionally strong, but the common sense they'd amassed up till then didn't allow for the sight of him holding a great sword in each hand so comfortably.

But…

He swung them around into a fighting stance so easily they might have been twigs. He cut quite a majestic figure.

"Momon…you're incredible…," Peter gasped, representative of everyone's shock. As a warrior himself, he'd just been instantly taught what kind of strength was possible, and it dawned on him how long he would have to train to achieve it. He'd had the vague notion that he and Ainz were on different levels, but having conclusive proof before his eyes gave him shivers that started in his toes.

Even goblins, with their lesser intelligence, seemed to realize they should be afraid. Their recklessly charging feet slowed, and they changed course to take a longer way around to Peter and the others. Only the ogres continued to barrel toward Ainz, too dim-witted to second-guess their strength.

As the distance closed, they raised their weapons. No matter how long Ainz's swords were, the ogres were still huge and had better range with their equally huge clubs. It looked like the ogres would get the first attack, but then Ainz rushed at them.

He was like a hurricane. Then, in an even faster flash of silver, the sword in his right hand flew through the air as if it were cutting space itself.

The attack was too magnificent. Regardless of the fact that they hadn't even been cut, everyone watching felt the sudden presence of death right beside them, so much so that every hair on their bodies stood on end.

It was over in that single swing.

Ainz targeted a new ogre, leaving the one in front of him. As if waiting for him to move away, the upper body of the now stock-still first ogre slipped to the ground, leaving the lower body standing. The spray of blood, slop of innards, and diffusion of an awful stench throughout the area were the signs that this was neither a dream nor an illusion.

He'd cut the monster in two with a single diagonal stroke.

Although they were in the middle of a battle, both friends and foes froze to observe the riveting scene as if time had stopped.

A deadly blow—and one that would slice a monster as meaty as an ogre in half.

A "whoa" escaped someone's lips. The battlefield had fallen so silent that everyone heard it.

"…I can't believe it. He must be a mythril plate or maybe orichalcum—no… Could he be adamantite?"

To cut an opponent in two—it wasn't an impossible move, per se. Someone who trained up a very targeted set of skills or who had a powerful magical weapon could probably pull it off. But to hold a gigantic, two-handed great sword in one hand and give it enough momentum to cut someone in half would be difficult. That was common sense. A two-handed sword was used with two hands and relied on mass and centrifugal force to cut—they weren't about slicing and dicing with physical strength.

So the only way to explain what Ainz had just done was to conclude that his sword was endowed with incomparable magic, that he had more strength in one arm than most warriors had in two, or both.

The ogres that had stopped in their tracks, shocked by the scene in front of them, began to backpedal with fear written on their faces. Ainz advanced one step to fill in the distance.

"What's the matter? Not going to attack?" His quiet, casual voice floated over the battlefield.

Even just that question scared the ogres—because they'd just seen how overwhelming the gap in strength was between Ainz and them.

Ainz moved in on a second ogre so quickly it was hard to believe he was wearing full plate armor.

"Uooogh!" The ogre raised a hoarse voice in what could have been either a shriek or a battle cry as it readied its club against Ainz, but anyone would have recognized it was moving too slowly.

As Ainz closed in, the great sword in his left hand moved as if he were going to lightly brush the ogre away. Its upper body went tumbling through the air to land somewhere completely different from its lower body.

He'd cut the monster in two with a single horizontal slice.

"Momon... Are you a monster?"

Witnessing another riveting scene, nobody had any objections to what Dyne had said.

"Okay, and as for the rest..." Ainz stepped forward, and the other ogres, ugly faces frozen in fear, moved farther back.

The goblins that had taken a large detour to the side got around and attacked Peter and the others. The Swords of Darkness had lost themselves in amazement but now had to spring into action.

Peter readied his broadsword and large shield and ran to meet the fourteen-plus goblins. The head of the one out in front went spinning off after a lunging swipe. Dodging the fountain of blood, Peter closed in on the rest of the goblins.

"Eat this!" A goblin bared its yellowed teeth as its foul, throaty scream filled the air. Peter easily took a goblin club strike with his shield. The hit that came from the side got blocked and repelled with a loud crack thanks to the magic reinforcing his armor.

"Magic Arrow!" Two glowing shots of magic nailed the goblin trying to hit Peter from behind, and it collapsed like a marionette whose strings had been cut.

Half of the goblins surrounding Peter ran at the remaining three Swords of Darkness. None of them went to attack Narberal, who was standing next to the gale-force wind of death named Ainz.

Lukrut had tossed aside his composite longbow and whipped out a short sword. Both he and the mace-wielding Dyne dashed into Ninya's line of fire to provide cover for him.

The fight between Lukrut and Dyne and five goblins was about evenly matched. If they paced themselves, they could probably beat them one by one, but it would take a while. Lukrut had taken a club to one arm and was tolerating the pain with an obvious grimace as he stabbed his short sword into a gap in a goblin's leather armor. Dyne had taken a bit of a beating, and although his movements had become somewhat sluggish, it didn't seem like any of his wounds were too critical.

Ninya, keeping a sharp eye on the situation, began to conserve magic. There was one ogre immobilized with a spell. If circumstances called for it, he would have to take it on.

Meanwhile, Peter was spending equal time on offense and defense against six goblins.

The eleven goblins' violence didn't overwhelm the adventurers, though, because there was hesitation in their attacks. Their morale had dropped significantly after witnessing Ainz's amazing one-hit kills, and they hadn't made up their minds yet if they should fight or flee.

Then, as if to crush their morale further, one of Ainz's swords swung in a huge arc. No one could hear anything but the sound of it slicing through the air and then something heavy falling to the ground—two things, in fact.

As everyone expected, the number of ogre corpses had increased. Now the only ogres remaining were the one trapped in the grass and the one cowering before Ainz.

Ainz's helmet moved to confront the final ogre. Perhaps because it had felt the gaze of Ainz's eyes from deep within the thin slit of his helmet, it emitted a bizarre groan and attempted to escape, dropping its club and racing back toward the forest faster than it had run over. But there was no way it would be allowed to get away.

"Nabe, get him." His icy voice rang out and Narberal, who had been standing by behind him, gave a quick nod.

"Lightning!" A bolt of lightning sent large vibrations through the air and shot through the fleeing ogre's body with a peal of thunder. Then it continued on through the ogre that was still tangled up behind him.

That was all it took to stop the beating pulses of two ogres.

"Let's get outta here!!"

"Run away! Run away!" The goblins that had been watching these events unfold as if in a trance called for a retreat and went to flee, but as might be expected, Peter and his crew moved faster. The demoralized goblins were not so tough anymore.

They were taken care of one after another in smooth succession. Ninya figured he didn't need to conserve magic any longer and added his powers to the fray. The goblins were killed in the blink of an eye.

Amid the reek of the dead bodies, Dyne tended to Lukrut's and Peter's wounds with Light Healing, while Ninya, with nothing to do, went around slicing the ears off the goblins with a dagger.

By turning items like those in to the guild, they would be compensated per monster. Of course, it wasn't always ears. A specific part was required from each kind of monster. That said, for subhumans like goblins and ogres, it was usually ears.

As he was removing the ears with a practiced hand, he saw that Ainz, accompanied by Narberal, seemed to be searching the vicinity where the ogres had fallen.

"Are you looking for something?"

Ainz looked up to respond to Ninya's question. "Yeah, just seeing if there are any drops...especially crystals."

"...Crystals? I've never heard of ogres carrying precious stones..."

"So they don't, huh? I was just thinking maybe on the off chance..."

"Oh yeah, it would be great if ogres carried treasure around," said Ninya, adeptly clipping off ogre ears. "But wow, Momon. I knew you had confidence in your abilities, but I didn't realize how strong you really were."

In response to Ninya's comments, the other three who were almost finished healing chimed in with more praise for Ainz.

"You were amazing! As a warrior, I hope I can be as awesome as you someday! How did you get so strong?"

"With Nabe along and all, I figured you were rich, but where are those fantastic swords from? I don't think I've ever seen more expensive-looking swords."

"Now I see that what you were saying at the guild was for real. You might be as strong as the oft-rumored-about strongest warrior in the kingdom. I'm impressed."

Nabe looked smug enough to snigger next to Ainz, but he demurred. "Nah, it just happened to work out."

"'Just happened to work out'…?" Peter smiled wryly. "…Really, the way you fought reminded me there's always someone stronger."

"I know you guys will get to the point where you can take care of small fries like that easily, too." Everyone's smiles got wryer.

Peter and his friends were working hard at getting stronger. And they didn't waste a copper of their rewards, only spending on things that would make them stronger. That's why they'd been able to work so well together so far, but even reflecting on how far they'd come, they didn't imagine they'd ever be able to reach Ainz's level. To the Swords of Darkness, Ainz's level was the furthest of extremes, which only a handful of people were allowed to access.

This guy they were traveling with would probably go on to be a hero whose name would be known by all. He was one of the greats who could stand at the pinnacle of adventuring. That was all they could think.

2

The party began pitching camp long before the sun would go down. Ainz took the wooden rods he was given and stood them up around the perimeter of their site. That said, they had to fit the cart inside, so it was fairly large—more than twenty yards across.

Once he hammered the four posts into the dirt, he would string a black silk thread around them to make an enclosure. Then, he would make a knot in the thread, pull it right near the opening to their tent, and hang up a big bell to finish it off. In other words, he was cordoning off their campsite and setting up a noisy alarm.

Narberal stood behind him as he was knocking in the posts. *Narberal was supposed to have something else to do… I guess it's fine if she finished that already? If that guy pissed her off again, I may have to have a word with him…,* Ainz had decided as he went to turn around, but then Narberal spoke in a dark voice as if she was suppressing her rage.

"…Mr. Momon, you shouldn't have to do such menial tasks as these…"

Seeing her anger, Ainz sighed slightly. Then, he looked around and lowered his voice. "Everyone is pitching in to set up camp. You think they would be okay with just me sitting around on my butt?"

"Didn't you show them your magnificent combat ability? Everyone has their strengths—this kind of work should be left to the weak."

"Don't be like that. Listen, we do need to stand out as powerful, but I don't want people to think we're arrogant. You need to keep an eye on your behavior, too."

Narberal nodded her understanding, but it was plain that she wasn't convinced, only taking his order. On the one hand, he was happy that her overwhelming devotion to him could beat down her own dissatisfaction, but he wondered if that was really sustainable.

Ainz was actually enjoying his stay in the outdoors. In the real world it had been impossible, of course, but he hadn't been able to do this even in the fantasy world of *Yggdrasil*, so it was all new and surprising. It also reminded him of going on quests in *Yggdrasil*, even though it did take a little too long to get from place to place here.

If instead of the Great Tomb of Nazarick it had been just me who got transported here, I would probably have just traveled around without a care in the world. He was undead, so he didn't need food or drink—he didn't even need to breathe. He could climb the far-off mountains empty-handed and dive to the deepest ocean depths, too. He would have simply enjoyed all the unfamiliar scenery the world had to offer.

But as long as his guildmates' precious creations were obeying him, he had to live up to their loyalty by acting as the ruler of the Great Tomb.

Shaking off his memories, Ainz devoted himself to his task once more. Once all four posts were sunk deep enough, he strung the thread tightly around them and returned to the marquee tent.

"Thanks."

"Oh, no problem."

Lukrut, who was inside, had addressed him without even looking up. It was perhaps lacking in courtesy, but it wasn't as if he were slacking off, either. He'd been digging a hole and building an oven around it for a while.

Ninya was walking the perimeter chanting some spell. Alarm was a spell one could cast as a precaution. He said it couldn't cover a very large area but was worth using just in case.

Ainz had squinted—this was magic that hadn't existed in *Yggdrasil*. Collecting spells that didn't exist in *Yggdrasil* was one of the jobs he'd given the others, but as a caster, unfamiliar magic awakened his greed.

The magic Ninya used was, like Ainz's, magical type. The spells even looked just like the ones in *Yggdrasil*. Ainz had been doing something only characters with the racial skill Black Wisdom could do to increase the number of spells he could acquire. *If I perform a sacrifice ritual, could I get spells that weren't in* Yggdrasil*? Or is there another way? There are so many things I don't know...*

Ninya had realized Ainz was staring, and although he had warmed up a little since they had first met, he still wore a forced smile when he came over. "You don't need to watch so closely! It's not such an interesting spell, is it?"

"I'm extremely curious about magic, so I take a great deal of interest in what you do, Ninya."

"Really? But Nabe is a way better caster than me!"

"But you can use spells she can't." Ainz saw Narberal lower her head slightly. He could tell from the corner of his eye that she was more jealous than embarrassed. "I'd like to be able to use magic like you can."

"You want to learn magic even though you're that good with a sword? You're a hard worker, huh, Momon? Although I suppose that attitude makes you a model adventurer."

Lukrut chimed in without looking up from the oven he was building. "Magic isn't something you can just learn overnight. First you gotta get this connection-to-the-world thing, but the only ones who can do that so easily are the ones who have a natural knack for it. I heard if you don't, all you can do is study little by little till you get the feel."

Ninya's smile vanished and was replaced by a serious expression. "Momon, I think you have the aptitude. I get the feeling you're different from normal people. There's something about you that...just doesn't exist among humans."

Ainz's nonexistent heart skipped a beat—it sounded almost like Ninya had vaguely realized he was an undead. He was using illusions and anti-intelligence magic, but it was plenty possible that unfamiliar spells or special abilities could strip off his mask.

He cautiously asked, "Oh...? I know I'm strong, but I don't think it's to a degree that is nonexistent among humans. I showed you my face, right?"

"Mm, it's not a question of looks... More just, that amount of power is not human. You were killing ogres in one hit...! I guess men are about power and not looks, huh? I mean, you got a babe like Nabe with you."

Considering Lukrut's remarks with a level head, it seemed like the illusionary face he'd created was being called ugly, and when he thought about the people he had met so far, he had to agree. *There's too much beauty in this world. You can look at anybody in the street, and they have nice, regular features. I used to consider my face worthy of a supporting role, but now I wonder if I'd even make the bill...*

"Faces aside, Lukrut is right. The ones they call heroes are on another level from ordinary humans. That really sunk in for me today."

"Er, I don't think I'm a...hero, though. I'm not fishing for compliments here." Ainz answered Ninya pretending to be flustered, while suppressing his sigh of relief.

"Would you like to come meet the person who taught me? My teacher has the talent of being able to tell how much natural aptitude someone has. For magical magic, it's apparently even possible to know what tier."

"Actually, there's something I've been wondering: Isn't that the same talent that the empire's head wizard has?"

"Yes, it's the same one."

Ainz couldn't let this chance pass. He could get more info if he pressed.

"…What kind of ability is it, exactly?"

"The way my teacher explains it, every caster has a magic aura. The more powerful they are, the bigger the aura. My teacher has the power to see those auras."

"H…hmm…" Ainz's voice was about to go too deep, but he controlled himself to reply in a normal range.

"My teacher collects kids with good auras and trains them." Ninya continued to say that he had been found in just that way. Ainz made appropriate feedback noises while inwardly cursing that there was such a talent—it could mean trouble.

"So if I think I'd like to use magic, what should I do first?"

"Maybe finding a proper teacher is a good place to start."

"…So maybe…I could be your disciple?"

"Mm, I think it'd be better to find someone stronger than me. But the thing is, in the kingdom almost all the schools are private, and if you're not affiliated with any of the magic-related guilds, you can't get in. And the people who do get in are usually kids, because their brains are still malleable. To get in at your age, you'd have to have someone pretty important pulling strings for you. In comparison, the empire has a solid magic academy and the theocracy also offers some fairly high-level education—in faith magic, of course."

"Aha. Is it pretty easy to get into the empire's magic academy?"

"It'd probably be pretty hard, actually. The academy is a facility mandated by state policy, so for a nonnational…"

"I see…"

"And about you being my disciple: My apologies, but I have something I want to do, so I don't have time to spend on that." Ninya's face darkened, and there was something sinister and threatening in his expression—a thinly veiled hostility.

Guess I should steer clear of that subject. Doesn't seem like there is any benefit to pressing him anyway. Just as Ainz made that decision, Lukrut casually interrupted.

"Hey, sorry to bug you in the middle of your chat, but food's almost ready. Could you go get the other three?"

"I'll go, Momon."

"Aww! You're leaving, Nabe? Wouldn't you rather make this meal the fruit of our love? Come cook with me!"

"Drop dead, centipede! Or do you want me to force-feed you boiling oil so you can't talk any more nonsense?"

"Would you give it a rest, Nabe? I'm going with you."

"Sir! Understood."

Ainz thanked Ninya before leaving the tent and walking over to where two of the others were sitting on the ground working a little ways away.

Peter and Dyne were completely absorbed in the inspection of the weapons they had used earlier. They applied oil to the swords so they wouldn't rust and checked all the weapons carefully to make sure they hadn't bent.

There was fresh damage to their armor, and the swords had dings from where they had clashed with the goblins' weapons. These makeshift repairs were standard, considering that one's life could depend on them. They were focusing so hard Ainz almost didn't want to interrupt.

After telling those two dinner was ready, they let Nfirea, who was tending to the horses a little ways away, know as well.

•

The sun was just about to disappear below the horizon… Its evening rays had dyed the sky crimson when dinner began.

Stew flavored with smoked and salted meat was ladled into everyone's bowl. That plus crusty bread and dried figs, along with walnuts and other nuts, made up the night's meal.

Ainz looked down at the salty-seeming soup in his bowl. He couldn't feel the heat of it through his gauntlets, but considering everyone was eating without waiting for it to cool, it must have been just the right temperature.

Now what? Ainz was undead with a body that couldn't eat or drink. He could create illusions to make it look like he had a body, but as long as he was made of bones and had a bottomless mouth, any soup he put in would spill right out. There was no way he could let them see that.

Unfamiliar food in an unfamiliar land… Despite how simple everything was, Ainz thought it a shame that he couldn't eat any. He had pretty much lost the desire for food entirely, but sure enough, when a bunch of tasty-looking dishes were laid out, his curiosity was piqued. He was rather frustrated he couldn't eat. It was the first time since coming to this world that he regretted being in his new body.

"Oh, is there something you don't like in it?" Lukrut asked, since Ainz wasn't touching his food.

"No, it's not that. There's a specific reason…"

"Oh yeah? Okay, then. Don't feel like you have to force yourself to eat it. Actually, it's mealtime and all, what about taking off that helmet?"

"…It's against my religion. There is a rule that one must not eat in a party of four or more on a day one has taken a life."

"Huh? You believe in some strange stuff, Momon, but I guess the world is a big place. I can't believe there's a teaching about how many people you can eat with on a day you kill something!"

Once they found out it was to do with religion, everyone's suspicious looks softened. *I suppose religion has the potential to cause trouble in this world, too.* Momon prayed to his nonexistent god to thank him for helping him out of that situation and then asked Peter a question to change the subject. "So, you guys are called the Swords of Darkness, but none of you have terribly dark-looking swords."

For his main weapon, Peter had a (not terribly) magical longsword, Lukrut had a bow, Dyne had a mace, and Ninya had a staff. Nobody had a black or dark-colored sword. Peter's sword and Lukrut's sub-weapon, a short sword, were close in shape but were nowhere near the right color.

By mixing special powder into the metal, it was possible to change a sword's color, so it would be easy enough to make a sword look dark—it was actually strange that none of them had one.

"Ohh, that." An awkward smile played across Lukrut's face, like he'd been reminded of some past embarrassment. Ninya's face was turning a shade of red distinctly different from the reflected light of the fire. "That's what Ninya wanted."

"Please stop. I was young and stupid."

"You have nothing to be ashamed of. It's important to dream big!"

"Dyne, would you give me a break? Seriously..."

The other Swords of Darkness chuckled warmly at him, and Ninya looked like he was about to start writhing from the awkwardness of it all. The name seemed to have some special meaning for the group.

"Uh, we're named after four swords that belonged to one of the Thirteen Heroes a long time ago," Peter declared, grinning from ear to ear. He didn't seem like he was going to add anything else.

That's great, but I have no idea what you're talking about... I know the Thirteen Heroes were super-powerful heroes who destroyed evil spirits that were terrorizing the land two hundred years ago, but I don't know who they all were and what kind of gear they had. Is that bad? Or should I just say, "Huh?"

While Ainz was wavering, Narberal spoke up from beside him. "Who were they?"

Nice! Ainz struck a victory pose in his head, but the Swords of Darkness seemed unsettled. The reality of someone not knowing magical weapons so famous they had named their whole team after them must have been a shock.

"You haven't heard of them, Nabe? Well, I guess you wouldn't have. Some people think of the Thirteen Heroes as evil or say they had demon blood. They were deliberately left out of the sagas... And people say the powers they had were insane..."

"The Swords of Darkness are four swords that belonged to one of the heroes called the Black Knight: Demonic Sword, Killineiram, that gives off dark energy; Canker Sword, Coroquedavarre, that is said to inflict wounds that never heal; Death Sword, Sufiz, that takes your life if it so much as scratches you; and Evil Sword, Humiris, the special ability of which is unclear."

"Hmm." Narberal seemed to have lost interest, and everyone smiled, embarrassed.

But Ainz cocked his head a bit. He had heard of those special abilities somewhere before. After thinking about it, a vampire came to mind. Shalltear Bloodfallen had a class called cursed knight that had skills just like that.

The cursed knight was a priest knight sullied with a curse and one of the more powerful classes in *Yggdrasil*. It was also heavily penalized, so it wasn't very popular. Among the skills it could acquire were the ability to give off a wave of darkness, inflict wounds that couldn't be cured except with the strongest healing magic, and cast an instadeath curse.

Ainz narrowed his illusionary eyes. It couldn't be a coincidence. It was possible that the Swords of Darkness were swords with effects that happened to match cursed knight skills, but there seemed to be a bigger chance that the hero who had wielded them *was* a cursed knight.

To meet the minimum requirements to be a cursed knight, one needed a cumulative class level of at least 60, which meant that this Black Knight person had to be at least level 60. No, to have all those skills he'd have to be at least 70.

That would mean that the evil spirits he fought must have been about the same level, but Nigun had been shouting about how the angel he'd summoned, the dominion authority, had defeated an evil spirit like it was some big deal, so Ainz wasn't sure how the power balance worked. If he went by the information he'd collected thus far, it made the most sense to assume that evil spirits came at all kinds of power levels, but he wouldn't know the truth unless he either got his hands on those swords or met the hero.

While Ainz was lost in thought, the party's conversation had continued. With a start, he turned his attention back to that. It would be a waste to miss the chance to get more information.

"—ultimate goal is to find them. There are a lot of weapons that are said to be legends, but these we know for sure exist. Well, I guess we don't know if they *still* exist, but..."

"Oh, I know of one person who has a Sword of Darkness." Nfirea casually dropped a bomb, and they all turned to face him as if he'd physically yanked them.

"Wh-who?!"

"Whoa! Are you serious?! So there's only three left?!"

"Hrm. Now there won't be enough to go around."

Nfirea responded timidly, "Er, it's the leader of that group of adventurers called the Blue Roses."

"Ugh, those guys? They're adamantite! I guess we should just give up, then."

"Indeed. There are still three left, so let's get strong enough to get all of those."

"Yeah. If one is real, the others must be, too! I hope they're hidden somewhere no one will find them before we do..."

"Ninya, write that in your journal so we don't forget."

"I will. But actually, my journal is personal, so couldn't you write it down yourself?"

"It's good to make a physical record for posterity!"

"I don't think that's the issue, Dyne..."

"Anyhow, we have that *other thing* already."

"'Other thing'?"

"This, Momon." Peter took a dagger with four small jewels inlaid in its handle out of his breast pocket and drew it. The blade was black. "The idea is to have this as our symbol until we get the real ones..."

"What if we called ourselves Blades of Darkness instead of Swords of Darkness? Then, there's no real or fake, and this thing can symbolize us properly."

"Hmm... For once, Lukrut, you have a point!"

The Swords of Darkness all laughed together like the group of good friends they were. Even Ainz smiled. They must have felt the same way toward that dagger as he did toward the staff that symbolized his guild.

Soon the conversation was of the idle sort suitable to mealtime. Since there were more of the Swords of Darkness, they took the lead and skillfully bounced topics off of Ainz, Narberal, and Nfirea.

Ainz participated, but he still felt some kind of wall between him and the Swords. He also felt like he was out of step because he always had to speak vaguely in order to conceal how little he knew about the world. Then, he ended up talking less—it was a vicious circle.

Anytime someone asked Narberal something, she would answer in a way that cut off all further discussion, so they gradually stopped bothering.

Nfirea was doing fine. There was the fact that he was a human who actually lived in this world, but Ainz felt the boy had social skills far superior to his own as well. He always found ingenious ways to keep the conversation moving. He had that knack for reading the mood.

Who cares? I have my old friends... Ainz sulked while he watched the harmonious bunch chat in the glow of the fire.

Perhaps it was only natural for people who risked their lives together, but they really did get along well. Nfirea also looked on wishing he could share in such a friendship.

Ainz thought of his old friends and got so jealous he loudly ground his teeth beneath his helmet. *It used to be like this before for me, too...*

"You all get along so well. Is that normal for adventurer teams?"

"I think so! Probably because we trust one another with our lives. It's dangerous to adventure with people if you don't know what they're thinking or can't tell what they'll do. So before you know it, you're all suddenly getting along."

"Oh yeah, and we don't have girls on our team. I heard if you do, you end up fighting."

"Yeah..." Ninya smiled with a nuance that was hard to pin down and continued, "If we did have a girl, I bet you'd be the first one to cause problems! But I think it has to do with our goal...well, I mean, that we have a solid one."

Peter and the others nodded in agreement.

"Yeah, that must be part of it. It's amazing how different it feels when everyone's aims are aligned."

"Huh? Did you used to have a team, too, Momon?"

Nfirea's curiosity put Ainz at a loss for words, but he realized there was no need to tiptoe around this topic. "Well, they weren't adventurers per se, but…" It was no wonder, as he remembered his old friends, that his voice started to sound a bit heavy and gloomy. Becoming an undead didn't stop all of his mental processes, and his strongest emotions were about those friends.

Sensing something in his reply, no one pushed further. A curtain of silence fell. It was so quiet it was as if there were no one else in the world. Ainz looked up at the stars that had come out at some point to twinkle.

"Back when I was weak, the one who saved me was a pure white holy knight with a sword and a shield. Under his wing, I made four more friends. Then we picked up three more weaklings, like I had been, for a total of nine. That was my first team."

"Wow…" Someone's impressed voice sounded among the crackling sparks, but Ainz didn't care who it was. He was reminiscing about the forerunner to Ainz Ooal Gown, the First Nine.

"They were wonderful comrades: a holy knight, a katana wielder, a priest, an assass— Er, a thief, a double-wielding nin— Er, no, a double-wielding thief, a sorcerer, a cook, and a blacksmith. They were the greatest friends one could hope for. I've been on many adventures since that time, but I'll never forget those days."

It was thanks to them that he knew what a friend was. Right at the moment he was despairing about being treated so badly even inside the world of *Yggdrasil*, those wonderful people reached out to him. And as their membership increased, the fun times continued.

That was why Ainz was willing to give up everything, to trample anything else underfoot, if he could protect and show off his precious guild. It meant the world to him.

"I hope someday you can make such great friends again!"

"That day will never come," snapped Ainz, annoyed by Ninya's consolatory words. His voice contained a surprising amount of hostility. Ainz stood, equally stunned himself. "…Excuse me… I'm going to go eat over there."

"I'll go with you."

"Really? Well, I guess if it's your religion…" Peter responded in a disappointed voice but didn't try too hard to make them stay.

Ainz saw that Ninya's face was gloomy, but he didn't have the will to say anything despite the fact that a simple "It's fine" would have been enough…

•

The two of them had gone to a corner of the corded-off area, and it seemed like they were beginning to eat.

When someone leaves a group, the conversation sometimes turns to the subject of that same person. And that day, the person on everyone's lips had just left. It was only natural that the conversation should move in his direction.

Just as the discussion was interrupted and silence had fallen, the fire popped loudly and sparks rose into the sky. Following the sparks with his eyes, Ninya mumbled, "I suppose I said something wrong…"

"Indeed. Something must have happened." Dyne nodded gravely, and Peter continued.

"I wonder if they got wiped out. People who've lost all their friends at once tend to have that sense about them."

"That'd be…really hard. Even in a world where lives are taken and lost every day, losing your friends must be…"

"Right, Lukrut. I should have thought harder about what I was saying."

"You can't reverse what you said. All you can do is give the person something to write over the top of it with."

Ninya said he would, but his face was cheerless. Then he mumbled, "I know how awful it is to lose someone, so why didn't I realize…?" and no one said anything in reply.

In the silence, a log popped and more sparks rose.

To change the topic to something less heavy, Nfirea cautiously began to speak. "…Momon sure was amazing in the fight today."

Peter jumped on the topic as if he'd been waiting for it. "Yeah, I had no idea he was that strong. Cutting an ogre in half with one swing…"

"Seriously, though!"

"Even I think it's amazing to kill an ogre in one hit, but about how impressive would you say it is that he cut it in half?" Nfirea asked, and the Swords of Darkness all looked at one another.

Nfirea, famous as a talent holder, was also an excellent caster. He had the potential to be a great success in the future, but it was hard for him to grasp how powerful Ainz was when he didn't have other warriors around for comparison.

Peter realized that and chose his words carefully to explain so Nfirea could understand. "Usually you use a large sword's weight to cut, but he made a severing slice. Achieving that with a large sword in one hand against a mass of muscle like that ogre would be extremely difficult. ...Well, there are some exceptions, but..." Nfirea seemed impressed and *hmm*ed, but Peter saw that he wasn't quite impressed enough, so he brought someone up for comparison. "Honestly, I think he's on the level of the captain of the Royal Select."

Nfirea's eyes nearly popped out of his head. He finally understood quite well how powerful the Swords of Darkness thought Momon was. "So you mean...he's an adamantite-rank adventurer? The strongest kind? A living legend? He's on par with one of the most elite humans there is?"

"Yes," Peter answered simply with a nod, and when Nfirea looked at the other party members, they all nodded as well.

He was dumbstruck.

A plate made of adamantite, a rare magic metal known for being the hardest, signified an adventurer at the peak of the profession. Naturally, there were very few who made it that far. The kingdom and the empire had two teams each—that was it. Their power was at the furthest end of human potential—in other words, they were *heroic*.

And Momon was their equal.

"That's amazing..." The whisper expressed a deep admiration.

"At first...when I first met Momon and saw he was a copper plate, I saw the fancy armor he was wearing and felt jealous, but now that I've seen that he has the skills to match, I can only accept that it makes sense—his armor is appropriate for his skills. Boy, I wish I were that strong…" Peter wore banded armor, which offered less defense than full plate armor. He hadn't selected it by choice; it was just the best protection his limited budget afforded him.

"What? Peter, you'll be able to buy even fancier full plate armor soon enough."

"That's right. And if you admire his strength, then all you have to do is make that your goal and put in the work. You should probably be grateful that you had the opportunity to witness such an inspiration."

"Yeah, what Ninya said! You just gotta try to work toward Momon's level. We'll support you—and we'll find our own role models, too!"

"That's right. Just take your time. The way he looked, he's been training far longer than you."

Nfirea reacted to what Dyne said. "You've seen beneath Momon's helmet?" Ainz hadn't taken it off a single time since meeting Nfirea. He had it on through all their meals; it was unclear how he even drank anything.

"Yes, we have. He was utterly normal, just…not from around here. He had the same black hair and eyes as Nabe."

"I see… Did he mention what country he's from?"

The Swords of Darkness all looked at one another—suddenly Nfirea was quite engaged in the conversation.

"No, he didn't say…"

"Hmm… Oh, uh, I was just wondering because if he's from a far-off country, maybe they have different kinds of potions there or something—apothecary stuff."

"Ah, right. It does seem like he came from the same place as Nabe, but they don't look alike at all! You wouldn't be able to call him good-looking even as flattery. But I guess she must be into that?"

"Looks don't matter so much when you're that strong. He's probably got any number of women coming after him."

Strong men were attractive. That is to say, given the existence of monsters, and humans being one of the inferior races, there were many women whose instincts caused them to be attracted very strongly to powerful men.

"Ahh, is this love of mine doomed, then?"

"Mm, no matter how you look at it, I'm pretty sure it was doomed from the get-go," Ninya said, laughing as he recalled Nabe's reactions to Lukrut's advances.

"C'mon, man! For now I'm just gonna keep push-push-pushin'. That's what it takes! And I mean, she's super gorgeous! If I can get her to return even a tiny fraction of my love, I'll be able to count myself among the winners in life."

"She *is* extremely beautiful, but…" Dyne was half through his sentence, wearing an austere expression, when he noticed the sour look on Nfirea's face. "Is something wrong, Nfirea?"

"Oh, nah. Er, it's not a big deal…"

"Hmm?" Ninya's and Lukrut's faces broke into indecent grins. "You don't have a thing for Nabe, do you?"

"No!" Nfirea quickly replied, practically shouting.

Peter sensed that there was something they shouldn't discuss behind that overreaction. "Lukrut, don't be rude. Think a little before opening your mouth." Lukrut apologized sincerely.

Nfirea didn't seem to know how to act in response. "No, uh, it's not that. I'm just a little anxious. …Do you think Momon is really that popular with women?"

"Well, I dunno about looks-wise, but with that strength, there's a good chance. And with that armor and those swords, he looks rich, too…"

"Ahhh…" Nfirea was looking slightly glummer.

Peter addressed him like an attentive big brother would, looking out for his little bro. "Did something happen?"

Nfirea opened and closed his mouth several times. Nobody intervened. There was no reason to force him to say something he didn't want to say. But finally Nfirea made up his mind and opened his guarded mouth. "Mm, there's someone in Carne who…I'd be upset if she fell for Momon…" Reading between the lines, the Swords of Darkness all smiled warmly.

"Okay, little guy. Let your big bro show you how it's do—" Peter stabbed Lukrut with a fist, and there was a strange slumping sound. Keeping only the corners of their eyes on the passed-out ranger, everyone had something to say to Nfirea, who was still in shock.

In the glow of the fire, he broke into a smile.

•

Meanwhile...

A forehead was pierced clear through the steel helmet protecting it. The body shuddered once and then collapsed to the ground like a marionette whose strings had been cut. The clatter of its metal armor echoed in the darkness.

Another man wanted to hope that someone might hear the racket and come running, but no one was crazy enough to come to a neighborhood of E-Rantel even the slum dwellers had abandoned. That's why they were meeting their requester here in the first place.

He glared at the woman in front of him but couldn't disguise that it was just a brave front. After watching her kill his three comrades in quick succession, his spirit was broken.

The woman whipped the stiletto she'd used to kill the others, spattering the ground with blood and restoring the blade's cold gleam.

"Nye-he-he-he! Looks like you're the only one left!" She revealed all her teeth in a big, carnivorous smile.

"Wh-why are you doing this?" He knew it was a stupid thing to ask, but this was all out of the blue to him.

The men were adventurer guild dropouts known simply as *workers*. Sometimes also called *dusk workers*, they would take on jobs that were borderline criminal or even actual crimes. So while there wasn't a total lack of reasons people would have something against them, they hadn't even done any jobs in this city yet, and they'd had no recollection of ever meeting this woman.

"Why am I doing *this*? Oh, I just thought I'd like to have you."

He blinked a few times in confusion and asked, "What do you mean?"

"The grandson of that famous apothecary is out, so I need someone to keep watch and tell me when he gets back. You think I wanna do a pain-in-the-ass job like that myself?"

"Why not just make that as a request, then? Wasn't that the point?" They were workers who would take on illegal jobs, so he had no idea why this woman had to kill him.

"Nah, nah, nah. Ya might betray me!"

"We don't betray anybody as long as we get paid!"

"Oh? Well, then let's say this: I adore killing people! It's my love, my passion!" She laughed and added, "Oh, and torture, too!"

The man's face screwed up in disbelief at this *thing* on which common sense had no effect. "What...the hell? Why are you so insane?!"

"Why?" The woman's expression suddenly changed, along with the tone of her voice. Her nonsensical attitude of just a moment before vanished. "Oh, I dunno... Maybe because it used to be my job to kill people? Or because I was always compared to my brilliant big brother? Or because our parents gave all their love to him? Or because I got abused when I was weak? Or because my friend died right in front of me? Or because I screwed up, got caught, and was tortured for days? Red-hot choke pears really hurt, ya know!" There was something childish about her then, but a moment later the adult had returned, grinning. "Just kidding! Those were all lies, lies, lies! None of that ever happened to me! But who cares, anyway? Even if you knew my past, it wouldn't change anything. Just a lot of junk happened, and here I am. But man, I'm really glad Khaj did the research for me, and I could contact you right away. It would have taken forever if I had to start from finding someone to work with!"

The woman let go of her stiletto. Pulled by gravity, the knife's tip sank into the earth far enough that it didn't fall over. That abnormal sharpness implied that it was made of not steel but some other metal.

"It's orichalcum! More specifically, orichalcum-coated mythril. That's not so common, ya know."

The rareness of her weapon spoke to her strength. In other words, the man realized he didn't stand a chance.

"Okay, next! If I give you too big of an injury, ya won't be any use to me... If only Khaj would use his faith magic so no matter how much I hurt ya we could heal ya back up... I'd be able to torture you forever! Wouldn't that be great?"

Chattering on about such horrible things, the woman took out another stiletto from under her robe. "This should work... Sorry if I miss...," the woman apologized, sticking out her tongue. Superficially, she *was* cute, but her true tainted nature was showing.

The man turned and started to run. Behind him, the woman yelped in what sounded like feigned surprise. He didn't stop to pay attention, just ran desperately through the darkness, employing the sense of direction he was so proud of. But he heard a jangling from behind him and the woman's icy voice, sounding like she wasn't even breaking a sweat: "Too slow!" And then a white-hot pain shot through his shoulder. As he realized he'd been stabbed with the stiletto, a haze washed over his brain.

Mind control... The man fought frantically, but the haze hanging over his consciousness was stronger.

After a short time, he heard the voice of his *new friend* behind him. "Heyyy. Are you all right? The wound isn't too deep, is it?"

"No, I'm fine." He turned around to smile at his friend.

"Oh, good!" The girl smiled a horrifying grin back at him.

3

The party set out as the sun was coming up and proceeded along the road hidden in the grass.

"Carne is just a bit farther."

Nfirea was the only one who had been to Carne before (well, Ainz had, too, but he was hiding the fact), so everyone nodded at this information. They didn't, however, do anything else besides walk along silently. Nfirea looked like he couldn't take it anymore.

Morale was extremely bad. *I messed up*, Ainz thought, hidden beneath his helmet. Ninya glanced over at him now and then. It bothered him, but it was his own fault, so he couldn't say anything.

In other words, they were still feeling the aftereffects of what he'd said last night. Ninya apologized again at breakfast, so forgiving him would have ended it; he just couldn't get out the words. He sensed that he was being petty, but he just couldn't let it go.

I guess I have to deal with this kind of thing even as an undead…

Since becoming an undead, stronger emotions were suppressed, but weaker ones didn't go anywhere. In other words, he was experiencing a slow-burning anger. That showed how important his old friends were to him. That part of it was a good feeling, but at the same time, he knew things couldn't go on like they were.

He just wasn't motivated to take the initiative and change the mood. It was a feeling that was difficult to describe; he knew he was acting like an ornery child and got annoyed at himself for being such a brat.

The only person who seemed unaffected by the bad morale was Narberal, walking next to Ainz—she was pleased as punch that Lukrut couldn't bother her. Everyone else just kept marching silently along at a fairly fast pace until they reached a place near Carne.

"So, I was thinking… It's such a nice view and all… Maybe we didn't need to form ranks…" Lukrut spoke, perhaps just to say something. Next to them was the dense forest, so it was a little puzzling what he meant by "nice view." And besides, not dropping one's guard just because of a nice view was one of the fundamentals of escort duty, so they were right to be in ranks.

However, it was clear that this time the reason they were marching silently in ranks wasn't the result of adventurer precaution.

"It's important to stay on guard! Let's keep—er, let's hurry on to the village," Peter said.

"Exactly! It's crucial to keep a constant watch so we don't get caught off guard," Dyne said, but his expression made it clear he didn't think that was true.

Ninya tossed out, "Plus, a dragon might fly over from super far away and suddenly attack us."

Lukrut bit right away. "Where'd that stupid idea come from? Use your brain, Ninya—could that really happen?"

"That would never happen. The last time a dragon was in the vicinity of E-Rantel was a long time ago, but that was just some made-up folktale; it said there was a dragon who could control natural disasters. You don't hear stories of dragon sightings nowadays. Oh, wait. There is that one about a bunch of frost dragons living in the Azerlisia Mountains. Pretty far up north, though, I think."

So there were dragons here a long time ago? I heard from the Sunlit Scripture captives that dragons were the strongest race on the continent...

Dragons could also be counted among the most powerful races in *Yggdrasil*. They had high physical attack and defense and seemingly inexhaustible health, plus countless special abilities and spells. They were very nearly overpowered.

Among *Yggdrasil's* monsters, named monsters, area bosses, and so on were the superpowerful World Enemies. These were balance-breaking monsters that were hard for even a legion (six teams of up to six players each) to beat.

One was the final boss of the so-so official story, Devourer of the Nine Worlds. Then there were the Eight Dragons, the Seven Sin Lords, the Ten Angels of the Sephirot, and then with the big update, "The Fall of Valkyria," the Sixth Master Angel and the Five Transcendent Ones were added for a total of thirty-two. The fact that dragons were one of the races represented there showed that the developers must have liked them.

If dragons still exist, then I should be careful. In Yggdrasil, dragons' lives don't end... Even just one could have more power than we can even imagine.

"Hmm, would you happen to know the name of that dragon that could control natural disasters?" Ainz mumbled, not quite bold enough to jump casually into a conversation with someone he was having a fight with. But it seemed like they'd heard him fine, and Ninya whipped around to face him.

It was as if they were a couple who'd had an argument, and he was looking for any possible chance to make up. (At least, that's how Ainz felt when he compared the situation to conversations of couples he'd seen in coffeehouses.)

Still, after Ainz spoke to him, Ninya was looking a little more cheerful, and the rest of the Swords of Darkness and Nfirea brightened up a bit, too.

The only one who seemed unchanged was Narberal—or rather, there wasn't the slightest indication that the awkward mood had registered for her at all.

"My apologies, but no! Shall I look it up once we get back to town?!"

Uh, you don't have to get so excited about it… And if you don't know, you can just say so… I was just making conversation. But he couldn't say those things. "Sure, Ninya. Please do, but only if you happen to have time."

"Okay, Momon!"

Ainz felt a tad shamed by everyone's content nods. If their positions had been reversed, it would have been fine, but as the oldest one in the party, he was embarrassed.

"Okay, we're just about—" Nfirea spoke in practically the first cheerful voice of the morning but abruptly closed his mouth.

Everyone's eyes looked at the village up ahead. It was a simple village right next to the forest. They didn't sense anything that would have caused Nfirea to clam up, and nothing about the scene bothered them.

"What is it, Nfirea? Is something wrong?"

"Oh no. Just…there didn't used to be such a sturdy fence there…"

"Oh yeah? Well, it doesn't seem like such a tough fence. Compared to the fences around the border villages, it's pretty shabby, actually. Wouldn't you think they'd have something stronger to protect against monsters with the forest so close?!"

"Well, maybe, but…they have the Wise King of the Forest, so they didn't even have this one before…"

Everyone looked at the village. The fence was made of thick logs that seemed difficult to break, and as far as they could tell, it surrounded the entire village.

"That's so weird… Did something happen…?"

Even hearing the concern in the boy's voice, Ainz said nothing, of course. The one who came here before was Ainz Ooal Gown the caster—this time it was Momon the adventurer.

Ninya spoke up with a sober look on his face. "Maybe I'm being paranoid, but I'm from a village, so I remember the lifestyle well, and two things stick out to me. First, at this time of day there should be people out in the fields, but there aren't. And second, I see that some of the wheat has already been harvested." Looking in the direction Ninya's finger pointed, the group noted that part of one of the wheat fields was indeed harvested.

"Oh yeah. You're right… I wonder if something happened…"

Ainz addressed the group as they exchanged worried looks. "Let us handle this, everyone. Nabe, go invisible and fly over the village to see what's going on."

After acknowledging the order, Narberal used an invisibility spell and disappeared. Then, they heard her disembodied voice chant the Flight spell and felt her presence move away. Everyone waited right there in the middle of the road, and it wasn't long before she returned.

"Villagers were walking around normally inside. It didn't particularly seem like they were acting under orders from anyone. And there are people working the fields on the other side of the village."

"Oh! I guess I was just worrying too much."

"There doesn't seem to be any problem for the moment, then. Can we… continue on to the village?" Peter asked Ainz and Nfirea, and they both responded in the affirmative.

The road narrowed, so the party walked toward the entrance to the village in single file. The fields on either side of the road were green with wheat that waved gently in the occasional breeze. From far away it would have looked almost like the party was waist-deep in a green sea.

"Hmm?" As the cart clattered along, Lukrut, walking second in line, made an odd noise and peered into the field. It wasn't even harvest season, but the wheat stalks were already more than two feet tall. Of course, just like the sea, it was impossible to see inside.

"What is it?" Ninya, walking behind him, asked nervously.

"Huh? Oh, maybe just my imagination…" Lukrut cocked his head for a moment and then sped up to close the gap with Peter.

Ninya looked in the same direction and then, having confirmed nothing was moving, hurried along to catch up with the other two.

The road was even partially covered with wheat as if the green sea were eroding it. They almost wanted to hack at the plants that stuck out to make more space to walk, but it would have been more trouble than it was worth.

"They should really take better care of the fields. This is such a waste." Peter was taking long strides out in front, and when the heads of the wheat collided with his leg armor, berries fell to the ground. Just as he was lamenting this, he was seized by the feeling that something was amiss.

The intuition forged by the life-or-death situations he'd encountered so far was whispering: *Would green berries really fall off so easily?*

Following his gut, he nonchalantly looked into the field—and saw a pair of eyes staring back at him. There was a little creature there that had wrapped its body in wheat to blend in. Its face was mostly covered, so he couldn't tell what it was, only that it wasn't human.

"Whoa!" He was so surprised that before he could alert his friends, the creature, a subhuman, spoke.

"Do yuh mind disarming?" The little subhuman had already drawn a blade and could probably stab Peter faster than he could do anything, no matter how quickly he moved.

"Not so fast! Drop yer weapons. And would yuh tell the people behind yuh, too? I wouldn't want to have to shoot them with my bow here." Another little voice came from somewhere else. When he turned to look, he found another subhuman waist-deep in a hole it had ingeniously dug in the field. It was also wrapped in wheat.

Peter hesitated; from the way they were talking, he felt like there was still room to negotiate. "…Can you guarantee our lives?"

"Of course. If yuh surrender, that is."

Peter wasn't sure what to do. He had to block the line of fire to the cart where Nfirea was and get a handle on how many enemies there were and their positions. And it was also important to find out what they wanted. Under the current circumstances, he couldn't submit to them or refuse to listen.

They must have noticed his confusion. With a rustling noise, two subhumans in the field stood up.

"Goblins…," Ninya murmured.

The race of the subhumans matched the one of the monsters they had fought the previous day. They had nocked arrows and were aiming with keen eyes.

Shall we? Ninya, Lukrut, and Dyne tried to read one another's thoughts from their eyes.

Goblins were inferior to humans when it came to physical ability based on height, weight, or muscle mass. They did have Darkvision, so attacking them at night was tricky, but in broad daylight the veteran Swords of Darkness didn't think it would be a terribly difficult fight.

And Ainz was with them. He could probably slaughter them like he had the others the previous day with no problem.

Peter was being held hostage, but everyone was certain they could rescue him from these goblins.

There was one reason they hadn't made up their minds yet—they could tell that these goblins were somehow different from the ones they had fought earlier. In a nutshell, these goblins had the air of trained fighters about them. And they were in good physical condition; the ones from yesterday lacked muscle tone, but these were covered head to toe in muscles.

That wasn't all. The posture of the goblin with the bow was perfect. If the other goblins had been children swinging clubs, this was an experienced warrior.

Last but not least, their gear was of decent quality. In fact, it might have been on par with what the Swords of Darkness were using, and everything had been polished meticulously.

Just as humans could train to get stronger, so could monsters. Even for subhumans like goblins, it was only natural. In other words, it was possible these goblins were far stronger than the ones the Swords of Darkness had fought before.

Suddenly a rustling came from the field that was different from the wind blowing through it. Lukrut whipped around to look at their rear.

"Eh-heh, yuh found me, 'ey?" A goblin poked its head out of the field and stuck out its tongue. Apparently it had been trying to sneak up behind them, but its skills weren't enough to fool ranger Lukrut. Still, just discovering them didn't mean the adventurers had gained the advantage.

Calmly looking out over the wheat fields, Lukrut could see movements indicating goblins lurking here and there. They were moving in to surround them, with the cart at the center.

The Swords of Darkness were at a complete disadvantage, and none of them could think of a way out.

Ainz stayed Narberal, who was about to open fire, with a hand and finished observing the goblins. His hunch had been right. "These are goblins and goblin archers summoned by the Goblin General's Horns." If these monsters were working for the girls he'd given the horns to, Ainz wanted to avoid acting in a way that could be perceived as hostile. If that wasn't possible, something would need to be done, but Ainz and Narberal could handle them no problem.

A goblin noticed Ainz looking around nonchalantly and called out to him, "Oy, full plate guy. If yuh could just not move, that would be great. We'd like to avoid combat if we can." He must have seen him reaching out to stop Narberal. It was the hard voice of someone taking strict precautions.

"Don't worry. As long as you don't attack us, we don't plan on moving."

"That's a big help. Those guys might be strong, but we're not scared of them. But yer different. And the lady, too. I'm getting some unfriendly vibes, like, if we got on yer bad side, who knows what would happen?"

Ainz just shrugged in reply.

"If yuh could just wait right there till our lady arrives."

"Who's your 'lady'?! Are you occupying Carne?!"

Dubious looks appeared on the goblins' faces in reply to Nfirea's threatening attitude.

"Nfirea, calm down. I don't even need to tell you who has the upper hand here. And if you think about what Nabe said after she looked at the village, there are still some things we can't explain. Let's avoid starting a fight before we know what's going on," said Ninya, but Nfirea wasn't able to hide his anger. Still, the expression that said he might pounce at any minute softened into frustration and a bit of the tension went out of his balled fists.

Seeing such a violent change in Nfirea surprised Ainz and even confused him a bit. *Of course, we've only been traveling together for a short while, so I wouldn't know his personality inside out, but I wouldn't have expected him to be this excitable. Does this village mean something more to him than just a place to stay while he's out gathering herbs...?* While Ainz looked at Nfirea with these questions in mind, the goblins were glancing at one another—it seemed like they'd been thrown off by the boy's rage.

"Hmm, something's not quite right here..."

"We're just guarding our lady's village because it was recently attacked by guys dressed like imperial knights."

"The village got attacked?! Is she okay?!" As if in response to Nfirea's shouting, a girl appeared at the entrance to the village escorted by a goblin. At the sight of her, his eyes widened, and he called out her name. "Enri!"

In response, the girl shouted back, "Nfirea!" It was the voice of someone calling a close friend, overflowing with kindness.

Then Ainz remembered something he'd heard before. "Oh, so the apothecary friend was not a girl but...a boy?"

Intermission

Demiurge walked through the ninth level of the Great Tomb of Nazarick. The clacks of his hard leather shoes were swallowed almost instantly by the silence. He had stationed several minions here for security purposes but was still unaccustomed to its mythical atmosphere.

He looked around and smiled. "Wonderful..." His admiration was addressed to the ninth level in its entirety. These were the appropriate surroundings for the Forty-One Supreme Beings, to whom he would be loyal even if it meant abandoning everything, so he loved this view.

Every time he walked the ninth level, his heart filled with joy, and his devotion to the Creators was renewed. No, it wasn't just Demiurge. Even rowdy types like clowns and musicians would find themselves pausing out of respect, trying to melt into the silence. If there was someone whose heart did not fill with joy at this sight, it meant they were either not loyal enough to the Forty-One Supreme Beings or they were *created that way*.

Demiurge thought on this as he turned the corner. He had almost reached his destination, the private quarters of the last remaining Supreme Being and ruler of the Great Tomb of Nazarick, Ainz Ooal Gown.

When the door came into view, it opened and some figures exited. They seemed to see Demiurge as well and waited
while he walked over. One was dressed like a butler, but all of his
clothes—except his white gloves—were black and more suited to
combat than to service.

He was one of Nazarick's ten male servants. But Demiurge
didn't know which one—he couldn't tell them apart because they
all wore ski masks like generic baddies in a superhero show and
only communicated in strange squawks.

Then there was the guy standing in front. Inane thoughts like
naked with a necktie flickered through Demiurge's head.

He was a penguin. There was no mistaking him—he was most
definitely a penguin. And wore nothing but a black tie.

"Long time no see."

In reply to Demiurge's warm greeting, the penguin grinned
(or something like that) and said, "Indeed, Master Demiurge."
Then, he bobbed his head.

Of course, he was no mere penguin—he was a type of gro-
tesque called a birdman, as well as the assistant butler, Éclair Éklair
Éklare.

Normally birdmen would, like the Supreme Being Pero-
roncino, have the head and wings of a bird of prey, as well as bird
parts from the elbows and knees down, but for some reason this
man was a penguin. Demiurge didn't question it.

"Is Albedo in there?"

"Yes, she is."

Albedo was in charge of the Great Tomb of Nazarick while Ainz was gone, but it was widely known that she couldn't be found in her own quarters and was instead holed up in Ainz's. Since she had Ainz's permission to be there, no one objected except for Shalltear Bloodfallen, who was about to leave the Tomb.

When Demiurge had suggested that a good wife's role was to guard the house and wait for her husband's return, she had retorted, "What's wrong with a wife guarding her husband's room?" so there wasn't much he could say after that.

Demiurge nodded an *I see* and chatted with Éclair. "It's rare for you to be out here, Éclair. Don't you generally work around the guest rooms?"

"Since Master Sebas is out, I need to perform his duties as well, so I was just meeting with Mistress Albedo to discuss some details."

"Oh yeah. If Sebas is gone, the ninth level depends on you."

"Exactly. I need to do a good job in preparation *for the day when I will rule the Great Tomb of Nazarick.*"

There was no change to Demiurge's smile, no matter how strange a thing was just said. It was widely known that Éclair was plotting to rule the Great Tomb, but that was because he was *created that way* by the Forty-One Supreme Beings, so there was no problem. Of course, if the order came down, they would liquidate him, but until then, there was no problem at all.

"Indeed, do your best. By the way, what are you going to do first?"

"Clean. What else is there? No one can clean so thoroughly as me. When I scrub the toilets, you can lick the bowl!"

Demiurge nodded in satisfaction at Éclair's overflowing confidence. "Wonderful. Your work is critical. If this floor were to become dirty, it could be taken as an insult to the Supreme Ones." He nodded emphatically and then asked a question. "I'm well aware of how important your work is now, but who is it that is in charge of administrative operations on this level while Sebas is away?"

"That would be the head maid, Pestonia; she's received orders from Master Sebas. 'Administrative operations' isn't such a big job compared to cleaning…"

"I see… Two NPCs built by the same Supreme One with a clear division of roles. …By the way, isn't it hard to clean with penguin hands?"

"It's precisely because I can do it that I am me." Éclair puffed out his chest to demonstrate his overflowing confidence and then continued, sounding slightly offended, "But Master Demiurge. That doesn't sound like something you, second in cleverness here only to me, would ask." He smoothed the golden decorative feathers growing on either side of his head with a comb he took from the male servant behind him. "The Supreme Lady Ankoro Mocchi Mochi created me as not just any penguin, but a proud rockhopper penguin. Make no mistake! And these are not hands—they are wings!"

"Do excuse me."

Demiurge bowed in apology, but Éclair told him not to worry about it and then turned around to give an order to the servant. "Carry me!"

"Eee!" The servant tucked Éclair under an arm.

Éclair's way of walking was to hop forward, and from a certain perspective, it was extremely slow. So whenever he had to go somewhere on foot, he had a servant carry him.

"Well, Master Demiurge, I take my leave."

"All right. See you again, Éclair." Demiurge glanced over once more as the assistant butler was carried away like a stuffed animal, and then he knocked on the door.

"It's Demiurge. I'm coming in." Of course, the master was not in. But what did that matter? To Demiurge, the rooms themselves were worthy of his respect.

There was no reply, and he entered. Looking around, he noted that, as expected, Albedo was not there, either. He sighed lightly and opened a door to go farther in.

The Forty-One Supreme Beings' private quarters were designed as royal suites. There were innumerable rooms including a large bathroom in the back, a living room with a bar and a piano, a master bedroom, guest rooms, a kitchen for their private chef to cook in, a dressing room, and so on. Out of all of these, the room Demiurge proceeded toward with no hesitation was the master bedroom.

He knocked and entered without waiting for a reply. There was only one bed inside, but it was a magnificent king-sized one with a canopy. Inside it was a bulge slightly bigger than one person, squirming.

"Albedo."

In response to Demiurge's disapproving tone of voice, the peerless beauty poked out her face. In fact, she was out to her shoulders and didn't appear to be wearing any clothes. Perhaps because she had been under the covers, her cheeks were flushed a delicate pink.

"…What are you doing in there?"

"When Lord Ainz returns, I would like for him to be enveloped in my scent." Apparently all that squirming was a form of marking.

Demiurge had no words; he just looked at this most elite NPC created by the Forty-One Supreme Beings, the captain of the floor guardians of the Great Tomb of Nazarick, and shook his head weakly. He didn't say, *Lord Ainz is undead, so he probably doesn't sleep in that bed*, or, *Even if he could sleep, I'm sure the sheets would be changed.* If she was satisfied, that was fine with him. "Well…don't overdo it."

"I don't know what you mean by 'overdo it,' but okay… Right, Lord Ainz?" Suddenly there was a face cheek to cheek with Albedo's. For a split second, Demiurge was shocked into silence—because he thought it was actually Ainz Ooal Gown. But it wasn't thick enough and didn't have even a fraction of the presence of their supreme lord.

"Is that a…body pillow? …And who made such a thing?"

"I did!"

At her immediate response, Demiurge cracked open his closed eyes. He didn't think she had that kind of skill.

"I may not look it, but I'm a pro at cleaning, washing, and sewing!" Delighting in Demiurge's surprise, she boastfully continued, "And I'm making clothes, including socks, for our child who will surely be born! I'm done with everything for the first five years!

"Tee-hee-hee," she giggled, grinning, and Demiurge wondered, a bit drained, if he should really leave her alone in this room.

"Boy or girl, either way! Oh! But what if it's intersex or sexless?"

Demiurge was once again at a loss for words and just watched as she moaned and groaned. To be sure, she was brilliant as the head of the Great Tomb of Nazarick's administrative operations—far better at that sort of thing than he was. But there were some doubts about her ability when it came to military affairs, such as handling defensive battles. That was where Demiurge came in.

There was no issue at present, when they hadn't detected any immediate enemies. Demiurge forced himself to swallow his anxieties and believe that. His departure was an order from their master; there was no way he could voice any objections. "Very well. I'm going to leave soon, as Lord Ainz commanded. That means the only floor guardians left in Nazarick at liberty to move freely are you and Cocytus. I don't think I need to remind you, but please take care."

"First Aura, Mare, Sebas, and Shalltear, and now you, huh? Yes, things will be fine. If it becomes necessary, I'll go to my sisters for support. And I'll have the Pleiades go all out. If I do all that, we'll be plenty able to buy time for everyone else to return."

"…Surely you would need Lord Ainz's permission to deploy your little sister, even in an emergency. And for the Pleiades as well. In the first place, two of them are out, so you can't even get the whole team together. If the situation is as dicey as that, why not just station Victim on a higher level?"

"Things aren't that bad… Anyhow, we've made preparations to take countermeasures, but if the time comes, please hurry back. More importantly, what are you going to do with the surviving members of the Sunlit Scripture? You got permission from Lord Ainz to be in charge of them, right? It's fine if you take them, but I just have no idea what you're planning…"

"Oh, them? Lord Ainz gave me permission to experiment." Demiurge smiled happily, and Albedo's shapely eyebrows crinkled. "First, a healing magic experiment. A severed limb will disappear if you cast a healing spell on a stub. So if you heal the stub after force-feeding a human an arm, what happens to the nutritional value? If repeated, would the subject starve to death?"

"Ah, I see."

"And that's not all! I had them vote on who will be eaten and who will be hacking off limbs with a dull saw—using their names!"

"And why would you do that?"

"It's obvious. It creates a hierarchy among the prisoners: food, cutters, and eaters. This, of course, causes hate to blossom between onetime comrades. Then, right when the critical level of hate is reached, I'll call out ever so sweetly to the food. To expose them. They're very hard workers, these creatures full of hate."

"See, that's just disturbing. Nazarick was created by the Supreme Beings; there's no way we could betray Lord Ainz. Yet humans would betray their master... They have zero loyalty."

"That's why they're so interesting. I think it might be good for you to have some fun with that side of them. Just think of them as toys."

"I don't understand that way of thinking one bit."

"That's a terrible shame. Anyhow, if I stand here gabbing, I won't be able to carry out Lord Ainz's orders on time, and we can't have that. If anything happens, get in touch and I'll come right back."

"Sure. I don't think there will be anything I can't handle, but if there is, I'll call you." She slipped a willowy arm out from under the sheets and waved good-bye.

"Then if you'll excuse me... Oh, but if you're making clothes for a male child, I should warn you: It seems as though the Supreme Beings dress boys as girls..."

"...Huh?"

Chapter 3   The Wise King of the Forest

Chapter 3 | The Wise King of the Forest

1

Clementine had returned to Khajit's hideout, the shrine beneath E-Rantel's graveyard, and her irritation was practically spewing forth as flames. Her gait was erratic, her brow knit. And her mouth was twisted into a frown that warped her shapely face so much she looked ugly.

Of course, her true nature was far uglier.

Khajit whispered in his head and sent the latest zombie off to the undead holding pen.

"Ohhh? A new zombie? We already have more than a hundred and fifty—the Jewel of Death's power sure is amazing!"

The number of undead a caster could create and control with the tier-three spell Create Undead depended on the caster's ability. Making more powerful undead meant being able to control fewer, but if they were bottom-of-the-barrel zombies, someone like Khajit, who specialized in controlling undead, could handle far more than normal—more than a hundred. And the reason Khajit was able to rule even more than *that* was the power of an item he possessed, the Jewel of Death.

"It's because you've been playing around."

"Sorryyy!" She gave a quick bow without seeming the least bit apologetic. "But why'd ya make all these guys who die so easily? You coulda tried a little harder…"

"Maybe if *you* hit them they die easily…"

"Adventurers won't go down without a fight, y'know."

"I'm not worried about adventurers. Regular people will die just fine... Is it a hobby of yours to go on and on about trivial things you already know?"

"Okay, okay, okayyyy. I'm sorry! I won't say any more, so please forgive me!"

Khajit clicked his tongue. "I can't trust you, but for now, don't kidnap any more humans—I mean it."

"Okayyy!"

Khajit wrinkled his brow at her lighthearted reply. He gave up on saying anything else because he knew it was futile, but he frowned as furiously as he could to convey his feelings. Of course, it went ignored.

"But I'm just so *bored*, ya know? I mean, where'd he go, anyway?"

"He hasn't returned yet?"

"Nope! Man! Maybe I should just kidnap the old lady after all?"

"Don't. That old lady may not look it, but she can use tier-three magic, not to mention that she has a prominent reputation in the city. There could be trouble if we meddle with her."

"Huh? But—"

Khajit thrust a hand into his robe and clutched a black stone. "Clementine...I've spent years preparing to turn this town into a city of death. I will not have your stupid games ruining my plan! If you make any more trouble for me...I'll kill you!"

"Spiral of Death, was it?"

"Yes. Our leader performed it."

There was a trend for stronger undead to be created in a place where there were many undead gathered. And when stronger undead were gathered, it was possible to create even stronger ones. Spiral of Death was a ritual that took advantage of that principle to build a series of stronger and stronger undead, and it was powerful enough to destroy a whole city.

It was a sinister ritual that had once turned a city into a place where the undead went unchecked. Khajit's objective was to turn E-Rantel into a second city of death and, by harnessing all the power of death concentrated there, turn himself immortal. And he'd been preparing for a long time. He wasn't about to have it all go up in smoke because of a girl who'd only showed up a few days earlier.

"Are we clear?"

Khajit caught the streak of brutality that flashed across her cute, puffy-cheeked, pouting face. A split second later she'd become a murderous storm wind and was charging toward him.

There had been plenty of distance between them, but she closed it in the space of one breath and her arm stretched out so fast it blurred. Held in the hand like an extension of that arm was a sharp blade, the gleam of which went straight for Khajit's throat—

The weapon she thrust at him was a sword made for stabbing called a stiletto. As a stabbing weapon, it didn't have very many attack patterns, which made it rather hard to use. But Clementine, who loved the stiletto above all else, had trained her muscles, selected her gear, and acquired arts all so she would be able to deal a single critical hit where it counted.

Before she knew it, having used the power she'd amassed to survive battles against both humans and monsters alike, Clementine reached a level of skill where normal people could no longer block her attacks. For someone who had enough inherent ability to deviate from the realm of normal humans in the first place, and then spent her entire life honing her skills, that was surely a matter of course.

But the man on the receiving end wasn't in the realm of normal humans, either. Khajit, one of the twelve leading disciples of Zurrernorn, would not be killed so easily.

—Something like a white wall came bursting out of the ground to receive the unblockable blade. It was a giant hand made of countless human bones, though it was also reminiscent of a reptilian claw. The claw wriggled, and the earth around it started to split. The huge thing was obeying Khajit's will, trying to jump out of the ground.

Satisfied by the powerful undead presence he could feel under his feet, he glared at Clementine. "Don't be stupid. Thanks to you, my control over the other undead weakened for a moment."

"Oops! Sorryyy. But I didn't mean it, I promise! I was gonna stop right before I stabbed ya!"

"Don't lie to me, Clementine. That's not the kind of person you are."

"Ooh! Busted, huh? Yeah, if ya hadn't blocked it, I probably woulda stabbed right through your shoulder. But I wasn't gonna kill ya—promise!"

Khajit twisted his face into an angry frown—because he saw an unpleasant smile spread across the face of the woman in front of him.

"But I can beat that thing, y'know. A caster might not have a chance, but I'm a warrior, so it shouldn't be too hard. I'm not so great at using battering weapons, but…"

"You're strong against living things with your deadly strikes, but I wonder how you'd do against the undead—none of their physiological systems are working in the first place. Besides, do you really think this is the final ace up my sleeve?"

"Hmm… Well…" Clementine eyed one of the passages, probably sensing the presence of the undead under Khajit's control that were lurking there. "I think I could win…although if it turned into an endurance contest, I'd lose, ugh. Heh-heh! Sorry, Khaj!" Clementine pulled the hand with the sword back under her cape. At the same time, the ground stopped shaking. "Ahh, I guess you didn't specialize in controlling undead for nothing, huh? Very nice!" Saying only that, she turned her back and started walking.

"Oh yeah, I won't lay a hand on that old lady till the very end, and I won't kidnap anybody else. That's fine, then, right?"

"…Yes…" He didn't unclench his hand until she left, not until she disappeared into the depths of the underground shrine.

"Psychopath!" he spat. *I have my issues, too, but not like Clementine.* "She's so skilled, you'd think— No, perhaps it's *because* she's so skilled that her personality is so warped."

Clementine was strong. Even among the twelve leaders in the secret society, there were only three who could defeat her. Unfortunately, Khajit was not among them. Even if he used the power of the item he had clutched, he only had about a 30 percent chance.

"So this is the former ninth seat of the Black Scripture... Socially dysfunctional people with hero-level power are quite bothersome..."

•

"Wow, that sounds awful..." Nfirea sighed heavily. He had known Enri's parents well. They were such wonderful parents that he was jealous of their two well-loved daughters. Nfirea had only hazy memories of the parents he'd lost when he was small, so whenever he pictured great parents, Enri's were the first to come to mind. He was full of rage for the "bunch of guys dressed like imperial knights" who killed them, and all he could think when he heard that those knights were mercilessly slaughtered was *That's what you get!* He was also upset at the higher-ups in E-Rantel who hadn't deployed any soldiers.

But he felt it would be wrong to express those feelings instead of paying attention to Enri, who had the most right to be angry and sad.

As he was trying to decide whether he should go over and comfort her or not, she wiped the tears out of her eyes and smiled. "But I have my sister! I can't stay sad forever!"

Nfirea had just started to get up but sat back down. He loathed himself for thinking even for a second that missing the chance to comfort her was unfortunate, but the feeling that he wanted to protect her remained. He wavered but then made up his mind. *I don't want anyone at Enri's side but me, even if the other guy is strong enough to protect her.*

He was scared, but the feeling that he didn't want to lose her overpowered his anxiety, so he decided to tell her what he'd been feeling since the first time he came to the village as a child. "So..." His speech clogged up as if it had gotten stuck in his throat. *Say it! Just say it!* he thought frantically, but his throat seemed to have a death grip on the words.

Enri and Nfirea were both at an age where it wouldn't be strange to get married. And with the money Nfirea made as an apothecary, he would be able to provide for Enri's sister as well. *Even if we had a baby...* He imagined the household he would create but shook his head to clear the fantasy before it got too out of control.

She was right there giving him a puzzled look, and that only made him more anxious. He opened his mouth—and closed it.

I like you.

I love you.

But he couldn't say either of those things—because he didn't want to hear her say, *Sorry, but…*

Then, how about something else that would close the space between them? *Wanna come live with me? It's safe in the city. I'll take care of your little sister, too. If you want to work, you can work at Grandma's shop. If you're nervous in the city, I'll be there to help you.*

That's all he had to say. She was less likely to reject that than a declaration of love.

"Enri!"

"Wh-what, Nfirea?" She jumped at the sudden loudness of his voice.

Nfirea continued, "I-i-if you ever need anything, let me know. I'll help out as much as I can!"

"Thanks! …You're a much better friend than I deserve."

"Ah, uh, okay—I mean, it's okay. We've been friends forever 'n all…"

He couldn't say anything in response to the smile that spread across Enri's face and cursed himself for being so pathetic. At the same time, he admired how cute she was as he listened to her reminiscence about when they were kids.

When the topic seemed exhausted for the time being, he asked her a question. "What are all these goblins?"

The goblins that called Enri "our lady" were vastly different from the ones they had met on the road; they had the air of veteran fighters. He had been even more surprised to find one inside the village who could use magic. What connection these goblins had to this mere village girl and how it happened, Nfirea couldn't fathom.

Enri gave a simple answer. "Ainz Ooal Gown, the man who saved the village, gave me an item, and when I used it, they came out. They listen to what I say and do all sorts of things for me!"

"Huh…" He acknowledged what she'd said, but her starry-eyed look left him feeling bitter.

Ainz Ooal Gown. The name had come up several times during her story. He was a mysterious caster who just happened to be passing by, and with his immense power, he saved Carne from the group dressed as imperial knights. He was a hero who had saved Enri, and Nfirea should have been grateful to him. But that was hard to do—because of the look on Enri's face when she spoke about him.

He knew it was natural for someone who had been saved to react that way, but jealousy welled up in his heart. He didn't want to lose, as a man, and he resented the fact that Enri didn't get that look on her face for him. All those sentiments mixed into an ugly cocktail of emotions.

He felt pathetic but tried to clear that away by considering the item Enri had told him about. It summoned goblins and was called a *Goblin something-or-other Horn.* Enri's rescuer had told her the full name, but after all the confusion, she couldn't remember it.

Nfirea had a strange feeling. He'd never heard of such an item before. And he couldn't imagine forgetting the name. This item was too special—anyone would remember the name after hearing it just once.

There *were* several types of summoning items and there was a tree of summoning magic, but the monsters that were summoned in those ways disappeared without a trace after a set amount of time. They certainly didn't stick around long enough to do odd jobs. If that were possible, it would rewrite magic history.

And then, how much would such an item be worth? Enri didn't seem to have realized its monetary value, but if she had sold it, it would probably have fetched enough to allow her to live the rest of her days in leisure. The reason she had used this rare item was to stop any more blood from being shed in the village.

The goblins summoned by Enri's wish (a wish that Nfirea approved of as befitting her) protected the village; they also looked up to Enri as their master and followed her orders—they'd even started tending the fields. Apparently they were even teaching the villagers how to defend themselves with bows and arrows, and so on. Given all that, they were now accepted as a strange sort of new villager.

Perhaps the fact that they had been attacked by fellow humans was behind their welcoming the goblins. A slight distrust of humans might have made it easier to embrace the goblins who had helped them out in a pinch. And it probably also helped that the one who had granted them the items was their savior, the mysterious caster.

"So this Ainz Ooal Gown—that was his name, right?—what kind of person is he? If I can meet him, I'd like to thank him personally."

Nfirea had never heard of anyone called Ainz Ooal Gown. Well, Enri hadn't seen under his mask, so even if it were someone he was familiar with, he wouldn't have a way of knowing. But this was the kind of guy who could give away an extraordinarily valuable item without another thought—if Nfirea had met him, he wouldn't be likely to forget.

When he told her that honestly, Enri was visibly disappointed. "Oh. I thought maybe you would've known him…"

Her reaction caused Nfirea's heart to leap into his throat for a moment, and his back oozed an unpleasant sweat. *Looks don't matter so much when you're that strong. He's probably got any number of women coming after him.* Those remarks from the previous night crossed his mind, and his breath grew ragged without him realizing it.

Desperately fighting back his terror, he asked her, "E-Enri, what's this about? You want to meet this Gown guy a-and then what?"

"Huh? I mean, I'd like to say a proper thank-you. There's talk of building a little bronze statue so we never forget our debt to him, but I should probably thank him personally, too…"

Sensing none of the emotion he had feared in her reply, Nfirea heaved a sigh and his shoulders relaxed. "Oh. Oh! Okay…phew. Yeah, of course you would want to thank him. If you can think of anything that would distinguish him from other people, maybe I can remember someone…and it would help narrow it down… Oh, hey, do you know what kind of magic he used?"

"Oh, magic. I-it was amazing! This bolt of electricity went *zap!* and the knight was killed in one hit."

"Electrici… He didn't happen to say, 'Lightning,' did he?"

Enri looked into space for a few moments and then nodded emphatically. "Yeah! …I'm pretty sure he did say something like that." She added that she thought it was something longer, so Nfirea figured he must have said something before casting.

"I see… So he used a tier-three spell, then."

"Is 'tier three'…that amazing?"

"Well, if I had to pick between 'amazing' and 'not,' I'd have to say it's pretty amazing! I can only use up to tier two. Tier three is the highest level attainable by normal human beings. Anything higher than that is the realm of people with inborn ability, et cetera."

"I knew it! Mr. Gown is amazing!" Enri nodded, impressed, but Nfirea had the feeling this caster was capable of more than tier three. And he could give away that magic item like it was nothing! He might even be able to use heroic fifth-tier spells.

What was a guy like that doing in a village like this?

As he puzzled over that, Enri dropped a bomb that blew all of his questions away. "And that's not all! He gave me this bright red potion—" Nfirea was so startled he practically forgot everything else they had talked about. He recalled a conversation…

"I'll pay, so will you get me some details about the guy who gave you this potion?"

Lizzy's question had caused the warrior Brita to furrow her brow. "So you get some details and then what?"

"Get connected, of course. If we get to know each other, maybe he'll tell me where he got that potion! Who knows? He might even just mention it in the course of a conversation. If he's an adventurer, I'd like to make a request. What do you think, Nfirea?"

*   *   *

That was how Nfirea ended up requesting Momon by name. He was supposed to make friends with him and get him to talk about the potion and/or see if he let any information slip while they were out gathering herbs.

Maintaining a level tone of voice so as not to let his inner agitation show, Nfirea asked her, "Uh, what kind of potion was it?"

"Huh?"

"Oh, you know, I work with potions, so…"

Enri told him everything about the potion she was given, mentioning several times along the way how amazing Ainz Ooal Gown was. A minute ago this would have made those ugly emotions come back, but now Nfirea's mind was full of other things.

Countless facts were suddenly tied up with a bow; it was as if a whole pile of veils had been removed at once to reveal what was beneath.

There was a very good chance that the potion in E-Rantel and the potion Enri drank were the same kind. And in both cases, a pair of travelers—a caster and a person in black full plate armor—was involved.

There's only one conclusion, but there are two people who could be Ainz Ooal Gown. He figured from the way Enri was talking that Ainz was a man, but he asked just to be sure. "Are you sure this Ainz Ooal Gown…person… wasn't a woman…?"

"Huh? Yeah! I mean, I didn't see his face, but the voice was a man's."

That still wasn't absolute proof. There were spells and even magic items that could change a person's voice. But Narberal as Ainz Ooal Gown seemed awfully unlikely. Her cruelty and slight airheadedness made her too different from the calm, intelligent hero Enri spoke of. The one who seemed more like Ainz was—

"Did he happen to mention that the name of the person in black armor was Albedo?"

"Y-yeah…"

Nfirea had heard that name before. There was his answer.

Momon was Ainz Ooal Gown.

If that was true, it was a shocking revelation—the caster who saved this village was also an incredibly strong warrior. There were warriors who trained in magic, but it wasn't possible to have the cake and eat it, too. If a magical magic-type caster wore heavy armor, they generally couldn't cast much of anything.

This guy could cast tier-three spells and knew his way around a sword well enough to be an adamantite adventurer. It sounded like a joke. If it were true, he was a hero among heroes.

But then why had he been asking so many questions as they traveled? The answer that made the most sense was that he had learned the magic of some far-off country and didn't know about the way things were here. If that were the case, it would explain why he had a potion made in some unheard-of way.

Nfirea couldn't keep his breath steady in light of how valuable all this information was, even though he knew Enri was staring at him.

He also had mixed emotions. When he thought of the man who had saved Enri by giving her a potion, he hated himself, who was trying to learn bit by bit how to make them. He felt like dirt. Enri would probably fall for the other guy. Thinking that made him want to throw up.

"A-are you okay? You're really pale all of a sudden."

"Y-yeah, I'm fine. Just…"

If he could save countless lives by learning how to make that potion, it might erase his guilt. But the probability of that happening was low, and he was armed with only his desire as an apothecary to find out. The one he was up against was a powerful warrior and superior caster accompanied by a gorgeous woman and in possession of unfamiliar potions—a chivalrous soul who saved damsels in distress. Nfirea despaired at the gap between himself and Momon—no, Ainz Ooal Gown.

"What's wrong? You're acting kind of weird."

"Ahh, nah. It's nothing." He smiled, fighting the nausea, but he wasn't sure if it was convincing, and from the look on Enri's face, it was not. "… What should I do? You don't like guys who do bad things in secret, right?"

"I believe there are some things that should stay with a person until they're called to be with the gods—especially if it's something that could hurt someone else. But it's different if you hide something and someone else gets hurt. Nfirea, I won't hate you, so if you committed a crime you should turn yourself in!"

"…No, I didn't commit a crime."

"Oh! …Yeah! Of course—I didn't think you did! You would never do something like that!"

Watching her force a laugh, he felt his shoulders relax. "But thanks, Enri. I know it sounds weird, but I feel better. For now, I'll just work toward getting on an equal footing…" *So I can hold my head high in front of you. So I can tell you that I like you, that I love you.*

Enri hadn't had any idea what he was talking about for a while now, but she reacted to his determination with a smile and a nod anyway.

2

"Huh…" Ainz looked at one part of the village and made a noise that might have indicated he was impressed. Several villagers had formed a line. It was a truly diverse mix of ages and sexes. There was a plump mother in her forties but also a boy who was just entering his teens. The thing they had in common was the earnest, even hostile, look on their faces. Nobody was there to play around.

A goblin holding a bow was speaking to them. Despite Ainz's superior sense of hearing, he couldn't make out what was being said at such a distance.

After a little while, each villager slowly nocked an arrow. The bows were plain, short ones. They looked shabby and awkward, like the villagers had cobbled them together themselves.

They drew their bowstrings all the way back. Their targets were bundles of straw made to look like humans set up a little ways away. The goblin must have given an order—everyone loosed at once.

Despite how sad the bows looked, the arrows flew admirably and burrowed into the bundles of straw. Not a single one missed.

"Not bad!" Ainz found himself uttering modest praise.

"Do you mean that?" Narberal's questioning voice came from where she was standing by behind him.

She probably doesn't understand why these achievements are worth praising. These villagers are like children playing with toys compared to the archers of the Great Tomb of Nazarick. Realizing how she felt, the illusion face under his helmet smiled wryly. "As you point out, nothing about their technique is particularly amazing. But these people never used a bow until ten days ago. They aren't out here because their spouses, children, and parents were killed, and they don't want to let another attack like that happen—they want to bare their fangs and fight when it does! That's worth praising, isn't it?" What was praiseworthy was the hatred that drove the villagers to do this, that was all.

"M-my apologies. I didn't think that far..."

"That's fine. It's not necessary for you to think that far. And truthfully, there is nothing whatsoever worth praising about their technique."

Watching another wave of arrows slice through the air and sink into the bundles of straw, Ainz suddenly had a thought. *How strong will these people be able to get?* And then, *How strong will I be able to get?* He had come to this world at the *Yggdrasil* level cap of 100, with his surplus experience points maxed out at 90 percent of a level. He wasn't sure, but he figured that since his abilities had carried over, that XP would, too. The question was whether it was possible to get that 10 percent and reach level 101 or not.

He had the feeling he was approaching the answer. *I can't get any stronger than this. This is my peak power.* Ainz's power was one that could not grow, whereas the villagers' weakness represented unfathomable possibilities. If by some chance, beings in this world had no cap and could advance past a level comparable to *Yggdrasil*'s 100, there would come a day when the Great Tomb of Nazarick would no longer be able to triumph. And that—

"It's definitely not impossible..."

The Slane Theocracy's Six Gods, whom Ainz suspected were players, appeared six hundred years ago. The gap between their arrival and his own was a mystery, but given that grotesques had no notion of a life span and the fact that some classes had special life expectancies, there was a fairly good chance they were still alive.

If the Six Gods were still behind the Slane Theocracy, the country might have been using them to power level (earn XP faster than usual by assisting a strong player) for the past six hundred years, in which case it wouldn't be strange if they had people over level 100.

But then why hadn't the Slane Theocracy taken over the world? Perhaps there was some comparable power out there. Or it was even possible that level 100 wasn't really so powerful at all. Thinking all of that made Ainz feel like he was being stabbed in his nonexistent stomach.

If the Six Gods really were players, in his current uninformed state, he needed to endeavor to make things proceed amicably. But according to the info he'd gotten from the Sunlit Scripture, the imperial knights who attacked the village were actually people from the Slane Theocracy in disguise, which meant that saving the village would have been an act of hostility against them.

"I wonder if it was a mistake to save the village…"

I really need to make gathering intelligence my highest priority. As he was absentmindedly thinking about those things, he noticed a boy running toward him. The eyes that were normally hidden behind his hair could be seen each time his bangs bounced, and Ainz noticed that he was looking squarely at him.

Something about Nfirea gave him a bad feeling—the way he was running reminded him of the headman from before.

"What's the rush? Another emergency? I swear, this village…," Ainz grumbled as Nfirea came to a halt in front of him.

Breathing heavily, his forehead slick with sweat, Nfirea pushed his damp hair out of his eyes and turned his serious expression to Ainz. As if he couldn't decide what to do or whether he wanted to talk to Ainz or Narberal, he repeatedly opened and closed his mouth. Finally, he seemed to make up his mind and addressed Ainz. "Momon, are you Ainz Ooal Gown?"

The suddenness of the question left Ainz speechless. Of course, he had to say no, he was not. *But would I be forgiven for denying the fact? It's the name my friends and I built up together. After taking it for my own, would it really be okay to deny it?*

His hesitation answered for him. "I see. Thank you very much, Mr. Gown, for saving this village and for rescuing Enri."

In response to Nfirea's bow, Ainz finally managed to mumble, "No. I'm not..."

Nfirea nodded that he understood. "I know you must have some reason for hiding your name. Even so, I wanted to thank you for saving the village—no, for rescuing Enri. Thank you so much for saving the woman I love."

Nfirea bowed again, deeper this time, and Ainz said nothing. He did have that *Love, huh? Live it up while you're young!* thought older guys tend to have and was feeling fairly nostalgic, but there was something more important on his mind. "Aw, geez. C'mon, raise your head." That response implicitly acknowledged that he was Ainz Ooal Gown, but no matter how many excuses he made, it was impossible to negate Nfirea's thinking on the matter anyway. Ainz was utterly defeated.

"Also, Mr. Gown, there's something I've been hiding as well."

"...Come with me. Nabe, stand by where you are."

After giving the order to Narberal, Ainz gave Nfirea and himself some room. He was worried that if the kid said something weird, Narberal would flip out. Once they were far enough away, Ainz faced the boy.

"Actually..." Nfirea swallowed hard. Then, he continued with a look of determination on his face. "That potion you gave that lady at the inn, you can't make it using the usual methods, Mr. Gown—it's very rare. I wanted to know what kind of person would have such a potion and how to make it, and that's why I made the request. I'm sorry."

"Ah, I see."

What a screwup. He had given a healing potion to Enri in this village. Then he gave someone the same type in E-Rantel. *That must be how he figured it out. Maybe I should get that potion back. I wish I had asked that adventurer woman her name. Well, regretting it now won't change anything.*

Ainz felt he had made the best move he could have in E-Rantel. When she had said, *You're wearing that fancy armor, so you must have at least a low-grade healing potion on you, right?* maybe she didn't mean anything in particular, but it narrowed down his choices a lot.

For example, say someone gets out of a luxury car. If it's easy to tell they poured a lot of cash into their appearance as well, then the car will be judged appropriate for its owner. But what about if the person looks poor? In that case, it will seem like they used their entire salary on their car, and they could end up the target of ridicule.

Ainz didn't want that to happen. If he had refused back there, he would have been envied for his fancy armor and for having such a beautiful companion, and there was the possibility that stubborn rumors would follow him around. Once people start talking behind someone's back, it doesn't ever stop, and lots of people love to pick at an open sore.

Ainz had come to the city to become renowned as an adventurer, so he had to avoid doing anything that could lead to disrepute.

He had given away the potion after considering all of those things. It had been a gamble, and it hadn't worked out, but he didn't regret it. It wasn't a fatal error; he just had to bounce back. He wasn't the kind of lucky guy who never slipped up.

Still, he didn't know why Nfirea was apologizing. "It's not like you did anything wrong."

"Huh?"

"It sounds bad if you say you were keeping secrets while shaking my hand with a smile, but you requested me for networking purposes, right? What's wrong with that?" He was genuinely puzzled.

"You're very understanding..." Nfirea seemed impressed.

Ainz was cocking his head in his mind, though. Networking was one of the basics of being a working adult; there was nothing wrong with making connections. But part of him did understand. *He probably feels like he was trying to get close to me to steal industry secrets.* "If I told you how to make the potion, how would you use that information?"

Nfirea yelped in surprise and then thought a moment before answering. "I didn't think that far ahead. I just have this thirst for knowledge, you know? I think my grandma is the same way..."

"I see. Then that's fine. If you had some kind of sinister plan, it'd be different, but otherwise there's nothing wrong with it."

"Wow. I can see why…people…admire you…" The sweat had dried, and the mumbling boy's hair had fallen over his face again, but behind it his eyes gleamed in adoration, like the way a kid who loves baseball would gaze at a pro player.

Perhaps the boy's reaction reminded Ainz of the awe he had felt when he first met his powerful friends back when he had been getting PK'd all the time. He suddenly felt a wave of self-consciousness, but it was suppressed.

Ainz was surprised he was so moved, but he composed himself and got down to business. First, there was something he needed to ask. "By the way, are you the only one who knows I'm Ainz?"

"Yes. I haven't told anybody."

"Okay, I appreciate that." Having gotten that far, he realized he had no idea what he could say to Nfirea to persuade him, so he just made his request point-blank. "Right now, I'm an adventurer called Momon. I'd like it if you could remember that for me."

"Sure. I kind of figured. I know I've probably made things awkward for you, but I still wanted to express my gratitude. Thank you again for saving Enri and the village." Nfirea thanked Ainz with all his heart, eyes earnest.

"Okay, that's enough. I just happened to be there."

"But if that was really all, you wouldn't have had any reason to give away those horns."

Ainz hadn't been trying to be particularly nice, but if Nfirea wanted to interpret it favorably, that was just fine. He didn't say anything else, just nodded quietly.

Before Nfirea turned to walk away, he again gave Ainz his heartfelt thanks for saving the village and mentioned, as a client, that they would be heading into the forest in an hour.

Ainz was watching Nfirea's figure recede when Narberal rushed around in front of him and flung her head down. "My apologies, Lord Ainz!"

"People can see us. Raise your head." As she straightened back up, he mumbled with an edge of irritation, "Yeah, it's all your fault for dropping

Albedo's name." *Actually it's not at all, but that was a big screwup. I can pin this on her so she doesn't mess up like that ever again—better to nip it in the bud. And here she is calling me Ainz, what the heck... Not that there's anyone around to hear her, but...*

"Allow me to apologize with my life!"

She didn't seem to be joking.

Everyone in the Great Tomb of Nazarick was like that. They called the forty-one members of the guild Ainz Ooal Gown "Supreme Beings" and worshipped them as absolutes. Devotion made them happy.

It was a bit much for Ainz, but he felt it was good if the beings he and his guildmates had created were overjoyed to be loyal to him. And he also figured that this was probably his fate as one of their creators.

So here was the NPC Narberal. If Ainz ever told her to kill herself, even as a joke, she would no doubt do it immediately. The fact that she was asking permission stemmed from her ultimate loyalty—her belief that her life belonged to her master.

"It's fine. Everyone makes mistakes. Just make sure it doesn't happen again. You can make mistakes, just don't make the same one twice. All is forgiven, Narberal Gamma."

She wanted to pay for her mistake with her life, but on the other hand, she was loyal to Ainz, who wouldn't allow it, and wanted to obey. These two contradicting feelings put Narberal between a rock and a hard place, but Ainz felt it when the scale eventually tipped.

"Thank you very much! I'll be careful not to commit this type of error ever again!"

"Well, don't worry too much. My plan to go undercover as Momon the adventurer hasn't failed yet, so we just have to be careful from now on. Of course, it may become necessary to do away with the boy..."

"I could do it this very moment."

"Ha, no. It would be bad for us to fail this job." Nfirea's grandmother was a famous apothecary in E-Rantel. Ainz had no intention of incurring her wrath. "Well...we'll play it by ear." Or rather, he just couldn't think of anything else to say.

3

Looking toward the woods, there was an open space about one hundred yards deep in stark contrast to the thick forest growth. It had been created when the townspeople, protected by goblins, cut trees to build the fence, but it looked like the gaping jaws of a giant magical beast.

That was where Ainz and company did their final check.

The client said, "Okay, we're about to head into the forest, so I'm counting on everyone to protect me. That said, once we get a little ways in, we'll be in the Wise King of the Forest's territory, so we should be less likely to be attacked by other monsters. The only thing is that the area we met those ogres in yesterday was also the Wise King of the Forest's territory. Something might be happening in the forest. I'm sure adventurers don't need reminding, but please be careful!" Nfirea's eyes flicked to Ainz for a moment and then to the Swords of Darkness. "Well, I think we'll be fine as long as Momon is here."

"If the Wise King of the Forest does appear, we'll cover the rear. I don't mind if everyone escapes ahead of us."

Everyone gasped at how confident he sounded. After the fight with the ogres and goblins the other day, they were more than aware of how much more powerful he was than them.

Every time someone said something like, *I wouldn't have expected any less!* Ainz's skin crawled a bit. He wasn't used to being praised, since up until recently he hadn't been. He was jealous of the proud attitude emanating from Narberal as she stood next to him.

"If you do need to run, can I ask that you move away as quickly as you can? If the Wise King of the Forest turns out to be a huge magical beast, we'll need to fight with all we've got and I don't want anyone getting caught in the cross fire."

"Understood. Then, if it comes to that, we'll take Nfirea and escape to the edge of the forest. Momon, don't try to do the impossible."

"Thanks. If things get hairy I'll escape right away."

"Um, Momon..." Nfirea trailed off but then seemed to muster his resolve. "Would it be possible for you to chase off the Wise King of the Forest instead of killing him?"

"...Why would I do that?"

"Well, the reason Carne hasn't been attacked by monsters is because the Wise King of the Forest makes this area his territory. If he gets defeated..."

"I see..."

"Momon can't do that! Like, I know he's strong, but he'll still have to give a hundred percent in a fight against a legendary magical beast! Who has the leeway to—?"

"Got it."

"What?!" Lukrut yelped in surprise. The other Swords of Darkness may not have vocalized their shock, but they wore it on their faces.

"It might be tricky, but I'll keep things at the shooing-away level."

It was as if they were frightened of his overflowing confidence, despite being fellow adventurers.

"But you'll be up against...a magical beast who's lived for hundreds of years..."

"Only someone very strong can get away with that attitude..."

"Knowing you, Momon, it's not pride or arrogance talking, so..."

In contrast to the Swords of Darkness, Nfirea, who knew a bit more about Ainz's strength, seemed relaxed. Ainz looked at him and smiled on the inside.

The boy's wish was that monsters not appear around the village of Carne. So he could fulfill it by deploying other monsters to guard the territory, i.e., even if he killed the Wise King of the Forest, he could just send over some minions from Nazarick.

"Okay! To jump right into things, the herb I'm gathering today looks like this. If you see some, please let me know!" Nfirea pulled some kind of wilted plant out of the big pouch around his waist.

"Oh, ngunak, huh?" To Ainz it looked no different from any old weed, but to Dyne the druid, it was apparently completely different; he knew exactly what it was right away.

At that, Lukrut and Ninya both nodded a few times, like it made sense to them; they must have known the name.

While Ainz was still trying to decide if he should pretend to know it, all eyes turned to him. "Got it, Momon?"

"Hmm? Oh yeah, that one. Understood." He nodded confidently.

If he didn't have undead-style emotions, his voice probably would've been shaking from the stress, but his expression was hidden under his helmet anyhow, so no one could tell how he felt. Behind his wall of steel, he was quite imposing, regardless of what was going on inside.

"Yes, this is used frequently in potions that contain herbs."

"Every adventurer knows ngunak!"

"Oh, so that's why. I was wondering why we had to come all the way to this forest to gather it. Wild herbs have stronger medicinal effects than cultured ones or something, right?"

"That's right. But the main reason is that we're proud to make all-natural potions! Of course, they are ten percent more effective, as well."

"That ten percent is pretty important to people who are out there fighting to the death. You offer a better product for the standard price... When you sell such high-quality potions, it's no wonder the Baleare name is so well-known."

Ainz let their conversation go in one ear and out the other as he pondered other things. In *Yggdrasil*, the basics of potion making required having a specific skill that only certain classes could get and knowing the spell you wanted to infuse into the potion. Although Ainz had never done it himself, he knew that synthesizing specific ingredients in an alchemical solution would then create the potion, but he'd never heard of anyone using herbs.

In other words, the potion-making method in this world was different from in *Yggdrasil*. When Nfirea said, *You can't make it using the usual methods*, this is what he had meant.

Ainz felt strongly that obtaining this world's potion-making techniques would strengthen Nazarick. It was just a matter of how to go about getting them.

As he was thinking, he realized that the conversation had returned to the task at hand, so he tuned back in.

"There's a clearing in the woods, so our plan is to aim for that. I've told Lukrut how to get there, so he'll be leading us." Lukrut responded casually with a "Leave it to me!" and Nfirea turned back to the group. "Then let's begin gatheri—"

"Might I make one proposal?"

"Go ahead, Momon."

"Nabe can use a spell similar to the Alarm one that we used on the campsite, so do you think once we reach our destination, she and I could go off on our own for a little while?"

Everyone including Nfirea furrowed their brows a bit out of anxiety that their strongest fighter would be leaving his post right when they would be in danger, but Nfirea spoke up the quickest. "Sure, that's fine. Just don't stay away too long."

"Of course. And it would be a problem if we got lost in the woods, so we'll use a rope. If anything happens, you can just pull on it."

"How about I chaperone? Just to make sure you guys aren't doing anything nasty out there…"

"Drop dead, cockroach. If I castrate you, will your horny brain start to work normally?"

"…Cut it out, Nabe. Lukrut, that won't be necessary. And Ninya, it would be useful if there were a spell that would let us find each other in case we got separated in the forest…"

"I've never heard of any magic like that, although it does sound like it would be useful."

Ainz acknowledged his negative reply with a nod. *There is a tier-six spell that allows the caster to probe for a specified object. Is he just ignorant of it? Or does it mean that just as this world has spells that aren't in* Yggdrasil, Yggdrasil *has some that don't exist here?* Ainz put aside his questions for the time being and gestured to Narberal with his chin that she should get ready.

In response, she focused on each of the Swords of Darkness members in turn.

"So, Momon and Nabe will go away for a little while, and once they return we'll start gathering." No one could complain if that was what the requester had decided. The Swords of Darkness all nodded once, twice, that they approved of the plan.

With the proposals and cautionary notes of the final check finished, Nfirea called everyone to go. The group shouldered their bags and stepped into the forest.

In the area where the villagers had cut trees, the ground was dry and walking was as easy as hiking a well-tended trail, but gradually their surroundings morphed into what one would be tempted to call a green labyrinth.

In the forest, where there were no landmarks, where it was impossible to even tell which direction they had come from, there was a sense of helplessness, as if they'd been swallowed up. That combined with the imposing presence of the towering trees would probably be enough to scare normal humans. But Ainz, aside from the faint vestige of a human clinging to his undead mind, was not afraid, so he calmly admired the splendid scenery born of Mother Nature.

He even found himself thinking, *The forests and other nature areas in Yggdrasil really were just game graphics.* His feelings were mixed, since he was proud of how well-made the Great Tomb of Nazarick was, but he hadn't realized a forest untouched by humans could be this moving. *I see why Blue Planet loved the outdoors so much…*

While appreciating the forest, he was on the lookout, of course, but detected no movement—it was very quiet. Far—quite far—away he could hear birds or some other animals twittering, but apart from that there was nothing that gave him the sense that there was anything alive in these woods.

He could see Lukrut walking cautiously at the front of the line, exercising all five senses to the fullest; the ranger seemed to have judged that there was nothing hiding in their vicinity.

But there is. Ainz thought proudly of the one who was probably silently tailing them at that very moment.

Perhaps because the sun couldn't penetrate to the ground, the forest was surprisingly cool. The party proceeded through it quietly and, minus two of them, nervously. The mental strain combined with the effort of walking over the uneven terrain had sweat beading on everyone's foreheads.

Eventually, they reached an open area about fifty-five yards in diameter.

"Here we are. This will be our base as we gather the herbs." Nfirea set down his bag and the others followed his example, but no one relaxed. They scanned the area and made sure they were combat ready, just in case—they weren't in human territory anymore.

"Okay, then allow Nabe and me to go out for a little while as we discussed earlier."

Upon receiving Nfirea's okay, Ainz tied a rope to a tree and stepped into the forest holding the other end. It was thin but well-made rope that wouldn't break from just friction with the ground.

Ainz and Nabe tried to go in as straight a line as possible. Normally that would be next to impossible because trees would get in the way, but since the rope showed the route they had come, even these two, who weren't accustomed to walking in forests, were able to go nearly straight.

Soon, about fifty-five yards into the woods, where their rope was running out, they stopped. Looking back, there were trees blocking the view, so there was no chance they'd be seen. There was someone nearby who could deal with anyone following them, so they didn't have to worry about anything.

"Here seems good."

"My lord."

"Now we can have our reputation-building meeting."

"…A question, if I may: What exactly are you planning to do? Bring back a huge amount of that herb they are looking for?"

Ainz looked at her without responding and then shook his head. "I'm going to fight the Wise King of the Forest." He could practically see the question mark over her head, so he explained further. "I want to make sure they understand exactly how strong I am."

"Surely the fight against the ogres was enough to do that…?"

"…That's true, but ogres aren't enough. There's a huge difference between them going home and telling everyone that the adventurer Momon halved an ogre in a single swing versus the adventurer Momon repelled the

Wise King of the Forest. It's obvious which rumor would spread faster and gain me a better reputation, hence the show I'm about to put on for them."

"Aha! Brilliant as always, Lord Ainz! That's a perfect plan, but how will you find the Wise King of the Forest?"

"That's already taken care of."

"And that means...?"

In response to Narberal's query, a third voice entered the conversation. "Hello! It means I'm here!"

Alarmed by the sudden voice, Narberal looked threateningly in the direction it came from, already aiming a spell with her right hand, but as soon as she saw who it was, she calmed down.

"Mistress Aura! Don't surprise me like that!"

"Sorry!" A dark elf girl peeked out from the shadows of a tree, giggling. It was one of the guardians of the sixth level of the Great Tomb of Nazarick, Aura Bella Fiora.

"How long have you been there?!"

"Hmm? Since you and Lord Ainz came into the forest." As a beast tamer and ranger, stalking was a piece of cake for her. Lukrut was a ranger, too, but there was too big a gap in their skill levels for him to detect Aura. "So I find the magical beast known as the Wise King of the Forest and send it after you, right, Lord Ainz?"

"Right. According to what we know, the Wise King of the Forest has a silver coat of fur, a long snakelike tail, and four legs. Does that description ring any bells?"

"Yes, no problem. I think I know who it is." Aura responded quickly in the affirmative, glancing up into the trees. "So should I just control it?"

"I thought about it, but no, let's not do that."

As a beast tamer, it would be a cinch for her to get him under her command, but things would get messy if it came out that the fight had been rigged. It was smarter to avoid as many worries like that as possible right from the start.

"By the way, Aura, how is the work on your orders proceeding?"

"My lord!" She dropped humbly to one knee.

Ainz didn't think it was very Aura-like, but he stayed in character as her master while he listened to her report.

"Work on your orders—'Explore the woodlands and get a decent understanding of what it's like in there. Check if there is anyone who would swear alliance to Nazarick, and set up a place to stockpile things'—is going well."

Ainz acknowledged her with just an "Oh, good." Before he left for E-Rantel, he'd assigned each of the guardians a job. Needless to say, the reasons he was having Aura (and Mare) investigate the forest were to guarantee Nazarick's safety and to acquire intelligence.

And the stockpile area, it was perhaps more correct to call it an evacuation shelter. They could hide there in the event they couldn't make it back for some reason, and building a fake base to keep Nazarick concealed seemed like a good precaution to take. Not that he wasn't planning on storing all sorts of different resources there as well.

Finding some kind of life-forms that would obey them would allow them to check whether power leveling was possible and also just learn how leveling worked in this world.

To fulfill all those duties, Aura and Mare, plus the minions who would be building the facilities, were dispatched to the woods. That was a gigantic abnormality for the forest to try to absorb. It had upset the power balance, which might explain why those ogres went so far as to venture into the Wise King's territory to get out.

"However, the stockpiling area will take more time."

"Well, that can't be helped. It hasn't even been that long since I gave you the order." They had brought golems, undead, and other minions who could work with neither sleep nor rest, but even so, there was a lot of work to get done; it wouldn't happen overnight. "Take as much time as you need and aspire to perfection. Equip it with defenses such that it won't fall in an attack."

"Yes, sir! Understood!"

"Okay, then, Aura. I'll leave the Wise King of the Forest up to you as we planned."

"Right!" Aura sprang to her feet.

•

After she parted with Ainz, as if on cue, a huge wolf with a gleaming coat of jet-black hair slowly appeared from behind a tree. Its fiery crimson eyes harbored a profound wisdom, which made it clear that it was no mere beast.

And that wasn't all. Curled around a different tree was a hexapedal monster that looked like a cross between a chameleon and an iguana. Its scaly skin was changing colors with such tremendous speed that it almost looked like waves were rolling over its body. It was just as big as the wolf.

"Fen, Quadracile. Worried about me, huh?" Fen the wolf rushed at Aura, snorting. Quadracile stretched out his tongue to pat her on the cheek. "Hey, hey, I gotta go do my job for Lord Ainz."

Aura was one of the weakest of Nazarick's floor guardians. There were even domain guardians more powerful than her—but that was her *solo* strength. Her true strength was in numbers. She controlled a hundred magical beasts at their level cap of 80, and with support from her skills, they were probably equivalent to level 90. Figuring in her pack, she could probably outdo any of the other individual guardians.

The familiars with her now were two of her favorites, divine beasts—an elite type of magical beast—Fen the fenrir and Quadracile the itzamna.

They both understood and stopped pestering her. "Okay, shall we go, then?" Accompanied by the two beasts, Aura raced through the forest. Despite all the trees, she moved as fast as the wind, never needing to slow down.

A little less than thirty minutes after she began her sprint, she reached her destination. A satisfied grin that clashed with her youthful features spread across her face. There was something innocent about it but also something cruel.

"I kinda wanted to keep it, but oh well, Lord Ainz's orders…," she said to herself, sounding more like she was talking about a piece of jewelry than a pet.

The reason she knew the location of its nest was that she had already been considering acquiring it. Compared to the other monsters she controlled, the Wise King of the Forest was extremely weak and not very valuable. Still, the idea of a completely unknown monster excited her collector's soul. She felt it was a shame she had to give up on that idea, but it was for her ultimate master to whom she had sworn her loyalty; there was nothing she could do.

"Let's see..." Aura changed the composition of the gas in her lungs. An exhalation of unnatural, recombined components escaped her slightly parted rosy lips. Now she had breath that was capable of manipulating emotions and more.

Usually it would just be a passive skill of, well, questionable utility, since it would only disperse throughout a limited area around her, but if she wanted to, she could combine it with a ranged skill to be able to strike a pinpoint at a distance of a mile and a quarter—even in the densest forest.

This time she didn't even have to go that far. She would keep her presence hidden and sneak up close to her target. Even a magical beast with exceptional senses couldn't register Aura now, much less normal wild animals. With her presence extinguished, she walked right up to the Wise King of the Forest and breathed on it, *phooo*.

The fear-inducing effect woke up the napping king immediately. With all its hairs standing on end, it hightailed it out of there, lickety-split. The quadrupedal beast, driven by terror to sprint at full speed, was oddly fast—but Aura, in pursuit, was faster.

She was like death incarnate as she pursued, guiding the beast to Ainz with a breath here and there.

"If it dies, I'm gonna see if I can get its pelt."

•

The forest stirred. Lukrut pricked his ears up at the change in the air and scanned the vicinity cautiously, a grim look on his face. "Something's coming!"

At that, the other Swords of Darkness, who had been helping gather herbs, drew their weapons and assumed fighting stances. A moment later Ainz grabbed his great swords.

"Is it the Wise King of the Forest?"

There was no response to Ninya's anxious voice as he began packing the herbs into a bag. Everyone just silently stared into the depths of the forest.

"Ahh, this is bad," Lukrut muttered, predictably sober considering the circumstances. "Something big is charging this way. I don't know why it's zig-zagging, but from the sound of the undergrowth being trampled, it seems like it'll be here soon. I just…can't tell if it's the Wise King of the Forest or not."

"We withdraw. Staying here is dangerous whether it's the Wise King of the Forest or not. Whatever it is, we've probably trespassed on its territory, so there's a good chance it'll come after us," Peter announced and turned to Ainz. "Momon. You'll take the rear?"

"Yes, leave it to me. We'll take care of it."

The Swords of Darkness peppered Ainz with words of encouragement and then took Nfirea and began their retreat to the edge of the forest.

"Momon, don't try to do the impossible, okay?" The trust Nfirea had in Ainz was audible, and his eyes sparkled under his hair. Ainz felt awkward and urged him to leave as quickly as possible.

As he watched them all depart, he was briefly made uneasy by the possibility that he and Narberal might not be able to find their way out of the woods, but he realized that when it was all over, he could have Aura lead them. The bigger problem was…

"Crap… This might not even be the Wise King of the Forest… Even if I take it to Nazarick, I need some kind of proof that I drove it off… Should I chop off a leg?"

"Lord Ainz!" A shadow loomed behind some trees in the distance where Narberal was looking. Since it was concealed, they couldn't tell what it was, and since the sun wasn't shining on it, it was impossible to confirm if it was silver or not.

"We've got company." *Or maybe we* are *the company,* Ainz quipped in his head as he moved in front of Narberal. Since they didn't know the Wise King of the Forest's combat ability (or what level he would be), protecting Narberal was an obvious thing to do; casters were at a disadvantage in hand-to-hand fights.

The moment Ainz stood in front of Narberal, he thought he could feel the air bend. In response, he shielded himself with one of his great swords. Then, a metallic screech echoed out, and one of his arms took some weight. It was the shock of something hitting his sword with a fair amount of speed.

Ainz saw an unusually long tail covered in scales like a snake withdrawing back into the trees. *So its tail can attack like a whip? But from the sound and feel when it hit me, it's like a whip made of metal… And the fact that its range is more than twenty yards is a pain… How does it even go about its daily life dragging that thing around?!*

Ainz didn't have any skills for frontline fighting, so he had no idea what to do short of moving in to make it a fight at closer quarters.

He exhaled. Of course, he didn't have lungs, so he only pretended to, but the tension went out of his shoulders, and he was more prepared to take up the chase if necessary.

In response, a deep, quiet voice came from behind the trees. "A magnificent job blocking my first attack, that it was… It may be…the first time I have met such an opponent…"

"*That it was…?*" Ainz screwed up his illusionary face and then remembered that the words he heard were translated. So apparently that was the closest his brain could get to the original.

"Well, invader of my territory, if you flee now, I'll refrain from pursuing you out of respect for your magnificent defense…but it's your choice, that it is."

"…Don't be ridiculous. I stand to gain from defeating you. …More pertinently, are you ever going to come out, or don't you have enough confidence in your looks? Maybe you're shy?"

"Well, you've got a mouth on you, that you have, invader! Very well—gaze in wonderment at my majesty and know fear!" The Wise King of the Forest slowly pushed through the bushes and revealed itself before Ainz.

The eyes of Ainz's illusionary face nearly popped out of their illusion sockets.

"Hoo-hoo-hoo. I can sense your terror and astonishment from under your helmet, that I can."

The beast's face twisted into a smile and her tail wriggled. There were strange markings almost like writing on her silver body—and she was big, probably as big as a horse, but not very tall. Wide from side to side, but flat.

The Wise King of the Forest began to slowly close the distance between them.

"What the heck…" Ainz was seized by a feeling that was difficult to describe. Since emotions would be suppressed by his undead mind if there was a big swing, he could assume this was not a very strong feeling. Still, it had been a long time (even including his *Yggdrasil* days) since he had faced a monster and felt like this.

"…I'd like to ask you something. What race are you?"

"I'm what you all call the Wise King of the Forest. I have no other name, no, I don't."

Ainz swallowed spit he didn't have and asked, "Are you a…Djungarian hamster?"

The Wise King of the Forest. She was the spitting image of a Djungarian hamster as far as Ainz could tell. Her hair was more snow white than silver, and her eyes were black and round. Altogether, she looked like a big ball of mochi.

Of course, hamsters didn't have long tails like that, and they didn't grow to be bigger than humans, but Ainz couldn't think of anything else to compare her to. *If you asked a hundred people, a hundred people would say she was a hamster—a giant Djungarian hamster or maybe a mutant Djungarian hamster.*

The Wise King of the Forest tilted her face (it was hard to tell where her head ended and her body began), nose twitching, and replied, "Hmm… I've lived alone ever since I was born, that I have. Since I know none of my kind, I cannot answer your question… Perhaps you know my race, do you?"

"Mmmm, I as good as know it, I suppose… A friend of mine once had a pet that looked just like you." Ainz recalled his guildmate who didn't log in to *Yggdrasil* for a week because his hamster died of old age. The admiring "ooh" from Narberal behind him must have been because it was information about one of the Forty-One Supreme Beings.

"What?! How dare someone make a pet out of a monster who looks like me!" The Wise King of the Forest puffed her cheeks into a pouty face.

Did I upset her? Or is that supposed to look threatening? Or...? All Ainz knew was that she didn't have food packed in there.

"Hmm...I would like to hear the details, that I would. As a living thing, I must ensure the survival of my species, that I must. If there are others like me and I don't create descendants, then I'm a horrible being, that I am."

By the Wise King of the Forest's logic, Ainz hadn't made any kids, so he was a horrible living thing. Mentally giving the excuse that he was already undead and not a living thing, he replied apathetically, "Well, it wasn't as big as you."

"Is that so, hmm...? Perhaps it was a baby?"

"...No. It was an adult and could fit in the palm of my hand."

The Wise King of the Forest's hairs drooped; she was probably a little discouraged. "Then it would be rather impossible, that it would... So I really am the only one, that I am..."

"If you were a cool race, that would be great, but...mm, yeah, you're a hamster. Not that I don't feel bad for you, but if you did have relatives, they'd probably multiply like mice—I think the world would end!"

The Wise King of the Forest's hairs stood on end. Her cute, round eyes stayed the same, but when she spoke, her anger was palpable. "Such impertinence! Ensuring the survival of one's species is a serious matter, that it is! And I've been living my whole life on my own, that I have! You would want to make some friends, too, would you not?!"

"H...rm... I don't *disagree*... Forgive me..." Thinking of his guildmates, Ainz apologized. Still, he wasn't sure how he felt about being reminded of them by, and apologizing to, this hamster.

"Well...I forgive you, that I do. Let's stop this pointless chatter—we shall fight to the death, that we shall. Now, then, invader, I'll turn you into my dinner, that I will!"

"Mm...kay..." Ainz felt less and less interested in continuing.

Even if the Wise King of the Forest's cuteness was an evolutionary advantage, Ainz wasn't motivated. When he imagined himself, the ruler of the Great Tomb of Nazarick, facing off against a giant hamster, it was just too shameful.

And if he killed her and presented the giant Djungarian hamster corpse, saying, "This is the Wise King of the Forest. It was a fierce battle and I couldn't drive her away," what would the Swords of Darkness think? No matter how optimistically Ainz considered the situation, awkwardly kind looks were the best he could imagine getting. Then, instead of killing her, he would capture her and extract her wisdom.

"Nabe, fall back." Ainz had forced himself to muster the will to fight, and upon his order, Nabe bowed deeply and withdrew to the edge of the clearing, confident her master would be victorious.

"Hmm? I don't mind if you both fight me at once, that I don't."

"Fighting a hamster with backup is too embarrassing!" Ainz spat as he readied his weapons.

Sensing that he'd moved into a combat stance, the Wise King of the Forest crouched. "...If you regret those words, it's too late to take them back, that it is! Here I come, that I do!" Then, she kicked off the ground with a *boom* and flung herself, in a ball, at Ainz. Anyone human size taking the Wise King of the Forest's body slam directly, without using any martial arts, would normally have been blown away, but Ainz blocked it with a great sword. It was a terrible amount of destructive power, but Ainz's strength was more than up to the task of enduring it.

"Argh, that I say!" Shouting in surprise that Ainz hadn't retreated so much as a step, the Wise King of the Forest raised her front legs with their unexpectedly sharp claws and began to scratch. Ainz beat back the attack with the great sword in his left hand and slashed with the other in his right. He didn't go all out, but it was still a hefty blow.

And it was repelled with a screech. The shock went up his arm. The Wise King of the Forest had brandished a foot to counter Ainz's attack. Their strikes clashed in midair and repelled each other.

"Magnificent, that it was! And how about this, hmm? Charm Species!"

Undead were generally immune to psychic attacks. Ignoring the spell completely, he stabbed with both of his great swords simultaneously.

A metallic screech rang out, and Ainz's swords were repelled once more. He squinted under his helmet. He wasn't trying too hard, but the Wise King of the Forest was repelling his attacks with her skin alone—it must have been harder than low-grade metals. *So she's not just a fluffy fur ball?* Ainz felt momentarily betrayed, but he realized that thought wasn't appropriate for combat and cleared it away.

Considering his physical attack strength by *Yggdrasil* standards, Ainz estimated that he would be equivalent to about a level-30 warrior, maybe a little higher. Of course, his magic and gear made a big difference, so he couldn't be sure, but if he used that as the bar and compared the Wise King's combat ability to it, they were probably close to equal. The illusionary face under his helmet twisted into a sinister smile. "Nothing wrong with that… This is a good chance to test out my close-quarters combat ability."

He judged that he would be able to win no problem if he put real effort into it. He couldn't let his guard down, but this opponent was a good one for practicing frontline swordsmanship.

Ainz brandished each of his great swords in turn. The Wise King of the Forest deftly blocked them with her front claws and then one of the markings on her body glowed as she cast a spell. "Blindness!"

Unlike the psychic spell Charm Species, Blindness would work on Ainz; however, he had a racial skill that neutralized all low-level magic, so the spell disappeared without having any effect.

The marking that lit up was a different one from last time… Seems like she can only use as many spells as the number of markings she has? In *Yggdrasil*, the amount of spells a monster could use varied a great deal depending on their level and race, but it was generally around eight. Ainz counted the markings on the Wise King of the Forest and it was about that number, so he felt like he was fighting a *Yggdrasil* monster.

Unconcerned by the resistance to her magic, the Wise King of the Forest closed in to fight with her front legs. Ainz blocked with one sword and kept attacking with the other.

The way some of his guildmates used to fight crossed his mind. Touch Me was one of the strongest warriors in *Yggdrasil* and used a sword and shield. NishikiEnrai had the highest attack power in the guild and wielded two katana named Amaterasu and Tsukuyomi. The Warrior Takemikazuchi who said "no second strike necessary," even though it wasn't true, used two different ōdachi, Imperial Sword Zanshin and Takemikazuchi Style Eight, for different purposes.

Then, he remembered someone he'd met more recently, the brave captain of the Royal Select, Gazef Stronoff. It was possible that the reason Ainz headed to E-Rantel in the guise of a warrior had something to do with him.

He sneered at himself for thinking such things in a corner of his mind. *You're in the middle of a fight! Even if I can afford to do it, thinking about stuff that off topic is just rude…even if she is a hamster…*

Ainz attacked over and over, trying to emulate the memories of his friends while deftly blocking the Wise King of the Forest's claws with the great sword in his left hand. It seemed like neither one of them would land a decisive blow, when suddenly Ainz managed to penetrate the Wise King of the Forest's defenses.

"What!"

The sensation of his blade piercing flesh was accompanied by the smell of fresh blood. The great sword in Ainz's right hand had made a small rip in the Wise King of the Forest's skin. A handful of hairs hung in the air.

Ainz tried to follow up with a blow from the sword in his left hand, but the Wise King of the Forest leaped backward as if she'd sensed it. Then, in a flurry of footfalls, she retreated to a position a little more than ten yards away.

He did say his hamster would jump and escape his cage…but wow, I had no idea hamsters could run backward like that! Ainz was letting his mind wander, feeling exactly like he was fighting a giant hamster, when the Wise King of the Forest suddenly got into a low crouch.

Ainz wasn't sure what to make of it. *What's she planning to do at that distance? If she's going to charge again like before, I should stick out my swords so she impales herself…but I suppose it's more likely that she casts another spell.* He didn't think the Wise King of the Forest's wriggling tail would reach, but—

"I was wrong!" He realized how foolish he'd been. The first tail strike had come from even farther away, i.e., he was well within range this time.

The bizarrely long tail did indeed strike, tracing a large arc through the air. He blocked it with the great sword in his right hand, but then his eyes widened: The tail turned at a right angle with his sword as the axis. "Ngh!"

He swung his sword sideways to shake off the tail, but he hadn't reacted fast enough, and he heard it graze the armor on his back at the same time as he felt the impact. Thanks to a racial skill, even if the tail had pierced his armor, he wouldn't have taken too much damage from an attack of that intensity. Still, it was like missing one shot in a level of a shoot-'em-up game.

"So we've each connected once, that we have…"

You damned hamster…, thought Ainz in a wave of mild irritation. *I can attack at range, too, you know.* He poured energy into his right hand.

As he was preparing to attack, the Wise King of the Forest expressed her heartfelt admiration. "Your armor…it's tremendous, that it is. But your strength, your sword—everything about you is astonishing. Truly magnificent, a superior warrior. You must be well-known in the human world, that you must."

All the energy drained out of Ainz's right hand. "You think I'm just a warrior?" he asked, with a hint of disappointment.

"What do you mean, hmm? What else would you be? A knight, hmm?"

"The Wise King of the Forest is…not so bright. I should've known this was a bust from the moment I saw it was a giant hamster…"

It was probably difficult to tell that Ainz was a caster when he was wearing full plate armor. But he wanted a monster with the name Wise King of the Forest to at least have had an inkling that something was off, even if she couldn't see through the disguise completely.

Did she think those spells were being neutralized through the power of sheer will alone? It's true that immunity and resistance had the same end result in Yggdrasil, but would it kill this thing to live up to her name as a "wise king"?

The name Wise King of the Forest is just not appropriate here. If she would have been called a giant Djungarian hamster, I wouldn't have bothered getting my hopes up. The blame lies squarely on the parent who named her. It's blatant false advertising—a misleading representation.

Ainz had completely lost the will to fight and let his sword droop.

"What do you think you're doing, hmm? You can't possibly…you wouldn't dare give up before the victor is decided, would you? Take me seriously, that you must! We shall fight to the death, that we shall!"

Every time the miffed Wise King of the Forest opened her mouth and missed the point, it chipped away at something in Ainz's brain. Taking into account the fact that any large mental swings would be prevented, he could probably still fight, but...

"Ugh...I'm done," Ainz uttered in a voice so cool it seemed to be accompanied by a frigid cold front. He pointed the sword in his right hand and unleashed an ability—Aura of Despair V.

A chance of instadeath was a tad overkill, so he went with the weaker fear-inducing tier I spell instead of tier V. A wind whipped up around Ainz, and a chill that only affected the mind radiated into the area.

The moment the chill made contact with the Wise King of the Forest, all her hairs stood on end, and she keeled over with astonishing force, leaving her soft silver belly completely unguarded.

"I surrender, that I do! My loss, that it is!"

"Ahh, so you really are just an animal...," Ainz replied in a hoarse, spiritless voice and walked over to the Wise King of the Forest to stare down at her belly while he contemplated his next move.

She's a monster from this world and all; it'd be a waste to shoo her away. Plus, she's a hamster, so maybe she could be like a pet... The only other option would be to make good use of her corpse.

One of the classes Ainz had acquired was necromancer. They could tamper with dead bodies to create undead familiars, but the strength of the undead that were created depended on the race of the corpse. The best corpses were powerful beings like dragons; humans and the like would end up zombies or skeletons. *What kind of undead would a monster that didn't exist in* Yggdrasil *turn into? A great zombie king of the forest, I guess?*

"Are you going to kill her?" a cheerful voice called out. At some point Aura had shown up and stood next to Narberal. "If you are, I'd like to skin her! She seems like she has a pretty nice pelt!"

Ainz looked down at the Wise King of the Forest's glistening black eyes and their gazes met. The monster quietly awaited her fate, so scared of what might happen to her that her whiskers were trembling. Ainz suddenly recalled their conversation—the one about friends that had struck a chord with him. He wavered but then sighed as he made up his mind. "My real name is Ainz Ooal Gown. If you'll serve me, I'll let you live."

"I—I thank you, that I do! In exchange for sparing my life, I give you absolute devotion, that I do—me, the Wise King of the Forest, to you, the great warrior Ainz Ooal Gown!"

Aura watched, disappointed, as the Wise King of the Forest jumped up and swore her loyalty.

•

When they emerged from the forest, everyone who had been awaiting their safe return gathered around to congratulate them on making it out in one piece. Lukrut was the only one who looked uneasy.

Nfirea's surprise and admiration got all jumbled together. "You don't even have a scratch! Did you manage to avoid a fight in the first place?"

As Ainz was about to answer him, Lukrut butted in. "Hey, Momon. You got somebody following you there... It's not charmed...?"

"I fought the Wise King of the Forest and forced her to surrender. Hey, get over here!"

The Wise King of the Forest, with her pearl-white hair, came out of the woods, slowly revealing herself. The Swords of Darkness, jaws dropped in awe, readied their weapons and fell back a step, shielding Nfirea.

Well, even if she is a Djungarian hamster, you don't usually see ones this huge...

Her round eyes may be cute, but at this size they're oppressive. It's only natural that the adventurers would take precautions to protect their client. Ainz made his voice purposely kinder. "Don't worry. She's completely under my command, so she won't be going on any rampages." Then, he moved closer to the Wise King of the Forest and ran a hand over her back, although the gesture seemed forced.

"Right you are, master! I, the Wise King of the Forest, will follow my master and do his bidding! I swear to him that I will not cause trouble for everyone, that I do!" The Wise King of the Forest professed her loyalty.

Right now, they might be wary because of her size, but she's still an adorable Djungarian hamster. Once they get used to her, they'll relax. The problem is how to get them to believe she's really the Wise King of the Forest... For that, Ainz was fresh out of ideas.

But it turned out that he was worried for nothing.

"So this is the Wise King of the Forest? Wow! What a magnificent magical beast!"

Huh?

Ainz looked first at Ninya, then at the Wise King of the Forest. He wondered if it was sarcasm, but Ninya's face was flush with amazement—he didn't look at all like he was joking.

"...Phew, the Wise King of the Forest... The name is quite apt! Even just standing here, I can sense how mighty she is." Dyne sounded like he was deeply moved.

What?! Mighty?!

"Man, ya really got me this time. If you can pull this off, then you're definitely strong enough to be going around with Nabe."

"If we'd have gone up against a magical beast of this caliber, we would've all been killed, but I'd expect nothing less from you, Momon. Amazing!"

Lukrut and Peter. Awash in everyone's praise, Ainz took another look at the Wise King of the Forest.

She's a huge Djungarian hamster. That was all he could think. Why did they find her menacing?

"But don't you think her eyes are adorable?"

The second he asked, everyone's eyes nearly popped out of their heads. Apparently he'd said something outrageous.

"M-Momon, you think this magical beast's eyes are cute?"

What else *would I think?* Ainz grumbled in his mind, nodded emphatically, and wondered if the Wise King of the Forest might have some kind of passive skill that was bewitching everyone.

"I can't believe it! But that's Momon for you. Ninya, what do you think when you see those eyes?"

"...I sense a profound wisdom and great strength. I don't think I could ever think they were cute."

"...?!" Ainz had no words. He looked at each party member, and it seemed that all present felt the same way. He felt the foundations of his worldview crumbling.

"Nabe, what do you think?"

"I dunno about strength, but I certainly sense power."

"What...the...?"

Everyone's eyes twinkled at Ainz as they peppered him with praise—for being so brave that he could declare such a fearsome beast's eyes cute.

Ainz looked at those eyes a few times and wondered where this "wisdom" was hiding. *Could it be that turning undead threw off my aesthetic sense?* If everyone else but him felt differently, it was certainly a possibility. Just to be thorough, he asked one more question. "By the way, do you think rats are amazing, too?"

"Rats... You mean giant rats? Not in particular, they're just your run-of-the-mill monsters..."

"They hang out in the sewers of E-Rantel."

"Giant rats carry scary diseases. And then there are wererats... You can't hurt them unless you have a silver weapon, so I guess that's pretty amazing."

Hamsters and rats look practically the same! Plus with her long tail, the Wise King of the Forest looks more like a rat than a hamster...

After racking his brains, Ainz's conclusion was, "This world is a bit strange."

As he was fretting about the differences between this world and the one he used to live in, Nfirea voiced a concern. "But if you take her away, then won't the territory free up? Won't monsters go attack Enr—Carne?"

Ainz jerked his chin at the Wise King of the Forest and the beast took the hint. "Carne is that village, is it not? Hmm...the balance of power in the forest is currently upset, that it is. Even if I stayed, I wouldn't be able to ensure their safety, no I would not."

"But..."

Ainz said nothing in response to Nfirea's shock—he just grinned in his head. *The King of the Forest may have been a bust, but I can make up for it here.* He could feel Nfirea's eyes on him while he plotted what direction to lead the conversation in. The boy was opening and closing his mouth like he wanted to say something. It was clear to Ainz that he wanted him to save the village again, but that sentiment was competing with the feeling that he didn't want to be a bother or fall back on him forever.

Behind him, the Swords of Darkness had begun bouncing ideas off of one another of how to save the village, but then Nfirea seemed to muster his resolve. "Momon," he said with a solemn expression on his face.

"What is it?" Ainz was practically licking his lips. Carne was valuable to him as a foothold; he'd been intending to save the village from the beginning, but it was important that they felt like they were relying on him. He could kill two birds with one stone here by getting Nfirea to feel indebted to him and collecting a reward. That was Ainz's plan and how he intended to compensate for his losses in the Wise King of the Forest affair.

But what Nfirea said was far afield of Ainz's expectations. "Momon! Please let me join your team!"

"Huh?!"

"I want to protect Enr— The village, but the way I am now I don't have the power. So I want to get stronger! I want you to teach me how to obtain even a sliver of your strength. I just don't have the means to hire such a brilliant adventurer as yourself, so please let me join your team! I'm pretty confident about my knowledge of medicine, and I'll carry your bags or do whatever you ask, so please, I beg you!" While Ainz was blinking his nonexistent eyes in shock, Nfirea continued, "I studied all my life to be an apothecary. My grandmother is one and my deceased father was one, so I didn't really consider my options before starting out... But now I know what I really want to do! And it's not be an apothecary!"

"You want to get stronger as a caster and protect Carne?"

"Yes!" The eyes of a man, not a boy, fixated on him.

In Ainz's *Yggdrasil* days, there had been a never-ending stream of people wanting to join his guild. The majority of them were considering the personal gains that could be had by joining one of the most elite guilds—not what they could do for their guild, but what the guild could do for them. There were even jerks who schemed to get in and steal intelligence or rare magical items. For that reason, after the early group had coalesced, new members were almost never admitted. They were wary of outsiders mucking up the things they worked so hard to build.

But the pure intentions of this boy who had never heard of the guild Ainz Ooal Gown (and so, despite the superficial resemblance, was unrelated to those earlier applicants) were charming.

"Ah-ha! Ha-ha-ha-ha!" Ainz burst into a cheerful laugh. It was an extremely amicable, invigorating laugh. But when he was done, he removed his helmet and made a deep, sincere, and respectful bow.

Narberal gasped audibly.

Perhaps it wasn't appropriate behavior for her master, the absolute ruler of the Great Tomb of Nazarick, but Ainz had felt he should bow, so he did without hesitation. He felt no shame for bowing to a boy half his age.

There was no malice in his laughter, but he still shouldn't have laughed. Even Ainz knew that. Once he'd straightened up, he told the stunned Nfirea, "I'm sorry I laughed. Know that I wasn't making fun of your determination. There are two conditions for joining my team, and you only fulfill one of them, so unfortunately, I can't admit you."

There was also a hidden condition, which was that the majority of guild members had to be in agreement with the addition, so even if he wanted to, he couldn't make any new guildmates. Even so, he continued in a good humor similar to the time all the floor guardians of Nazarick professed their loyalty to him. "I understand your feelings well enough. I will always remember you as the boy who wanted to join my team. And as for protecting Carne, I think I can give you a hand with that, but I may need your hel—"

"Yes, please!"

"Okay, then, okay." As Ainz was nodding, his eyes met Ninya's for a moment. It made him uncomfortable to be gazed at with warm fuzzies. "Wellll, let's continue that conversation a bit later on. First, I have an exciting proposition for you—now that I've bent the Wise King of the Forest to my will!"

Chapter 4   Twin Swords of Slashing Death

Chapter 4 | Twin Swords of Slashing Death

1

They spent one night on the road back to Carne and one night in the village. And then they left for E-Rantel early in the morning to complete their two-night, three-day itinerary; when they arrived, the city was just beginning to put on its evening face. On the main street, Continual Light lamps threw white glows, and the people walking were gradually changing to a different sort. Young women and children were gone—most of the pedestrians were men on their way home from work. Lively voices and warm light spilled out of the establishments lining either side of the street.

Ainz took it all in. It didn't seem like the city had changed in the two days he'd been gone. Well, he'd left for Carne the day after he arrived, so he didn't have the knowledge of or fondness for it to be able to tell. Even so, he felt that there was nothing different about the peaceful cityscape.

One road behind the main street, the party halted for a moment. They would surely have been in the way, stopping in the middle of the street, but there was no one close enough to complain. That is to say, people were steering clear of them.

Ainz peered at them feebly, with his back rounded. Almost everyone going by stared at them—no, they stared directly at *Ainz* and whispered to one another. He could hear them, and he felt like everyone was having a laugh at his expense, but that was just his paranoia. Actually they were all speaking highly of him, expressing their surprise—and fear.

But that didn't quite assuage his paranoia.

Ainz looked down—at the pearl-white hair. Yes, he was mounted atop the Wise King of the Forest.

All the passersby were amazed at the majestic (though Ainz had his doubts on that point) Wise King of the Forest and saying things like "My, what a noble magical beast that warrior is riding!"

Ainz wondered if he should be proud. He knew he should—everyone was saying what a splendid magical beast the Wise King of the Forest was. But Ainz felt like he was on some kind of sketchy game show. The closest thing he could think of was if an older dude was riding a merry-go-round with no girlfriend or family, looking straight ahead and deadly serious.

Knowing how to ride a horse was no help at all. The hamster's shape was entirely different, so Ainz had his butt stuck out and his legs spread wide. If he didn't assume perfect gymnastics vaulting form, he couldn't keep his balance.

Obviously it hadn't been his idea to ride the monster. The Swords of Darkness and the Wise King of the Forest herself had suggested it, and then Narberal chimed in that a ruler shouldn't have to walk, so he found himself thinking it might not be that bad. How wrong he was.

I shouldn't have gone along with this… It's like someone set a trap for me… Riding a hamster was like something out of a fairy tale, which would have been fine if he'd been a little kid—or *maybe* a woman, but that was a stretch. It certainly didn't suit a robust warrior in full plate armor, but everyone said he was the weird one for thinking that.

Is my sense of aesthetics off or theirs? Or maybe the whole world's? Needless to say, the answer was clear. If the majority of people said something was beautiful and Ainz felt otherwise, then it had to be Ainz's sense of aesthetics that had gone haywire. That was why he couldn't put up a proper resistance to the idea of riding the Wise King of the Forest, especially if doing it would distinguish him and help Momon the adventurer carve out a sturdy position in the social order of this world. Still…

Why the humiliation play…? His mind would suppress any emotional wave of a certain strength, but there wasn't any sign of that happening. In other words, he wasn't feeling *too* humiliated—a fact that taught him something about himself. *If I have a high tolerance for shame, that means…! Could I be a brilliant masochist…? I always thought I was more of a sadist, but…*

"Well, we made it back to the city, so the request is fulfilled."

Peter and Nfirea were talking, oblivious to Ainz as he agonized over his kinks while comparing his current mental state to the videos and images of *that persuasion* he had collected.

"Yes, you're right—request complete. So, the agreed-upon reward has already been arranged, but I'd like to give you the extra reward I mentioned in the forest, so could you come with me to my shop?" Behind Nfirea, the cart was crammed full of medicinal herbs. Not only that, but there was also tree bark, strange fruits that had been hanging from the branches of the tree, mushrooms that seemed bigger than Nfirea's arms could get around, and long grasses—i.e., a whole bunch of miscellaneous loot. For someone not in the know, it looked like just a pile of plants, but for someone with the right knowledge, it was a sparkling mountain of treasure.

The reason they'd made such a haul was that the Wise King of the Forest, at Ainz's command, had escorted them around her territory so they could gather things safely. In return for the extremely rare herbs and other useful potion ingredients, Nfirea had promised them all a handsome bonus on top of the original reward.

"Okay, Momon, you're off to the Adventurers Guild, right?"

"Oh, right. Any magical beast in the city needs to be registered at the guild, huh?"

"It's a pain, but that's how it is."

"What's the plan? We defeated those ogres, so should we all go and collect for that, too?"

"Hmm… No, Momon held our hands through every step of this trip. Let's go to Nfirea's place and at least help him unload the herbs and whatnot. If we don't do *some* work, I'd feel bad taking an equal share of the reward."

The Swords of Darkness nodded in agreement, but Nfirea tried to politely decline. "Oh, you don't need to—"

"Well, there's the extra reward you promised us, too, so just consider it a favor." Peter was so casual about it that Nfirea gave in to their kindness.

"Okay, then, I'll give you guys a discount when you buy potions at my shop."

"Wow, that's awesome. Okay, Momon will go to Nfirea's after he swings by the guild. And the rest of us will go straight to Nfirea's, help out with odds and ends, and then head to the guild to settle up. We'll apply for the ogre compensation and then we can pick up the reward tomorrow, so I'm sorry to trouble you, but do you think you could meet us at the guild again tomorrow? Around the same time as when we first met?"

"Sure thing." That was just what Ainz wanted to hear. He'd managed to nonchalantly ask how beast registration worked, but he was glad he was able to avoid the situation of having to ask them to read or write for him if they had come. There was a chance that something like that would make all his efforts so far come to nothing.

"Okay, see you later, then!"

With a shallow bow of his head, Ainz, still riding the Wise King of the Forest, accompanied by Narberal, took leave of the Swords of Darkness and proceeded to the guild. Once they were far enough away, Narberal sidled up to him and asked with some suspicion in her voice, "Are you sure it's okay? To trust them like that?"

"…I'm fine with it. Even if they betrayed us, all we'd lose is the reward for the ogres. I imagine we'd lose more if we obsessed about such a small sum and gave the impression we were greedy."

Ainz had come to this city to get famous. Having a reputation as petty would be a huge hurdle to his plans.

A warrior may not be able to eat, but he'll still pick his teeth. Remembering that saying, Ainz put a hand in his pocket and fingered the small pouch containing his change. It was flat as a pancake and he couldn't feel much of anything hard inside, so it was depressingly easy to tell how little it contained. It was still somehow enough to get two people a room for the night.

If paying for food had been necessary, they would have come up short, but since Ainz was undead and Narberal wore a ring that made eating and drinking unnecessary for her, they were able to save quite a bit of money. The idea behind having one of her two rings be something so boring was to take precaution against poison, but it ended up coming in handy in this unexpected way.

But this thing eats, Ainz was thinking, looking down at the Wise King of the Forest, when Narberal continued their conversation.

"It *would*...be strange for a Supreme Being such as yourself to cling to such a paltry sum. Please excuse my lack of thought, Lord Ainz."

Ainz grunted a response and fingered the pouch again; his spine wasn't breaking into a cold sweat, but it sure felt like it was. *Why am I making things harder than they need to be? And again with the "Lord Ainz"... Whatever, Narberal, it's fine. As long as nobody is listening, I don't care.*

As Ainz was inwardly slumping, Narberal chattered on cheerfully. "Oh yeah, those crane flies were bowing down before your awesome power, my lord."

"I hardly think they were 'bowing down.'"

"So modest, Lord Ainz! I'm sure that ogres and the like are below worms in your eyes, but you still put on a display of first-class swordsmanship for us. I was impressed."

Ainz could feel the Wise King of the Forest trembling strangely beneath him. Ignoring that, he said, "That? I was just swinging it around..."

"One-hit kill" made him sound good, but really he wasn't. The motions of Gazef in the battle he'd witnessed earlier had a flow to them. Meanwhile, when Ainz thought back on his motions, they were as lame as a kid recklessly swinging around a sword. Everyone's praise was only due to the overpowering destructive power that stemmed from his extraordinary physical power. His technique was nothing compared to that of a real warrior like Gazef Stronoff.

"Not that I expected I'd be able to move like an actual warrior."

"...So why not use magic to become a warrior?"

Wearing armor, Ainz was capable of using five spells. One of them would take his level as a caster and make that exact number his warrior level. In other words, Ainz could temporarily become a level-100 warrior.

There were pros to this, like being able to use gear that only certain classes could use, but naturally, there were also big cons. For starters, during that time, he wouldn't be able to use any magic. Also, while he would become a warrior, he wouldn't acquire all the warrior skills, and the recalculation of his ability points would place him lower than a warrior who had been one from the beginning. Essentially, he'd be transformed into a half-assed warrior. Maybe he'd be able to defeat a priest knight or other quasi-warrior class in a sword fight, but against someone who'd collected pure warrior classes, it was doubtful.

Still, he'd be far stronger than he was right now. The problem was—

"There are too many drawbacks. If I was suddenly assaulted by another warrior and couldn't use any magic for even a short amount of time, I would undoubtedly be defeated. Even if I could use a scroll and cast a spell that way, considering the amount of prep that takes, I'd be at too big of a disadvantage."

At the present time, when they didn't know if there were enemy players out there, he couldn't let his guard down. There was no point in going to the trouble to use that magic just to give himself a weak point.

"Well, this warrior thing is just an act to hide who I really am, so it's probably not worth getting so upset about."

The Wise King of the Forest jumped with a gasp and turned to look up at Ainz. "I've been listening to your conversation... Y-you're not really a warrior?!"

Ainz looked her in her black eyes and answered in the negative with a confident shake of his head.

Narberal explained, her voice oozing superiority, "Lord Ainz is just pretending to be a warrior. It's like a game. If he were to use his true power, he would rend the heavens and split the earth!"

Faced with her absolute faith, her belief that him being capable of so much was a given, Ainz couldn't get himself to say, *No, that would never happen.* "...Mm, yeah, pretty much. You're lucky you didn't have to fight me for real, Wise King of the Forest... If you had, you probably wouldn't have survived more than a second."

"I-is that so, master? I, Hamusuke...will be even more loyal to you!"

Hamusuke. That was the first thing that had popped into Ainz's mind when the Wise King of the Forest asked him for a name. He'd given it to her that very moment, and the Wise King of the Forest was happy with it, but he realized it was totally lame. *Yeah, Hamusuke was a hasty decision... Creampuff—that would've been more witty. Even all my old guildmates used to tell me I had no sense for names...*

So it was that Ainz, full of regret, trundled along to the Adventurers Guild atop the Wise King of the Forest, also known as Hamusuke.

●

Nfirea pulled the cart around to the rear of the house and parked right outside the back entrance. He hopped out of the driver's box carrying a lantern lit with magic, and then unlocked and opened the door. He banished the darkness of the room inside by hanging the lantern on the wall. Several barrels appeared in its glow. The smell of dried herbs coming from them indicated that this room was used to store medicinal herbs.

"Okay, then. Sorry to trouble you, but do you mind carrying in the herbs?"

The Swords of Darkness gave a willing reply and carefully took the bundles of herbs off the cart and put them in the storage room. As Nfirea gave directions on where to deposit each item, he had a strange feeling.

"Grandma must not be here?"

She was getting on in years, but her eyes and ears were still sharp, so she should have heard them clattering around and come in to greet them. That said, when she was focused on making potions, she didn't let little noises interrupt her. Nothing seemed out of the ordinary, so he didn't raise his voice to call her or anything.

It wasn't long before all the bundles of herbs had been put in the appropriate places. The Swords of Darkness were looking a little out of breath. "You must be tired! There should be some cold fruit water in the main building. Would you like some before you leave?"

"Sounds great!" said Lukrut happily. A few beads of sweat stood out on his forehead. The other Swords of Darkness nodded their agreement.

"Right this way, then." Just as Nfirea turned to lead them to the main building, the door across the room opened.

"*There* you are. Welcome *home!*" Standing there was a cute woman, but there was something troubling about her. Her short golden hair swung with each step she took. "I was so *worried* about you! Because you were just gone! What horrible timing you have. I've been waiting this whole time, wondering when you'd get back!"

"…Uh, umm… Who might you be?"

"Huh? You don't know her?!" Peter yelped, surprised they weren't on at least acquaintance terms given the woman's familiar tone of voice.

"Hmm? Eh-heh-heh-heh! I'm here to kidnap you! I want you to use the spell Undead Army to summon a legion of zombies, so come be my pawn! Pretty pleeease!"

Sensing the malicious mood, the Swords of Darkness immediately drew their weapons. She kept talking even as they all assumed fighting stances.

"A seventh-tier spell. Tricky for a plain old person to use, but doable with a Crown of Wisdom. Furthermore, though it's impossible to *control* all the undead that are summoned with it, they *can* be *led!* Perfect plan, don't ya think? Awesome, right?"

"…Nfirea, get back! Get away from here!" said Peter in a hard voice, focused on the woman with his sword at the ready. "The reason she's rambling on and on is that she's a hundred percent certain she can kill us. So as long as you're her aim, the only thing that can change the current situation is you running away."

When Nfirea panicked and fell back, the Swords of Darkness formed a wall in front of him.

"Ninya, you should also fall back!" Dyne shouted, and then Lukrut spoke up as well.

"Take the kid and run for it! You have something you need to do. It doesn't seem like we'll be able to help you…but we can at least buy you some time."

"But—"

"Oh, your story's a real tearjerker, huh? You're gonna make me cry, yup. But I can't have ya runnin' away on me. I wanna play with at least one of ya."

She laughed delightedly at Ninya as he bit his lip in hesitation and slowly pulled a stiletto out from under her robe. As if timed for that moment, the door on the other side of the room opened, and a man like a sickly pale, bony undead appeared.

The Swords of Darkness's faces turned grim when they realized they were caught in a pincer.

"…You've played enough."

"Ohh, whaddaya mean, Khaj? You made it so no one outside will hear their screams, right? Can't I play with at least one?"

Her toothy grin sent chills up Nfirea's spine.

"Well, there's nowhere to run now, so let's get to it, shall we?"

2

The actual registering of Hamusuke went smoothly enough, but they got caught up for an hour and a half. The part that took the longest was the sketch—the time it took to draw Hamusuke. It would have been faster if they'd done it with magic, but Ainz would have had to cover the fee, so he passed.

Of course, he didn't want to seem tightfisted, so he was forced to come up with a random excuse. "It's too late now, but 'I'm interested in drawing' was a bit forced, huh? …Well, whatever. So now we head to Nfirea's?" he said to Narberal in front of the guild after the registration was taken care of. Then he went over to Hamusuke.

He was already used to it. Or rather, the merry-go-round was not a ride for only the affluent (lovers and families). What was wrong with solitary older dudes getting on? Ainz no longer cared what anybody thought.

Making full use of his high physical ability, with movements as graceful as a celebrated gymnast, he sprang onto the Wise King of the Forest. He had neither saddle nor harness, but his few hours of experience had turned him into a fine equestrian.

The passersby who witnessed the spectacle oohed and ahhed. Some women even squealed. The looks from adventurers were particularly intense—and incredulous once they'd checked the plate hanging around his neck.

I'm the one who can't believe it! What happened to your concept of aesthetics? he grumbled in his head and was about to give the order to depart when a voice called out to stop him.

"Say, aren't you the one who went to gather herbs with my grandson?"

He turned toward the elderly-sounding voice and found an old woman standing in the road. "…Who are you?" He already had a guess. If what she said was true, then there was only one person she could be.

"My name is Lizzy Baleare. I'm Nfirea's grandmother."

"Oh, so it is you! As you say, I escorted Nfirea to Carne—I'm Momon. And this is Nabe."

Nabe bowed, and Lizzy smiled at her. "What a beauty! I can hardly believe my eyes. And what is this magical beast you're riding?"

"This is the Wise King of the Forest, Hamusuke."

"I'm Hamusuke, I am, and very pleased to meet you!"

"What! This mighty beast is the Wise King of the Forest?" Lizzy's shout caused all the eavesdropping adventurers to look even more surprised and voice their shock among themselves: *Is that really the legendary magical beast?*

"She is. We ran into her on the way to gather herbs. I forced her to surrender."

"Wow… The Wise King of the Forest…" She was seeing stars. "So… where is my grandson now?"

"Ah, he took the herbs and went home a little while ago. We're actually on our way to your place to pick up our reward."

The old woman was visibly relieved to hear as much. Then, with a strange look in her eye, she said, "Oh, I see… Why don't we go together, then? I'm very interested in hearing about your adventure."

Her offer was music to Ainz's ears. "Gladly!"

Lizzy guided the group through the streets of E-Rantel.

*   *   *

"Okay, let's go in." They'd arrived at the shop, and Lizzy had taken the key out in front of the door when she cocked her head. She pushed and the door opened silently without any resistance. "…That boy! So careless…," she grumbled as she entered, and Ainz and Narberal followed.

"Nfirea! Hey! Momon's here!" she shouted toward the back, but a deep quiet reigned over the shop. There was no sign anyone was there. "Where could he be?"

Ainz gave a short answer to the puzzled query. "Well, this is trouble." Ignoring the uncomprehending Lizzy, he placed his hands on the hilts of his great swords. Narberal knew immediately what that meant and removed the sheaths.

"Wh-what is it?"

"Just follow me." With that curt reply, he fully drew his swords, gripped them properly, and strode toward the back of the shop. He threw open the door and turned right down the hallway. He was in a stranger's house, but there was no hesitation in his footsteps.

When he came to the door at the end of the hallway, it took a moment for Lizzy to catch up. Then he asked her, "What's behind this door?"

"I-it's where we store the herbs. And the back door is there, too…" She didn't know what had happened, but she could tell something was wrong.

Ainz ignored her and opened the door. The smell that assaulted their noses was not medicinal herbs but something more foul—the stench of blood.

Peter and Lukrut were near the door, Dyne farther away. And all the way in the back was Ninya. All four were slumped against a wall, legs splayed, arms flopped limply at their sides. And all across the floor was a puddle of dark blood—enough that it looked like every drop in their bodies had been bled out.

"Wh… What in the…?" Lizzy tottered toward the threshold in shock, but Ainz held her back by her shoulders and entered swiftly ahead of her.

All of a sudden, Peter began to make a jerky attempt to stand. But more quickly than he could, with not a split second of indecision, a great sword sliced through the air. Peter's head landed with a thump and rolled across the floor. Then, as Lukrut was trying to get up, the sword returned in one fluid motion to slice off his head as well.

Lizzy could hardly believe the horrors occurring before her eyes while Dyne managed to get upright. The face he turned to them was not the face of a living thing. From its bloodless pallor, clouded eyes stared them down. There was a hole in his forehead, and one glance was enough to tell it had been fatal.

There was only one reason the dead would walk—they'd been turned into undead.

"Zombies!" Lizzy screamed, and Dyne lurched toward them with a hostile groan. Ainz hastily stabbed with his great sword and the huge blade went through Dyne's neck. His destabilized head wobbled loosely as he sank to the floor.

No one moved anymore. In the silence, Ainz looked at Ninya in the back, who didn't so much as twitch.

"Nfirea!" It finally dawned on Lizzy what had happened, and she ran off to look for her grandson.

Ainz glanced at her briefly before turning to Narberal with an order. "Guard her. My passive skill Immortal Blessing doesn't detect anything, so we can assume there aren't any more undead around, but there may be some live enemies hidden somewhere."

"Understood." Narberal gave a quick nod and ran after Lizzy.

After seeing that both of them were gone, Ainz turned his attention back to Ninya. He slowly knelt down before him and patted him down lightly. Satisfied there was no corpse booby trap like he used to use when PK-ing in *Yggdrasil*, he raised Ninya's head. Needless to say, he wasn't unconscious but dead—probably beaten to death with a blunt object.

His face was swollen up and in such rough shape that the word *pomegranate* was perhaps the most apt metaphor. If Ainz hadn't known it was Ninya, it would have been difficult to tell who it was. His left eye had been crushed, and its vitreous humor had run down his cheek like tears. Every bone in each of his fingers had been smashed; the skin had split, revealing the bright red flesh beneath. In some places, even the flesh was mangled.

When Ainz loosened the youth's clothes and looked underneath, his eyes widened; he put them back the way they were and cleared his throat. "I see... All over, then..." His body had been beaten into a state just as gruesome as his face. Internal bleeding had discolored his skin, and it was hard to find anywhere that wasn't damaged.

Ainz silently closed Ninya's eyes. No one heard him whisper, "It's just a little...unpleasant."

"My grandson! Nfirea isn't here!" Lizzy returned, practically screaming.

Ainz, who had just finished gathering all the bodies into one corner of the room, answered her calmly. "I went through their things, and there's no evidence that someone was looking for anything in particular. That must mean their aim from the start was to kidnap Nfirea."

"Agh!"

"Take a look at this." Ainz pointed to some writing scrawled in blood on the wall behind where Ninya had been. If he hadn't moved the body, they probably wouldn't have found it.

"The sewers...? Does that mean they've taken him into the sewers?"

"Hmm. The people behind this atrocity could be trying to mislead us. We shouldn't rule that out. And I don't know how big the city's sewer system is, but...I think it would take quite a while to search it. What'll we do about that?"

"Look, there are numbers written before the words! Two-eight! That must mean something!"

"That's even more suspicious. It's not clear what those numbers stand for, but...one idea would be that they divided up the entire city into a square grid of eight or more boxes to a side, and those numbers indicate an intersection. Or it might indicate some sort of address, but...would Ninya even have had the energy to think that far? Even if Ninya wrote it, do you think the culprits would really let that much information slip? It seems altogether too convenient."

Even more wrinkles appeared on Lizzy's wrinkled face. She seemed just about ready to explode in anger at how awfully coolheaded Ainz was. Then her eyes moved to the corner where the four bodies were laid out.

"Who are these people?!"

"Adventurers who undertook your grandson's request along with me. We had parted ways; they were supposed to be unloading the herbs..."

"What? Then, these are your friends?!"

Where another adventurer might have nodded, Ainz shook his head. "No, we just happened to be traveling together." Lizzy blanched at his cold reply. "More importantly, faced with their corpses, I've been thinking about a lot of things, but what do you make of the fact that they were turned into zombies?"

"Create Undead. That means they have someone who can use at least tier-three magic, right? What else could it mean?"

"Here's what I think: You should take care of this as soon as possible."

"That's a given...but what do you mean?"

"These guys could have manipulated them with mind control, or they could have hidden the bodies—there were other options, but instead of taking them, they set up this little game. Maybe they didn't care if they were found out? Or were they just that confident that they could get away? Hmm...it has to be one of those. If they were going to go to the trouble of making zombies, they could have taken them with them."

If their aim was strictly to kidnap Nfirea, they could have gained plenty of time just by concealing the corpses. The fact that they didn't do that meant that either they had some secondary aim or they wanted to force Lizzy to do something. The latter was a simple matter, but the former would mean that Nfirea's life and powers had value to them. And probably, whatever they wanted could be completed in a short amount of time. Would these brutal killers send him home safely when they were done?

Lizzy's face, as she understood what Ainz was getting at, went past pale to white as a sheet. To figure out where in this huge city they'd gone, and then begin searching from there—it would take way too long. The only clue they had was the sewers, but Momon was voicing doubts. This time slipping through their fingers was the waning light of Nfirea's life.

Ainz made a quiet suggestion. "How about making a request?" His icy voice continued. "This is definitely the sort of thing you should hire an adventurer to take on." A light in Lizzy's eyes seemed to indicate that she had grasped his meaning. "You're in luck, Lizzy Baleare. Standing before you is the best adventurer in town. I'm the only one who can bring back your grandson. If you make a request, I might even take it on. But…it'll cost you! I can tell what a tricky job this is going to be."

"But yes, you could… You had that potion…and you must be strong if the Wise King of the Forest obeys you. I'll do it. I'll hire you!"

"I see…and you're prepared to compensate me?"

"How much will it take?"

"Everything."

"What?"

"I'll take everything you have."

Lizzy's eyes grew wide and she shuddered.

"Everything you have. If Nfirea comes home safely, give me everything."

"You…," Lizzy murmured, backing away as if she were frightened. "You don't mean money or potions by this *everything* of yours, do you…? They say a demon can grant a wish in exchange for your soul. You're not demons, are you?"

"Even if we were, does it matter? You want to save your grandson, don't you?"

Lizzy said nothing, just nodded once, biting her lip.

"Then there's only one answer, right?"

"Yeah…I'll hire you. I'll give you everything I have. Save my grandson!"

"Okay, the deal is sealed, then. To get right down to business, do you have a map of the city? If you do, I want to borrow it."

She seemed dubious but went to get him a map right away.

"Okay, now we're going to find out where Nfirea is."

"You can do that?!"

"This time, I can. Either our enemies are idiots, or…" As his sentence trailed off, he looked at the four bodies. "Well, we're going to get things under way in here, so go look in the other rooms and see if you can find anything that might lead us to Nfirea's kidnappers. Things'll get hairy if this was just a diversion. Anyhow, this is your house, so you know it best."

Having made up some reason to get rid of Lizzy, Ainz watched her go and then turned to Narberal.

"What are you going to do?"

"It's simple. Look, their plates are gone. It was probably the kidnappers who took them. The question is, why would they take those when they didn't take any of the more valuable items? What do you think?"

"My apologies. I don't know."

"They're—"

"*Lord Ainz!*" A slightly shrill voice sounded in his head—and some kind of squeaking noise layered over it like a second audio track.

"Entoma?"

"*Yes, sir.*" Entoma Vasilissa Zeta was, like Narberal, one of the Pleiades. "*There's something I need to talk to you abou—*"

"I'm busy right now. I'll contact you when I get some time."

"*Understood. Then, please contact Mistress Albedo when you have time.*"

The spell vanished and Ainz continued his conversation with Narberal, who was looking at him curiously. "Trophies. They're hunting trophies. The criminals must have taken them as mementos. But that was a fatal mistake. Narberal, use this." He reached into an Infinity Haversack and pulled out a scroll. "It's Locate Object. I'm sure I don't have to tell you what we're looking for."

"Understood."

The moment she unrolled the scroll and was about to cast the spell, Ainz grabbed her hand. She was caught by surprise. "...You fool," he declared icily.

His level tone made her shoulders jump. "M-my apologies!"

"When you're using intelligence-gathering magic, preparing adequately to guard against your enemy's potential counterspells before casting is an iron rule. Considering your opponent could be using Detect Locate, protecting yourself with Fake Cover and Counter Detect is the most basic of the basics. Then you have—" Ainz had prepared ten scrolls. He went on to explain the rest of them to Narberal as if he were lecturing at a university.

When collecting intelligence using magic, it was necessary to take elaborate defensive measures. That was fundamental.

When Ainz Ooal Gown was going to PK someone, they first collected any information they could get about the player and then sneak-attacked to win in one fell swoop. That was their basic strategy, *No Fuss PK-ing*, developed by guild member Squishy Moe, who declared, "The battle is over before it begins!"

That was why Ainz was teaching Narberal now—so that in the future, when they encountered players, she would be able to fight with an advantage.

"—and that's it. Really, it's also basic to use skills for boosts and counters, as well, but we probably don't need to go that far against these guys. If they had casters able to do anything stronger than this, they wouldn't have cast such low-level spells on those corpses. Okay, Narberal, do it."

Finally free to act, Narberal unfurled each scroll in order, naming each spell as she went. The scrolls burst into heatless flames and burned up in a matter of seconds to release the magic sealed inside.

Once she had used them all and was protected by numerous defensive spells, she cast Locate Object. Then, she pointed at the map.

"They're here."

Ainz couldn't read what was written there, so he searched his memory to remember what was in that area. "…The graveyard? So there's a good chance it's not the sewers."

The graveyard in E-Rantel was in a league of hugeness all its own, partially because the city was used as a military base. The magic was pointing to the location farthest in.

"Okay, then next use Clairvoyance. Cast Crystal Monitor at the same time, and show me what's going on over there, too."

Narberal used the two scrolls, and they saw countless human figures on the screen that appeared in the air. But something was strange about the way they were moving—many of them were jerking awkwardly. There were also countless figures that were definitely not human.

And in the center of it all was a boy. He was dressed differently, but there was still no mistaking him.

"Got him. And the plates are in this area… An undead mob, huh?"

The place was occupied by a huge swarm of undead. They were all lower tier, but there were lots of them.

"…What will you do? Should we teleport in to attack all at once? Or take them by storm from the air with Fly?"

"Yeah, sure, we can wrap it up on the down low—don't be stupid." Narberal looked confused, so he explained. "They have this huge mob of undead, so they must be trying to do something big. If we can put a stop to that while saving Nfirea, it'll be great for our reputation. If we deal with this in secret, all we're likely to get is the reward from Lizzy."

Of course, if they didn't deal with it as soon as possible, Nfirea could be killed. Even Ainz couldn't summon and control that many undead at once, so there had to be some trick to it. *Maybe it's somehow dependent on Nfirea's life?* But if that were the case, then he wanted to know that trick, even if it meant sacrificing Nfirea. Ainz was most concerned with strengthening the Great Tomb of Nazarick. If letting Nfirea die would benefit Nazarick, he would choose that.

"Well, we can't gather much more intelligence as we are, and it would take too long anyways…," Ainz murmured as he proceeded to the door. Flinging it open, he shouted, "Lizzy! We're done! And we're going to the graveyard!"

"What about the sewers?!" she screamed from somewhere, and they could hear her footsteps rushing over.

"They were just misleading us. Their real aim was the graveyard. And as a bonus, there's an undead army numbering easily in the thousands."

"What!"

He'd just taken a guess. It wasn't like he was going to count them all.

"Don't be so surprised. We're going to break through. The problem is what happens if the undead overflow the graveyard. Please tell as many people about this as possible, that we need people to stop them as they start escaping. It's not a very convincing story, but you're famous here, so people will listen to you, right? If the undead overflow the graveyard and no one is ready for them…there'll be trouble."

Ainz frowned under his helmet. He needed people to make a fuss. The bigger the fuss, the better his reputation would get at the end. Telling her to spread the word was a strategic move.

"That's enough chitchat. Time is running out, so we're leaving."

"Do you have a way to break through the undead army?!"

Ainz looked calmly at Lizzy and pointed at the great swords on his back. "…It's right here, isn't it?"

3

Taking up about a quarter of the area inside E-Rantel's outermost wall in a huge block that occupied most of the western district was the E-Rantel Public Cemetery. Of course, other cities had cemeteries, but not as gigantic as this one. They needed it to prevent undead from spawning.

How undead spawned was still a mystery in many ways, but they often appeared, with their impure "life," in places where a living thing had met its end. If the person died a tragic death or went unmourned, the chances of undead appearing were much higher. For that reason it was very common for them to spawn in ruins or places where battles had been fought.

Since E-Rantel was close to the sites of the battles with the empire, they needed to build a huge cemetery—a place to mourn—so that their dead wouldn't turn undead.

This went for the empire as well, so the two sides arranged it so that even though they were at war with each other, they would both make sure the other could properly mourn their dead. Even if they were killing each other on the battlefield, they knew that the undead who attacked the living out of hatred were the common enemy of all life.

There was another problem with undead. If they were left alone, the probability that a stronger undead would spawn went up. That's why adventurers and guards swept the graveyard every night and took out any undead while they were still just lower tier.

The graveyard was surrounded by a wall. It was the boundary between the world of the living and the world of the dead. At about thirteen feet, it wasn't as tall as the city walls, but it was fairly thick, and it was possible to walk along the top. The gates were sturdy, too. This was all as a precaution against the undead that spawned inside.

Flanking the gates were staircases that led to lookouts. Five men to a side exchanged yawns while keeping watch.

Although it was nighttime, light posts lit with Continual Light kept the place bright. That said, there were still pockets of darkness here and there, and gravestones impeded visibility.

One guard with a spear, gazing absentmindedly out over the cemetery, said to the fellow next to him through a yawn, "Quiet night."

"Yeah. Just those five skeletons so far? Seems like the spawn rate went way down all of a sudden."

"Yeah. Maybe everyone's souls were called to be with the Four Gods. If so, we lucked out!"

The other guards joined in.

"As long as it's skeletons and zombies, we can handle 'em...although skeletons are a pain to get with spears..."

"The worst one I ever saw was a wight."

"Mine's a skeleton centipede. If the adventurer on guard nearby hadn't run over I'd a been a goner."

"A skeleton centipede? The ugly ones only come out if you overlook weak ones. Just wipe 'em out while they're wimpy, and we won't have to deal with the strong ones."

"Exactly! The liquor the squad patrolling the tombs sent us the other week after our leader gave them what for tasted great, but I never want to go through an ordeal like that ever again."

"But when you think about it like that...doesn't it kinda give you the creeps that nothing has spawned lately?"

"Why?"

"Well, like, maybe we're missing them or something..."

"You worry too much. Supposedly there aren't usually that many to begin with. There's talk that the reason we had such a high rate of appearance was because we were burying people who died in battles against the empire. In other words, maybe this is what it's like when there's no fighting."

The guards nodded at one another. Villages buried people just like they did, but they'd never heard of a place with so many undead.

"Supposedly the Katze Plain is just a mess."

"Yeah, the undead that spawn there are on a whole 'nother level."

The plain where the kingdom and the empire clashed was known as a region with frequent undead outbreaks, so adventurers requested by the kingdom and knights from the empire worked together to clean it up. Sweeping the area was so important that the kingdom and empire both sent goods to maintain a little town built out there to support the people suppressing the undead.

"I heard a rumor that—" one of the guards started to say and then closed his mouth.

One of the others got anxious. "Hey, if you're trying to scare us—"

"Quiet!" The one who had closed his mouth was looking toward the graveyard as if he could pierce the darkness if he stared hard enough. The others followed his line of sight and looked, too.

"...Do you hear something?"

"Probably just your imagination."

"Nah, I don't hear anything, but it smells kinda like dirt. Like when we had to dig that one time? It smells like that."

"Okay, not funny. Cut it out."

"...Huh? Ah, hey! Look over there!"

One of the guards pointed out into the graveyard. Everyone turned to look.

Two guards were running frantically toward the gate. They were both breathing heavily, eyes wide and bloodshot, hair plastered to their foreheads with sweat.

The guards in the lookout had a bad feeling. Patrols went out in groups of at least ten. Why were there only two? Running that desperately with no weapons, they could only be running *away* from something.

"O-open up! Open the gate!"

A guard ran down the stairs in response to their panicked screams and opened the gate. The pair tumbled out of the graveyard as if they couldn't wait for the door to open. "What the heck—?" the guard started to ask, but the two patrollers, faces white as sheets, interrupted him, shouting with what little breath they had left.

"C-close the gate! Hurry!"

Frightened by how upset they were, the guards all helped shut and bar the gate.

"What the heck happened?! Where are the others?"

The guard who looked up to respond had terror written all over his face. "Th-they were eaten! By undead!"

Learning that eight of their comrades had been killed, the guards looked at their squad leader. He responded with orders.

"...Hey, someone go look from up top!"

One of them sprang up and started running up the stairs but froze partway.

"Wh-what's wrong?"

Trembling uncontrollably, the guard screamed back, "It's undead! A huge mob of them!"

If they listened closely, they could hear a kind of squirming noise coming from the other side of the wall. Everyone followed the first guard, and one by one they were rendered speechless by the view.

A number of undead for which there were no words was coming across the graveyard, heading straight for them.

"What the heck? How are there so many...?"

"It's not even a hundred or two... There's gotta be...at least a thousand?"

There were so many even just in the areas the light reached that they couldn't count them. Figuring in the human shapes wriggling in the darkness, their number was unfathomable.

The undead shuffled their swaying way toward the gate in a horde, accompanied by the smell of rot. Among them were not only skeletons and zombies but also stronger undead—though not as many—such as ghouls, ghasts, wights, swollskins, and corrupt dead.

All the guards were shaking now.

The city proper was behind another wall, so unless that was breached, no residents would be attacked. But they weren't sure they could take this mob, even if they called for a general mobilization of all the guards. They may have been called "guards," but they were just burlier versions of regular citizens. They weren't confident they could subdue this many undead.

And some undead possessed the ability to turn anything they killed into the same type of monster. One wrong move and they'd be getting attacked by their undead comrades. On top of that, there weren't any flying ones now, but they knew that if they didn't wipe these out soon, some fiendish fliers would show up, and that terrified them even more.

The flood of undead reached the wall.

Bam-bam…

Undead with low intelligence made use of their inability to feel pain to senselessly beat on the gate. They must have known they'd get to attack some living things if they broke it down.

Bam-bam…

The repeated pounding sound, the squeaking of the hinges, the moaning of countless monsters.

They didn't need a battering ram. The mob of undead that rushed the gate without even considering if they could break it or not performed as well as any siege weapon.

The cold sweat that drenched the guards' backs when they saw that was like a bucket of ice water.

"Ring the bell! Get help from the garrison! You two, alert the other gates that this is an emergency!" The squad leader returned to his senses and started commanding. "The rest of you, use your spears to stab the undead near the gate from above!"

His voice reminded the guards what they were supposed to be doing, and they began plunging their spears into the throng of undead below. There were so many they couldn't even see the ground. They could stab at random and still skewer one. Thrust, wind up, thrust again.

Murky blood spilled, the reek of decomposing bodies numbed the guards' noses, and the repetitiveness of their frantic motions made them feel almost like zombies themselves. Several undead lost their un-lives, tumbled to the ground, and were trampled by the ones behind them.

Since they were so lacking in intelligence, they didn't even try to counterattack. Lulled by the repetitive task, the guards gradually began to relax.

But just as if the monsters had been waiting for that to happen—

"Wah!" Someone screamed, and when the others turned to look, one of the guards had something long wrapped and wriggling around his neck.

It had a slimy pink gleam to it—intestines. At the other end was an egg-shaped, yet human, corpse with its front split wide open vertically. Inside the gaping cavity were more entrails than one person could ever possibly have, writhing like parasitic worms. It was an undead called an organ egg.

The squirming intestines yanked on the guard. "Yaaagh!" Faster than anyone could move to save him, he yelped and fell. "H-help! Someone! Aaarghghyaa!" he shrieked at the top of his lungs.

The other guards had no choice but to witness their comrade's fate. Undead piled onto every part of his body and began to eat him alive. The armor protecting his torso and the efforts he made to protect his head only prolonged the brutality. First his fingers went, then his calves, then his face was chewed apart…

"Fall back! Retreat behind the wall!" ordered the squad leader, seeing that the organ egg's innards were wriggling again.

Everyone rushed down the stairs. The pounding behind them grew stronger, and the screeches made it plain that the door was about to give.

The sense of tragedy gradually mounted. It didn't seem very likely that the door would hold until reinforcements arrived, and the undead that appeared would only grow stronger. If the gate opened, a torrent of death would come flooding out and who knew how much damage would be done?

The moment all the guards' faces had turned a sickly shade of despair, a metallic clank sounded. Everyone instinctively turned to see where it had come from.

It was a warrior in full plate armor astride a magical beast with wise black eyes. Next to him was a woman so pretty she looked out of place.

"H-hey! It's dangerous here! Hurry up and—" Having said that much, the guard noticed the metal plate hanging from the warrior's neck.

An adventurer!

But when he saw that it was copper, his slightly raised hopes deflated. *There's no way an adventurer of the lowest possible rank will be able to turn this situation around!* Disappointment shone in all the guards' eyes.

The warrior sprang lightly off the beast, as if he didn't weigh a thing.

"Didn't you hear me? Get away from here!"

"Nabe, my swords." The warrior's voice was soft compared to the guard's yell, but strangely, it could be heard clearly over the symphony of noise the undead were making. The beautiful woman ran over to him, and the warrior drew a great sword.

"Hey, look behind you. Better watch out!"

The guards whipped around as if repelled by the sound of the warrior's voice and faced The End.

A shadow loomed taller than the thirteen-foot wall. Countless corpses had gathered together to form an undead titan, a necroswarm giant.

"Wahhhh!" As the guards screamed and went to flee, every man for himself, an unexpected scene unfolded before their eyes.

The warrior held his sword like he was about to throw a javelin.

To do what?

The next moment answered that question. He threw it and at an unbelievable speed. Turning quickly back around to watch where it flew, they saw something even more unexpected.

The necroswarm giant—a colossal undead monster they would have never thought could be beaten—got knocked back as if it had taken a blow from an even bigger giant; it was defeated. As proof the giant had fallen, a colossal *thud* sounded over the squirming noises.

"That thing was in my way," was all he said before striding forward with his other sword drawn. "Open the gate."

For a moment the guards didn't realize what he'd said. They blinked a few times, and the warrior's words finally sank into their brains.

"D-don't be stupid! There's a huge mob of undead on the other side!"

"Oh? The name's Momon. Does that have anything to do with me?"

The guards were all overawed by the black warrior's overflowing confidence and couldn't say anything.

"...Well, if you don't want to open the gate, I guess I can't blame you. I'll just let myself in." The warrior took a running start, kicked off the cobblestones, and vanished over the wall. He'd leaped over a thirteen-foot wall in a single bound—while wearing full plate armor.

Were they seeing things?

Unable to process what had just happened, they all stared gape-mouthed at the space where no one was standing anymore.

The beautiful woman who was left behind floated lightly into the air and was about to soar over the wall when a voice called out to stop her.

"Please wait, that I beg you! Take me, too, that I ask!" The voice's owner was the robust magical beast the warrior had been riding. She sounded just as dignified as she looked.

The beautiful woman frowned slightly—not that it compromised her beauty one bit—and told the beast, "...Take those stairs. Don't tell me you're gonna break your legs falling from that height."

"Of course not! Then away to my master's side I go! Master, wait for me, that I ask!" The huge magical beast scampered past the guards, agilely ascended the stairs, and jumped down to the other side of the wall.

Then it was silent.

It was as if a typhoon had gone by. How long did they stand there, dumbfounded? Then one guard realized something and said, his voice trembling, "Hey... Can you hear it?"

"What?"

"The noises the undead were making."

Even if they strained their ears, they couldn't hear a sound; silence had swallowed them up. All the pounding on the door had stopped.

Awestruck, the shivering guard murmured, "Wow, can you believe it? That warrior...went in there against all those undead...and he actually broke through the mob...and is still going."

The guards were overcome by amazement and admiration. The reason the noises had stopped was that all the undead in the area had been drawn away toward a new target. And the reason the noises didn't return was that the battle was still ongoing, so the undead hadn't come back.

The guards ran to the top of the wall in disbelief. Could this be real? They gasped.

"What…! That warrior, what the…?"

There were bodies everywhere. A mountain of them. There were so many corpses lying around that the guards couldn't see the ground. Some of them, twitching, hadn't completely lost their negative life, but none were able to fight.

As they thought, the sounds of a far-off battle drifted over on the putrid-smelling breeze.

"You gotta be kidding me… He's still fighting?! He made an enemy of that whole mob…and broke through?! There's no way…"

"Who the heck is that guy?!"

"…He said his name was Momon, right? That copper plate has to be a lie, right? He's gotta be one of those adamantite plates you hear rumors of, don't ya think?"

Everyone nodded to someone's muttering. There was no way that was a copper-plate adventurer. He was a hero who had to have the highest-ranking plate. That was all they could think.

"We may have just seen a legend… The Dark Warrior… No, the Dark Hero…"

The others all nodded in agreement.

•

Every time his right arm moved, undead went flying. Every time his left arm moved, undead were sliced in two.

Ainz had advanced like a tornado of one-hit death, but now he stopped. "You guys are such a pain." Holding both great swords he'd remade with magic, he scanned the crowd of undead surrounding him with fed-up eyes. He addressed his sword, grimy with bodily fluids, to the monsters.

With a flurry of flinches, the undead tried to squirm away from him.

Undead shouldn't have been able to feel fear, but they sure seemed scared of Ainz.

"...I apologize for the trouble, that I do." The voice came from above Ainz—quite a ways above. The Wise King of the Forest was floating floppily, four legs splayed, in the air. Her hair drooped and her voice was cheerless.

The one she was apologizing to wasn't Ainz. "Could you...not move around? You're so soft and fluffy it's hard to hold you." Narberal's voice came from somewhere around the Wise King of the Forest's belly. It wasn't the king who was flying—Narberal, half sunk into her squishy body, was holding her up using Fly.

"I'm sorry, that I am..."

The lower-tier undead with their subpar intelligence didn't immediately treat Ainz as an enemy. Their senses were keenly attuned to *life*, so they took Ainz to be one of them.

But they weren't going to miss the *living* Wise King of the Forest. As a result, Ainz was drawn into a brawl, and to avoid the albeit medium-low possibility that the beast would be injured, Narberal had to heft her out of the undead's reach.

Ainz took a step forward. The undead mob took a step back. The distance between them didn't change one bit, and the circle remained intact.

The circle moved according to how Ainz moved. They seemed to be looking for openings to attack, but if they set one foot inside the circle, they'd be destroyed in one hit. That's why they simply encircled him and none were attacking. It was the result of the low-intelligence monsters finally learning, after a ridiculous amount of repetition, that they would be annihilated if they made a careless approach.

"But I'm not going to get anywhere at this rate..." Ainz was only grumbling about the annoying amount of undead still remaining. If he were to make a serious attempt at getting by, he'd plow right through this mob. But if he barreled ahead and the undead spread out, the guards back there might be killed. If that happened he would lose the witnesses who would testify that he resolved the incident; to minimally guarantee their safety, he needed to draw off at least a good chunk of the monsters. It did slow his progress, though.

But Narberal took his comment at face value. "Then let's call the army from Nazarick, my lord. With a hundred minions or so we could eliminate all in this graveyard who oppose you in the blink of an eye."

"…Don't be stupid. How many times do I have to tell you the reason we came to this city?"

"But Lord Ainz, if your aim is to gain a reputation, would it perhaps not be better to wait until the undead had breached the gate and racked up scores of human casualties?"

"I've already considered that. If I were well-informed as to the aim of our enemy, the war potential of this city, and so on, I may have taken that route, but as it is, we know barely anything, so I'd like to avoid losing any more initiative. I don't want things going according to their plan. It's also possible that another team would swoop in to steal our show while we were standing around."

"I see… Brilliant, Lord Ainz. I should have expected that a Supreme Being would have thought everything out. I'm struck anew by admiration. By the way, I apologize for still being so ignorant, but I wonder if you might tell me if you don't think that sending in some minions who specialize in stealth abilities, like eight-edged assassins or shadow demons, would have been a better plan? Then you could just stand back and watch the fight, unless anything major changed, to gauge the best timing…"

Ainz said nothing and just looked up at her. The undead took the silence as lowered guard and stepped into the circle. And were hastily cut down. "…I-if I tell you everything, how will you ever learn to think for yourself?"

"Yes, sir! My humble apologies!"

Shaken, albeit slightly, Ainz whipped around to see how far from the gate they had come and to check if the guards could see them. "But! That said, time is short. I have no choice—I'll have these guys slice through for us."

Ainz unleashed a power. "Create Middle-Tier Undead: Jack the Ripper,

Create Middle-Tier Undead: Corpse Collector." As the skill was used, two undead appeared.

One wore a trench coat and had its face covered with a laughing mask. Its fingers turned into oversize, sharp scalpels partway through.

The other had a robust enough physique, but its body was covered in pus and wrapped in yellowed bandages. At the ends of chains anchored to its flesh by several hooks were moaning skulls.

"Get 'em."

Taking Ainz's order, the two undead sprang at the surrounding monsters. There were only two of them, but their power was overwhelming. While the Jack the Ripper sliced off limbs with its scalpels and the corpse collector ripped off heads with its chains, Ainz took an added measure.

"Those plus these should be good. Create Lower-Tier Undead: Wraith, Create Lower-Tier Undead: Bone Vulture." He summoned a few of each and gave them all orders. "If anyone enters this graveyard, chase them out. I don't care if you kill adventurers, but leave the guards."

The wraiths drifted into the air, and the bone vultures flapped their bone wings. Ainz chuckled to himself in satisfaction that his preparation was complete. He'd dispatched the lower-tier undead to make sure that no adventurers stole this great job out from under them by using flight magic to swoop in and defeat the ringleader.

"Now, then, shall we?" Thanks to the two undead Ainz had sent out, the mob had thinned out quite a bit. Ainz gripped his swords and jumped in.

Accompanied only by Narberal, Ainz reached the mausoleum farthest back and saw a group of suspicious-looking people doing something in a circle outside. The black robes concealing each member were not dyed very well, so there were patches of lighter and darker areas. Black triangular caps covered their heads except for the eyes. A strange pattern was carved into the ends of the wooden staves they held. The figures were all different heights, but judging by their silhouettes, they were all male.

Only one man, standing in the middle of the circle and looking a bit like an undead himself, had his face uncovered; the impression he made was not so shabby. In his hand he clutched a black stone, and it seemed like he was focusing his spirit on it.

The wind carried the sound of undulating murmurs to where Ainz stood; sometimes they were high-pitched, sometimes low. The harmonizing undertones sounded almost like a prayer, but this was no solemn service for the dead. It was more like some kind of blasphemous, evil ritual.

"Should we launch a sneak attack?" Narberal spoke softly so only Ainz could hear, but he shook his head.

"That won't work. It seems like they've already noticed us." Because neither of them had stealth skills, they walked right over. They'd avoided the lights, but if their opponents had Night Vision, they'd be able to spot them as if it were the middle of the day. And in Ainz's experience, there was a mental connection between summoned monsters and the summoner. There was no way their approach hadn't been sensed after they'd killed that many.

There were actually a few people looking right at them. Ainz guessed the reason they didn't attack immediately was that he wasn't the only one who wanted to talk, so they walked straight toward them.

When they reached the light, the members of the group braced themselves, and one of them spoke to the man in the center. "Lord Khajit, they're here."

Welp, now we know they're idiots… Or I guess it could be a fake name. I'll take it with a grain of salt. "Hey there, isn't it kind of a waste to perform a boring ritual on such a beautiful night?"

"Hmph, I'm the one who decides what night is appropriate for a ritual. More importantly, who are you? How did you break through that mob of undead?" The man in the center of the circle—Khajit, if it wasn't a fake name—did seem to be the highest-ranking one among them and addressed Ainz on behalf of the group.

"I'm an adventurer who undertook a request. I'm looking for a certain boy… I'm sure I don't even have to say his name for you to know who I mean." As the members of the group shifted into subtly more defensive positions, Ainz whispered, "Okay, then," under his breath. The possibility that they were innocents who had just gotten mixed up in the incident vanished.

As Khajit scanned the area, Ainz smiled wryly at him from under his helmet.

"Are you the only ones? Any others?"

Ha-ha, what? Who asks that? I get that you're worried about an ambush, but maybe you should think a little more before you start chitchatting. This guy must just be another pawn. Ainz seemed to have lost interest, and his shoulders slumped. Then he replied, "It's just us. We flew in a straight shot."

"That's a lie. That can't be."

Sensing something in those words of conviction, Ainz countered, "Whether you believe it or not is up to you. More pertinently, if you return the boy unharmed, you won't have to die, Khajit."

Khajit glanced at the foolish disciple who'd said his name. "What's your name?"

"Tell me something first. There's someone besides you guys, isn't there?"

Khajit shot Ainz an icy stare.

"We're it."

"It's not just you guys! You must have someone with a stabbing weapon…so you're trying to hide him? Or is *he* hiding because he's scared of us?"

Suddenly a woman's voice came from inside the mausoleum. "Aha, so you investigated those corpses, I seeee. Nicely done." She slowly moved into view, jangling with each step.

"You—"

She heard the harshness in his voice and smiled guiltily. "Ehhh, they figured it out already. There's no point in hiding. Plus, I can't use Conceal Life, so I really was just hiding."

Even though Ainz had told them what he was after, they weren't holding Nfirea for ransom. He was considering the possibility that he'd already been killed when the woman spoke to him.

"So, hey, can I get your name, Mr. Guy? Oh, I'm Clementine. Nice to meet ya."

"…I don't think there's any point in you hearing it, but it's Momon."

"I've never heard of him…have you?"

"I dunno him, either. I collected all the info on high-ranking adventurers in this town, but there was no Momon. How'd ya even find this place? I left ya those dying words about the sewers!"

"The answer is under your cape. Let's see it."

"Whoa, pervert! You dirty lech." Having said that much, her face twisted into a grin that sliced across her face ear to ear. "Just kidding. You mean these?"

Clementine flipped open her cape to reveal something that looked like gleaming scale armor. But Ainz, with his superior vision, saw what it was right away. Those were not the tabs of metal used to make scale armor.

She was wearing countless adventurer plates: platinum, gold, silver, iron, copper. There were sparkles of mythril and orichalcum among them. These were the marks of all the adventurers she had killed, her hunting trophies.

The rubbing of metal on metal was almost like innumerable resentful voices.

"Those told us where you were."

Clementine pulled a face that said she had no idea what he was talking about, but Ainz wasn't in an explaining mood.

"...Nabe, you take Khajit and the rest of those men. I'll get this lady." Then he dropped his voice and told her to keep her eye on the sky.

"Understood."

Khajit's face was something between a bitter smile and a sneer.

Narberal shot him a chilly look that implied how bored she would be.

"Clementine, how about we go kill each other over there?" He strolled away without even waiting for her response. He was sure she wouldn't object, and the footsteps following leisurely after him confirmed it.

After they'd taken some distance, an explosion of lightning flooded the area near Khajit and Narberal with a blinding glare. As if that was their cue, Ainz and Clementine stared each other down.

"So were the adventurers I killed in that shop your friends? Are ya mad 'cause I killed your buddies?!" She continued in her mocking tone, "Ah-ha-ha-ha! That caster really cracked me up—believing to the very end that someone would come. There was no way to survive my attacks until help arrived with *that* flimsy physique! ...But maybe you were the one who was supposed to save them? Sorry—killed 'em all!"

Ainz shook his head in response to Clementine's taunting laughter. "Eh, there's not really any need to apologize."

"Oh? Bummer. Getting people who are all pissed, like, *How could you?!* to surrender is hilarious! Why aren't you mad? That's no fun! They weren't your friends?"

"...I might have done something similar under certain circumstances, so it'd be pretty hypocritical to come down on you for it." Ainz slowly moved into a fighting stance. "However, they *were* tools I was using to build my reputation. They were supposed to gossip about my exploits to other adventurers when we got back to the inn—about how I'm a hero who, with just one other party member, repulsed the Wise King of the Forest. The fact that you upset my plans is extremely displeasing to me."

Perhaps picking something up from his tone of voice, Clementine grinned. "I see. *Oh noooo, you hate meee!* By the way, coming over here was a mistake. That pretty lady's a caster, right? Then she'll never beat Khaj. Maybe if the pairings had been reversed she'd've had a chance, but... Well, nah, she wouldn't be able to beat me, either!"

"Oh, I'm pretty sure Nabe could beat you."

"Don't be ridiculous! A caster couldn't win against me! I just swoop in and *shoonk*! That's how it ends! Always is!"

"Ah, so you're a very confident warrior, then..."

"Ya, of course. There aren't any warriors in this country who can beat me! Well, almost none, anyway!"

"Okay, then, I have an idea. I'll give you a handicap. That'll be my revenge on you."

Clementine narrowed her eyes; it was the first time she looked uncomfortable. "According to the intelligence gathered by the Flurry gang, there are only five people who could put up a decent fight against me: Gazef Stronoff, Gagaran from the Blue Roses, Louisenberg Arbelion from the Drops of Red, and then Brain Unglaus, and Vesture Kloff Di Laufen, who's retired. But ya know, they don't really have a chance—even if I did throw away the magic item my country gave me..." She looked at Ainz with her lips drawn so far back her smile was disturbing. "I dunno what kinda piece of shit ya got for a face under that helmet, but Clementine doesn't lose! I've entered the hero realm!"

Compared to Clementine's fury, Ainz was infinitely calm. "That's why I'm giving you a handicap. I refuse to take you seriously."

4

"Twin Max Electrosphere!" Two electrospheres double their normal size appeared in the palms of Narberal's outstretched hands. She fired them simultaneously.

—Impact.

The electrospheres with increased destructive power swelled to scatter their electric shocks over a huge area. The graveyard was illuminated with a dazzling white light. The magic shocks disappeared a moment later, but their destruction was absolute. Khajit's underlings were all sprawled on the ground. In their midst stood a single shadow.

"Argh. If only you were as easy to squash as the caterpillar you are... Did you cast Electric Energy Immunity or something?" As soon as she asked, she noticed a scorch mark on his cheek. That meant it must have been something weaker than Electric Energy Immunity, maybe Electric Energy Protection.

Narberal was a little disappointed she hadn't wiped them all out in one shot but comforted herself by deciding the offense was forgivable. Besides, ending it all at once would be no fun.

"So you're not just an idiot, you're an idiot who can use tier-three magic!"

"...An idiot? A human mite like you dares to call me an idiot?!" Her eyebrows twitched.

"What's wrong with me calling the fool interfering in my plan an idiot?! But you're going to be dead before you can even recognize my strength for what it is! My preparations are already complete! I've gathered enough negative energy—behold the power of this supreme jewel!" Khajit held up the stone in his hand.

It was a plain jewel with a gleam like black iron, neither polished nor cut. *Raw ore* were probably the words that came closest to describing it. Narberal thought she saw it pulse.

Suddenly, six of the leading disciples who should have been burned to a crisp sluggishly stood up. These motions were not willed by life but ruled by death. They moved on unsteady feet to stand between Narberal and Khajit.

Narberal looked on quizzically. "You're making me fight *zombies?*"

"Wa-ha-ha-ha-ha! That's exactly what I'm doing. That will do! Attack!"

Zombies were the lowest tier of undead and had no magic ability. The former leading disciples came clawing at her, but she cast a spell. "Electrosphere!"

Another sphere of white light scattered shocks throughout the area, swallowing up all of the leading disciples. When the electric flash died down, the disciples collapsed to the ground once again. Although she had mopped them all up with ease, Narberal's face was somber.

Create Undead didn't have the power to turn multiple corpses into undead at once. *Did he use some kind of supporting skill?* Her eyes flicked to the black lump in his hand. It was probably that item that allowed him to create and control multiple zombies at once.

Wasn't that language a bit presumptuous for such a wimpy effect? The Forty-One Supreme Beings who ruled the Great Tomb of Nazarick and created Narberal and the other NPCs were the ones worthy of the word *supreme.*

Those were the unpleasant things on Narberal's mind when Khajit shouted with joy. "That's plenty! I've absorbed enough negative energy!"

The black lump in Khajit's hand looked like it was absorbing the darkness of the graveyard and giving off a faint glow, and it was pulsing more obviously than before, beating quietly like a heart.

There'll be trouble if I let him do much more, Narberal decided. Just as she was about to make her move, she heard something—something slicing through the air. Remembering her master's words, she jumped clear.

Something enormous buzzed the spot where she'd been standing before pulling up to hover in front of Khajit and landing slowly.

It was an agglomeration of human bones around ten feet tall. Made up of countless pieces, the form it took on had a long neck, four legs, and wings—a dragon. Its tail, composed of innumerable bones, gave the ground a heavy whack. It was a monster called a skeletal dragon.

Level-wise, it wasn't so strong compared to Narberal, but it did have one trait that was potentially fatal for Nabe. For the first time in this fight, her face registered surprise and annoyance.

"Wa-ha-ha-ha-ha!" Khajit's unhinged laugh echoed throughout the area. "Skeletal dragons have absolute resistance to magic! Casters are helpless against them!"

Nabe's magic wouldn't be able to do anything against the skeletal dragon. *In that case—*

She took out the sword her master had instructed her to carry, still in its sheath. The sword was bound to the sheath with a cord, so it wouldn't come out so easily.

"—I'll clobber it to death!" She charged.

The dragon tried to counter by stomping with its front legs, but she slipped neatly past them. Her hair waving in the gust of air created by the attack, she dove for its chest. She took a focused swing using every muscle in her body.

The skeletal dragon may have been ten feet tall, but it went flying. A moment later the vibrations of its impact reached them with a giant thud.

"What?!" Khajit was astounded.

Skeletal dragons were lighter than they looked, since they were made of bone. *That's still* lighter, *though.* Knocking it back was not the type of feat a caster who had spent their days in the pursuit of magical-type magic should be able to perform.

Hastily moving behind the skeletal dragon for cover, Khajit screamed, "Wh-who are you?! A mythril—no, orichalcum—adventurer?! I didn't think there were any in this city—are you after Clementine?!" He gnashed his teeth so hard it seemed like they would break.

Narberal sighed. "It's 'cause you get all worked up like that that you're a click beetle!"

"Wh-why you—" He'd used up a huge amount of negative energy and spent two months performing a huge ritual to create this skeletal dragon. Was it going to be defeated this easily? In the final stretch of his multiple-year plan?

As Khajit's face grew blotchy with rage, the skeletal dragon slowly creaked and squeaked its way to its feet. There were large cracks in the bones making up its chest, and broken pieces were crumbling out. He couldn't let her hit it again.

"No! You can't! I won't let you! Ray of Negative Energy!" A black beam shot out of Khajit's hand and hit the skeletal dragon, rapidly healing the wounds with negative energy.

"You were talking so big about its absolute resistance to magic, but you can still use magic to heal it, huh?"

Khajit ignored her quip and cast a series of spells. "Reinforce Armor! Lesser Strength! Undead Flames! Shield Wall!" All of them were buffs for the skeletal dragon. Its bones grew harder, its strength was magically increased, and its body was enveloped in black flames that would drain life energy. Then, an invisible wall formed to cover one side of its body like a shield.

"Two can play at that game! Reinforce Armor! Shield Wall! Negative Energy Protection!" Narberal cast a handful of defensive spells.

Once they had both protected themselves well enough, they returned to fighting as if the bell for round two had rung.

Narberal brandished her sword. While beating on the skeletal dragon's front legs, she furrowed her brow. Things had gone well before, but she couldn't call the present situation good. She wasn't built for physical clashes, and her weapon was lousy.

Since the dragon was made of bones, stabbing and cutting weapons didn't do much damage. A battering weapon would've been the most effective, but Narberal didn't have one. That's why she was using her sheath. But although she was on the offensive, she wasn't balanced well when she swung, so it didn't seem like she was dealing damage very effectively. An actual warrior might be able to keep their balance, but Narberal was a caster—she wasn't performing very well in that department.

The skeletal dragon swung a front leg and missed as Narberal ducked. Part of her caught the dragon's black flames, but Negative Energy Protection blocked them and they disappeared immediately. If she hadn't defended herself, she would've probably taken damage despite dodging the attack.

"Ray of Negative Energy!" Khajit sent a beam to heal the dragon's wounds.

This was another cause of Narberal's brow furrowing. Even if she managed to hurt the monster, Khajit would just heal it from his position in the rear. Why didn't she attack Khajit first? She couldn't because of the skeletal dragon he'd stuck right between them.

Even if she used a piercing spell like Lightning, the dragon's absolute magic resistance would block it. An area-of-effect spell like Electrosphere would have almost no effect because of the defensive spells Khajit had cast. *Then how about mind control?* Barring resistance, it would let her win in one shot.

"Charm Person!"

"Undead Mind!"

Narberal and Khajit both cast at the same time—Narberal, a spell that would charm humans on Khajit; Khajit, a defensive spell that would block psychic magic on himself. The result? Khajit flashed a triumphant smile, and Narberal frowned and practically clicked her tongue in disgust.

Was she too distracted by Khajit's smile? A shadow fell over her face.

Her entire field of vision was taken up by a white mass.

Evasion seems difficult.

Her mind was immediately racing—she brought the point of her sheathed sword to her opposite shoulder and held the whole thing across her body like a shield. The impact sent numbing vibrations through the sword to her hands, shoulders, and whole body—which went soaring into the air. A tail attack aimed right at her face had sent her flying.

"Hup, okay." Balance intact, Narberal nimbly landed on her feet and retreated farther away.

It would have been the perfect time for the skeletal dragon to follow up its attack, but it didn't. It had to protect Khajit, so it couldn't stray too far. Keeping an eye on the dragon, Narberal tried to shake the numbness and pain out of her trembling hands.

Then, Khajit peeked out from behind the monster. "Acid Javelin!"

"Lightning!"

His green spear went flying straight at Narberal. Normally she would have been wounded by the spray of acid, but it was repelled a couple inches away from her body and disappeared. At the same time, the bolt of lightning that sprang from Narberal's finger was nullified when the skeletal dragon moved to block it.

The two adversaries glared at each other.

"…You cast a defensive spell? What a pain."

"…A pain? That's my line, bagworm moth. Why don't you quit hiding and come out here?"

"Why should I have to do that?"

"Won't your plan go haywire if you're tied up fighting?"

She was right. Khajit narrowed his glare while Narberal just smiled.

"…I see I have no choice." Having made up his mind, Khajit squeezed the strange sphere once again. Then, he held it up high. "Behold the power of the Jewel of Death!"

Narberal lost her balance—proof that the ground was shaking. It was a sign that something big had arrived. A moment later, the ground cracked open and something white slowly climbed out.

"…Another one?"

"Hmm! I'm already out of negative energy. But if I kill you and your friend and then spread death throughout town, I should be able to get quite a bit back!"

Narberal was unfazed, but Khajit was yelling furiously. She exhaled sharply and broke into a run—a run far faster than any normal person could run. Khajit was caught off guard and didn't have time to react.

As Narberal entered the skeletal dragon's range, it tried to attack her with its front legs. She twisted her body to slip past the stomps on her right, but then the other dragon's tail came to sweep her feet out from under her.

She jumped clear and not a second too soon. Right below her, the tail plowed noisily through the spot she'd been standing. Then, it changed directions and whipped into the air to swing down at her.

The tail strike shook the ground, but Narberal had managed to dodge to the left, except the dragon on the right closed in to hit her with a front leg.

"Guh!" She took the forceful hit with her sword. It was *not* very light, but she stopped the foot and then shoved it back. The attacking skeletal dragon retreated, creating another brief interlude in the fighting.

"What are you?! To be able to block those attacks without using a martial art… How did you get so strong?"

"I was created by Supreme Beings whose powers surpass even the gods!"

"I won't buy that, you idiot!"

"You can't recognize the truth when you hear it and call *me* an idiot? This is why humans are nothing more than planarians!" Narberal flashed her eyes at Khajit.

It was such a strong gaze that it gave him the chills, and he took a step back. As if to shake himself free of his fear, he gave an order. "Get her, skeletal dragons!"

The dragons, maintaining proximity to Khajit, attacked Narberal again. She dodged one blow and tried to move in but lost her chance while evading a second. In the midst of that back-and-forth, Khajit made a decisive strike.

"Acid Javelin!"

The magic spear flew straight at her face, and Narberal moved her head, without thinking, to dodge it. That was a mistake. It wouldn't have done anything if it had hit her, so she should have ignored it. But since it was aimed at her face, her instincts had taken over. This was an error only a caster who hadn't concentrated their efforts on melee combat would make—and she paid for it.

With a screeching noise, Narberal's view abruptly changed—everything flew by sideways. After a moment of weightlessness, she crashed into the ground. She'd taken a swipe of a skeletal dragon's tail to her left upper arm, but still tumbling over and over, she couldn't tell what had happened.

The multiple defensive spells she had cast meant there wasn't much pain. She was flat on the ground, but before her eyes were two skeletal dragons. Both of them were brandishing their front legs.

It seemed like the end of the line. Normally, it would be.

"If you surrender, I'll spare you!" Khajit, sure of his victory, grinned sadistically. Surely he had no intention of sparing her. That grin spoke louder than his words—he would simply savor the look on her face as he crushed her after she'd pleaded for her life.

Narberal had sat up, and her face was twisted in anger. "…an… sc…m…"

"…What?"

She glared at him. "Human scum, don't talk that shit to me, you piece of garbage!"

Eyes bulging, Khajit shivered and screamed a panicky order. "Crush her, skeletal dragons!"

As the feet began to move, Narberal smiled. She couldn't miss the voice of the one she worshipped, no matter how far away it was coming from:

"Narberal Gamma! Show them the might of Nazarick!"

"…As my lord wishes. Then, I shall face them not as Nabe, but as Narberal Gamma!"

She was still on the ground, and the dragon legs seemed like they were about to crush her. One blink of an eye and she'd be stomped flat. Then she cast a spell—

"Teleportation!"

Her view changed instantaneously—to one from more than 1,600 feet in the air.

Naturally, having no wings, she plummeted toward the ground.

The wind roared past her, and the ground grew closer. She cackled. "Fly!" Gradually slowing, she eventually came to a stop hovering in the air. Looking down, she saw the battlefield she had just been on, Khajit, and the two skeletal dragons. They glanced around restlessly, no doubt bewildered by her sudden disappearance.

●

"Ahh! I'm tired!" Clementine commented loud enough that Ainz could hear. After several minutes of action, Ainz's great swords hadn't so much as grazed her. "But ya know, ya do seem pretty strong. You're probably pretty proud of that, but—" Her smile turned carnivorous. "—are you some kinda dummy? You're just swingin' that thing around with brute strength. There's no technique—you're like a kid swingin' a stick around. I mean, it doesn't do ya any good to have a sword in each hand if ya can't use 'em right; it'd be smarter to use just one. I dunno if you appreciate the complexities of being a warrior!"

"Then maybe you should attack me. All you've been doing this whole time is evading. You're the one who's deeper in trouble the more time goes by, right?" Ainz sneered.

Clementine scowled. It was true that she hadn't attacked him even once; she'd just been dodging. Faced with his superior physical abilities, she hadn't been able to find an opening. In other words, she wasn't having such an easy time, either. Her irritation at herself stemmed from her earlier bragging.

"I thought there weren't any warriors who could beat you! Where'd that confidence go?"

"…" Finally, allowing Ainz to provoke her, she drew a weapon. From the four stilettos and a morning star she had hanging from her waist, she had selected a stiletto.

Noticing with his extraordinary vision that the morning star was caked with what looked like meaty blood, Ainz clenched both of his great swords with his full strength.

Just as both of them were about to step forward, the ground shook.

In combat mode, Clementine couldn't shift her gaze too much, but she did take a look to see what was going on—there were two dragons made out of bones over where Narberal was fighting.

"Skeletal…dragons…?"

"Bingooo! That's right—ya know your stuff, huh? They're a caster's worst nightmare!"

"I see. So that's why you say Nabe can't win."

"Exxxactly." Having regained composure with the appearance of the skeletal dragons, Clementine returned to her previous mocking tone.

The illusion face under Ainz's helmet grimaced. Skeletal dragons were a tough opponent for casters. And against two of them, Narberal *the way she was now* had as good as no chance at winning.

Perhaps sensing his frustration, Clementine made a subtle move. It could have been a feint, but it wouldn't be *only* a feint. If a warrior showed a talented adversary a weak spot, they could bet that advantage would be taken.

Pushing Narberal to the edge of his consciousness, Ainz thrust his left hand's great sword out like a spear as a threat and held the one in his right hand over his head.

Clementine's weapon was a stabbing weapon; it didn't have the variety of attacks a cutting weapon did. Stab—that was all it could do. And her stilettos were delicate, not sturdy enough to clash with a great sword.

So with his left sword up, making it difficult for her to approach, he just waited for her. But she realized what he was up to.

"Do you have a way to close that distance?"

"Oh, I dunno…" Her casual attitude, relaxed appearance, and flippant smile told him she wasn't lacking ideas.

Slowly her posture changed. It was as if she were crouched and on her mark but standing up—an odd posture. In a way, it was kind of a funny pose, but it definitely wasn't a stance that could be taken lightly.

Then, she moved. To Ainz's alert eyes, she was like a spring that had been compressed to its limits and sprung. She was racing directly at him at a speed that was hard for Ainz to believe; it seemed beyond what flesh was capable of.

Like a storm moving in to swallow everything up in a moment, Clementine closed the distance in the blink of an eye and slipped past the pointed great sword without losing speed.

Her movements were like a snake going in for the kill. Startled, Ainz swung his right arm with his immense strength. The mighty attack seemed to cut the very air and was accompanied by unimaginable destructive power.

He had less than a split second but noted the fissure-like smile on her face intensify.

"Impenetrable Fortress!"

Beholding something that should be impossible, Ainz shivered in astonishment. The slim stiletto had taken the full force of the blow from his great sword, more than ten times its weight.

That sword taking Ainz's glorious attack should have snapped in half, or even if by some miracle it didn't, Clementine should have gone flying. On the contrary, Ainz's sword bounced hard, as if he'd hit a tremendously solid castle wall.

Clementine jumped at his wide-open chest like a lover slipping into an embrace. Her well-formed features and the smile widened across them loomed large in his field of vision.

The attack came well before he could retreat. Uniting her full-throttle sprint with the strength of all her muscles, she took advantage of her body's momentum to deliver a strike that deserved the word *meteor*.

The sparkle of a flourish and the awful *kreeeee* of metal scraping metal echoed loudly through the graveyard. Ainz hastily swung his left great sword, but Clementine jumped aside.

He knew her trick. "A martial art?" They were moves to be careful of—skills that didn't exist in *Yggdrasil*, warrior magic. *It must protect her sword and give her physical indomitability.* That had to have been how she'd repelled Ainz's attack.

"...Tough stuff! What's that armor made of, adamantite?"

There wasn't any pain at all, but at the time of that abrasive noise, he'd felt something with a sharp point stick into the area near his left shoulder. Shocked, he looked at his shoulder and discovered a slight dent. It may not have had any special magical powers, but this was still armor made by a level-100 caster—and it was proportionally hard. The fact that Clementine had managed to damage it spoke volumes to her destructive power.

"Well, whatever. Just the next time I gotta hit somewhere less heavily protected. Aw, but I wanted to chip away at ya till ya couldn't move and torture you! Too bad—what a shame."

Hearing that she attacked his shoulder not by chance but because she was aiming to incapacitate his arm caused Ainz to respect her—a bit—for the first time.

Ainz always ended up swinging with causing damage in mind. That was sufficient enough when one sound hit would kill his opponent, but against a tougher one, he had to think about how the battle would play out. *A good lesson to learn...*

"Okay, here I go!"

While he'd been admiring her, Clementine had once again taken the odd bent-over posture from before. In response, Ainz raised the great sword in his right hand. But this time he didn't thrust out the left sword.

Seeing that, Clementine smiled and rushed forward. She was moving so fast, even Ainz's dynamic visual acuity couldn't make her out. If she hadn't been coming in a straight line, he might have lost sight of her.

She flew at him like a sinister arrow, and in response, he carried out his planned attack. The great sword in his right hand swung and—

"Impenetrable Fortress!"

—bounced back against the same martial art from before. But he'd expected that. The previous time he had swung as hard as he could so the rebound had broken his stance. This time he didn't use as much force.

The shock felt like hitting a hard wall, but he overcame it with the strength of his arm and then swung his left great sword. He was confident she couldn't withstand two of his transcendent full-power blows.

But before he could connect, she used a different martial art. "Flow Acceleration!" It made something mind-boggling happen.

It was almost as if she had manipulated time. In this sluggish space where everything moved as if it had fallen into a highly viscous fluid, Ainz's great sword moved at a snail's pace.

Only Clementine maintained her speed in this quiet world; she easily evaded his counterattack and slipped right in front of him.

Perhaps it was in Ainz's head. He was wearing rings against time manipulation and that hindered movement to prevent external forces from slowing him down—not that this couldn't be something new...

It must have just been her sudden acceleration causing him to perceive things that way in his heightened battle mode. After all, he'd seen this martial art before, and it hadn't affected him like this.

"Gaze—" It was a martial art Gazef Stronoff had used.

Before he could get the shout out, the stiletto stabbed at him. She'd aimed for the narrow slit in his helmet—his eyes.

Ainz shook his head away and avoided getting it stuck in the slit, but the sound of metal grating on his helmet was horrible. Before he could feel any relief at having dodged, he caught Clementine in the corner of his vision holding her stiletto back, as if she were coiled and ready to spring.

"Tch!"

Even taking into account their difference in strength, Clementine's direct line of attack was faster than the arc of Ainz's sword. This time she didn't miss, and her sword stabbed into the slit of his helmet.

"Huh?"

"Guh!"

The puzzled question and flustered grunt occurred at the same time.

Pressing his helmet with the hand that held his sword, Ainz retreated quite a ways without countering.

Watching him from the corner of her eye as she looked curiously at the tip of her stiletto, she joked, "Better stop talking about handicaps—if ya don't start fighting for real, you're gonna die!" Ainz didn't say anything, so she asked a question to clear up her doubt. "But how did ya not take any damage from that attack before? I thought for sure it'd be a pain parade!"

"Sheesh. I've learned…a lot during this fight—first about a new martial art, and then about how important it is to use your whole body for balance and not just swinging your weapon around."

"Huh? Are you stupid? You figured this out now? Some warrior you are! Well, you're gonna die now, anyway, so it doesn't matter. But I did want you to answer my question… Was it a defensive martial art?"

Sensing her annoyance, Ainz smiled wryly under his helmet—about his qualifications as a warrior, she was right. "Ah, I really came underprepared. I apologize. But we're running out of time. Let's stop playing games." Ignoring the confusion on Clementine's face, he raised his voice. "Narberal Gamma! Show them the might of Nazarick!"

Ainz spun the hilts of his swords till their blades pointed down and thrust them into the ground. Putting his empty hands out in front of him, he beckoned her gently. "Now come at me like you're ready to die."

•

"…So it wasn't a bluff, 'ey? You can actually use Fly. But how did you dodge that attack? I couldn't see because I was behind the dragon…"

The voice directed at Narberal as she slowly descended back to earth was cautious. He couldn't fathom why she hadn't used Fly to run away. Especially having encountered two skeletal dragons, who wouldn't pull out if they could?

"Hmph. You think you have a chance at winning? Against skeletal dragons with absolute magic resistance?"

"There are any number of ways for me to win, but first…" Narberal grabbed the shoulder of her robe and tore it away. "Rejoice, human scum, for you have received the honor of facing Narberal Gamma of the Pleiades, combat maids loyal to the absolute ruler of the Great Tomb of Nazarick, Supreme Being Lord Ainz Ooal Gown!"

All of her gear had transformed. She wore vambraces and greaves of silver, gold, and black metal, armor like a maid outfit from a manga, and instead of a helmet, a white lace headpiece. In her hands she gripped a staff of silver-coated gold.

The performance of custom items in *Yggdrasil* could be changed by changing their data-crystal makeup. Narberal's robe had the quick-change crystal, so she could change her whole gear set without spending any time swapping pieces.

The robe was put "away" into space.

Khajit blinked several times at the maid who'd just appeared before his eyes. Then he finally grasped the situation—"What?!"—and shouted in disbelief.

Sure, it was perfectly normal for the caster in front of him to turn into a maid.

Her outfit was a joke and made him uncomfortable, but the exceedingly calm look on her face made him panic, and he ordered the skeletal dragons to attack. The two dragons approached Narberal with surprising agility. One of the huge bony monsters went to crush her with a foreleg, but when it was a hair's breadth from whacking her, she cast a spell.

"Dimensional Move!"

"Not again!"

Narberal vanished once more.

Trying to see where she went, Khajit remembered last time and looked up in the sky. But this time he would learn where she'd gone via pain.

"Gyahh!" His shriek echoed across the graveyard. A white-hot sensation suddenly shot through his left shoulder and a dull pain radiated through his body with each beat of his heart. Stupefied, he looked at the spot and saw a sharp point jutting out.

The next second, the blade was ripped carelessly out, creating a new wave of acute pain. "Gah! Gyah!" The vibrations of his bone being sawed propagated through his body, combining with the pain to increase his discomfort. Blood glubbed out of the puncture, soaking his black robe. In so much agony he was drooling, he spun around to see what had happened.

Narberal was standing there with a puzzled look on her face. "Does it hurt *that* much?"

"Ngh!"

She was toying with a freshly bloodied black-bladed dagger in the hand that didn't hold her staff.

Khajit was in so much agony he couldn't even speak.

Because he was a caster, he was never out on the front lines, and he was waited on by so many people that although he had occasion to give pain, he was rarely on the receiving end. As a result, he had low tolerance.

As clammy sweat coated his forehead, inside his head, he gave orders to the skeletal dragons. Narberal leaped away—Fly was faster than running.

The dragons inserted themselves into the open space. Behind them, Khajit, who, having secured a safe location, had regained a shred of composure, finally understood the significance of Narberal's previous spell.

It was—

"Teleportation magic?!"

Dimensional Move was a tier-three spell, but it was generally thought of as an escape spell used to quickly put distance between the caster and their opponent.

But that was in the case of a physically inferior caster. If one had strength that could put a warrior to shame, the spell could be just as valuable as an attack spell—no, since it was unblockable, it was actually *better* than lesser attack spells.

Holding his shoulder, he scowled at Narberal. "I see. So your ace move is teleporting in for the kill! And that's also how you evaded that attack earlier!"

It was certainly a pesky ace. If magic didn't work on the skeletal dragons, she could kill the summoner. An obvious strategy. And if she made effective use of teleportation magic, there was a good chance he wouldn't be able to stop her.

But Narberal scoffed lightly in reply. "I don't think so!"

Khajit's eyelids fluttered for a moment as he failed to comprehend what she was saying.

Then, to clarify, she began to move. "I just demonstrated *one* way I *could* easily kill you!" Narberal had been at an overwhelming disadvantage, but the moment she seemed to reveal the way she would turn the tables, she renounced it instead.

Khajit had no idea why she would do that. "Are you insane…?"

"I get that you're a flea, but what kind of reply is that? It'd be nice if you'd use your head a little more!"

Her frigid glare made his whole body tremble—not from anger but from fear. Anxiety flickered through his mind.

"Let's end this soon. It's rude of me as a follower of Lord Ainz to keep him waiting… You seem to think magic won't work on skeletal dragons, so allow me to create a learning opportunity for you, pond skater. The lesson fee is your life."

She dropped her staff, and the sound of her hands clapping together rang out. When she pulled them apart, white shocks arced between them. Reacting to the lightning writhing like Chinese dragons, the nearby air sparkled as it discharged. It was like she was enveloped in a white light.

"…Gah…" Khajit's eyes nearly popped out of his head. He had no more words. He knew she was casting a spell far beyond anything he was aware of. Within the white light frying his eyes, he could see her faint smile. Recalling the huge skeletal dragons standing between them, the clamorous alarm bells in his head made him scream. "Y-you can't defeat skeletal dragons with magic! They have absolute resistance! Go! Kill her!" he ordered in a trembling voice that betrayed the fear he couldn't hide.

As the dragons approached, Narberal smiled like a cruel instructor who was about to educate a foolish pupil. "Absolute resistance? They *do* have resistance, but the power they have is to nullify spells from tier six and below."

It took a little more time for the dragons to reach Narberal, during which Khajit realized, with an awfully level head, what she meant by that.

"In other words, I, Narberal Gamma, can use more powerful magic than that, so they won't be able to nullify my attack!"

She wasn't lying—Khajit's gut told him that.

Which meant that this woman's magic could slay the dragons and then kill him, too.

"Why?! You're going to destroy the fruit of more than five years of labor in less than an hour?!" Khajit squawked. Scenes of his past flickered before his eyes like the shadows of a revolving lantern.

Khajit Dale Badantel.

Given life as the only child of a father with a robust physique forged by village labor and a gentle mother in a remote Slane Theocracy village, he had a "normal" childhood.

He started down the path from then to his current self when he found the remains of his mother.

That day—the sun had been low on the horizon—Khajit had been racing toward his house. His mother had told him to be home early, but he was late for some reason he couldn't even remember anymore: He'd been on the outskirts of the village looking for cool rocks; he'd picked up a stick and pretended to be a hero—some stupid thing like that.

Thinking his mother would scold him, he'd flown into the house—and seen her sprawled on the floor. Shocked, he'd panicked, and even now he could remember the warmth he'd felt when he touched her.

You've got to be kidding me. His expectations had been betrayed.

His mother was dead.

The clergyman said the cause of death was "a lump of blood that formed in her brain." In other words, it was no one's fault. No one was in the wrong. No, Khajit felt there was one and only one person to blame—himself.

If he had gotten home sooner that day, would he have been able to save her? There was a huge number of the Slane Theocracy's faith-magic casters, including several in his village. If he had gone to them for help, would his mother still be alive and smiling?

The face of his precious mother twisted in pain…was a crime he had perpetrated.

Khajit made up his mind. He would live to right his wrong, i.e., to bring his mother back to life.

*   *   *

The more magic and knowledge he acquired, the bigger the obstacles he faced.

There was a resurrection spell on faith magic's fifth tier, but he couldn't bring his mother back with it. During the resurrection, the deceased consumed a vast amount of life force; if the body didn't have enough, it would be impossible to resurrect and turn to ashes. His mother didn't have the life force in her for that.

But he didn't have enough time to develop a new resurrection spell. So, he would give up being human and turn undead to buy the time. That was the conclusion he came to.

He abandoned the faith-magic path he'd been walking and turned down the path of using magical magic and becoming an undead, but he was confronted with another wall.

It would take an extremely long time to plow ahead as a magical-magic caster, quit being human, and become a powerful undead. Then, there was also the hurdle of talent and ability—it was possible he wouldn't be able to become an undead.

The breakthrough plan he conceived was to gather a vast amount of negative energy—yes, the amount that killing every person living in a city and turning them into an undead would generate.

Why, at the moment his desire would be realized, was there someone getting in his way?

"Why should you have the right to make my five years of preparation in this city, the feelings I can't forget even though it's been more than thirty years, all for nothing?! You just came out of *nowhere*!!!"

The response to Khajit's howl was a sardonic smile. "I'm not interested in your feelings. But I do have something to say to you for all your laughable hard work… *You made a lovely stepping-stone for Lord Ainz.* Twin Max Chain Dragon Lightning!" Lightning writhing like a dragon shot out from each of Narberal's hands.

The skeletal dragons' giant white frames trembled when the lightning bolts, each thicker than a human's arm, met them. The lightning that coiled like Chinese dragons around the skeletal dragons' bodies burned up the false life that made the dead bones move.

The result was immediate.

The skeletal dragons, who were supposed to have absolute resistance to magic, were turned to rubble by magic lightning.

Even after they had completely crumbled, the lightning didn't disappear. The two electric dragons raised their heads as if searching for their next prey and raced through the sky to their last remaining target.

Khajit's entire field of vision filled with pure white electric light. There was no time to beg for mercy, no time to scream. The tears that welled up in the corners of his eyes vaporized in an instant, leaving nothing behind but a whisper: "Mother…" Khajit was devoured by the lightning.

His muscles went into convulsions, and his body writhed where he'd stood, as if he were doing a strange dance. After rapidly burning through his insides, the electricity vanished, and Khajit fell to the ground, smoking from his burns.

The stench of cooking flesh wafted throughout the area.

Narberal shrugged and called out to Khajit, whose body had curled up into a ball as his muscles burned up. "Even worms smell good grilled… Might make a nice souvenir for Entoma." Dropping the name of her fellow Pleiades member who preyed on humans, Narberal sneered.

●

The warrior before her opened up his arms as if he were going to hug her.

"What're ya doing? Ya give up?"

"No, what? I just figured that since I gave Narberal the order, I should probably settle this pretty soon as well."

"Huh? Are you serious? How can you win against me with no martial arts or any decent skills? How much more annoying can you be?"

"You talk a lot of crap for a wimp."

You're the wimp! she nearly raged but instead calmed her seething heart. The man before her had little skill as a warrior, but his physical ability easily exceeded the realm of ordinary humans. As far as she knew, it was surpassed by only two demigods: the Black Scripture's extra seat and its captain, who occupied the first seat. But because of that, he swung his sword around however he felt like, which made both his offense and defense sloppy, which meant he was in danger of being dealt a fatal blow.

Clementine put on her usual sneer and taunted him. "...Welllll, I do agree that we should settle this."

Momon the warrior merely shrugged in reply.

She coolly observed the way he carried himself. He was full of holes, but that couldn't be true. It had to be a trap.

But she didn't have a choice. What she'd said a moment ago had sounded like a joke, but she'd meant it. She figured she could escape if she could borrow a skeletal dragon, but she couldn't afford to lose any more time. Even if it was to throw off the Flurry Scripture members who had come to the city, playtime was going a little long.

She slowly moved into a crouch and tightened her grip on her stiletto. She wanted this critical clash to be short—if possible, over in one hit. She didn't have time, but the other thing was that the warrior seemed to be gradually getting the hang of things. It was safer to crush him before he grew into a monster she couldn't handle.

With a sharp exhalation, Clementine charged. "Stride of Wind! Greater Evasion! Ability Boost! Greater Ability Boost!" She used the same four martial arts from before all at once to get her physical ability even a little closer to his. Regardless of how Momon had fought so far, there was still the possibility he could use martial arts.

In her accelerating world, she could see her opponent's every move. He was going to take his swords out of the ground and attack. Or use a martial art, or hand-to-hand combat, or a hidden weapon—no, a throwing weapon. She could think of a zillion ways he could attack her, but she was confident she could prevail over any of them. Then he betrayed her expectations.

He's not doing anything?!

The dark warrior just stood there, arms open, as if he was welcoming her attack.

A chill ran up Clementine's spine—fear of the unknown; he was acting completely outside the scenarios she'd imagined. *Should I keep charging or retreat?* Those were her only two options.

Clementine was cold-blooded and cruel, but she wasn't stupid. In the split second left, she calculated out countless possibilities and countermeasures. What gave her the push to continue was self-confidence and pride in her abilities.

Even though she'd betrayed them, she was a member of the Slane Theocracy's strongest special-ops unit, the Black Scripture, and she could count the number of *warriors* powerful enough to defeat her on her fingers. There was no way she could run from this Momon character who had no reputation and little skill.

Once she'd made her decision, the rest happened quickly. Her hesitation vanished, and having regained the cool composure befitting a top-class warrior, she leaped in close to Momon's chest.

"Die!"

The stiletto she thrust, mobilizing all her body's muscles, stabbed into the slit in his close helmet. Then, she twisted it. She increased pressure to reach the back of his skull and then wiggled the blade to break the nearby blood vessels so the wound would be fatal beyond a doubt.

An armored arm wrapped tightly around her body, but she paid it no mind and followed up with another attack. Responding to her desire to kill him dead, the magic power contained in her stiletto was unleashed—Lightning.

Electricity coursed through Ainz's entire body.

Clementine's weapon was invested with the power of Magic Accumulation. The magic was drained in one shot, but it was possible to load up all different spells over and over. One could prepare according to their specific needs, so it was a really easy power to use.

She'd stabbed to the back of his skull and left him a lightning souvenir. *He's definitely dead.*

But—

"I'm not done yet! Flow Acceleration!" Clementine accelerated, whipped out another stiletto, and stabbed that through his helmet slit as well. On top of that, she unleashed the Fireball spell it contained. She hallucinated Momon's flesh burning up from the inside out and had the feeling she could smell the meat grilling.

Instead, her eyes widened in shock at how wrong she was.

"Hmm. *Yggdrasil* didn't have magical weapons like that. The more you know!"

As he spoke at leisure with a stiletto still sticking out of each eye, she realized that it hadn't been a coincidence that there wasn't blood on the blade when she'd stabbed him earlier.

"No way! This can't be happening! Why won't you die?!" She'd never heard of a martial art that made the user invincible. Was there something protecting him from stabbing? Even then, how did he block the magic follow-up? Even the veteran warrior Clementine didn't know the answer.

"?!" She was pulled in close. Their bodies bumped together, and her adventurer plates jangled.

"You want to know if you got the answer right?"

The raven-black armor—*poof*—disappeared, revealing Momon's horrifying face. It was a skull with neither flesh nor skin. Stilettos were stabbed into both of his vacant orbits—through his mirrored shades—but he didn't give any indication he was experiencing any pain.

That appearance rang a bell for Clementine. "An undead... An elder lich?!"

"...? Well, I sure have some questions for you, but meh. Let's just say you're close. And then..."

She shouldn't have been able to read an expression from a face with no skin or flesh, but she had the feeling he was wearing a wide grin.

"So, how does it feel fighting a caster with a sword? How does it feel to not have it end with a swoop and a *shoonk?*"

"D-don't make fun of me!" Clementine struggled violently to get away, but it was as if she were bound to him by sturdy chains, and she couldn't.

An elder lich was certainly a mighty undead, good at using magic and so on, but it shouldn't have much in the way of physical ability; in a comparison with Clementine, she should come out on top. But...

"Wh-why?!"

I can't get away.

Her entire body went cold when it dawned on her that his incredible power and physical ability wasn't due to some magical effect in his armor. The image that ran through her mind was of a butterfly caught in a spider's web—a helpless creature.

"This was the true nature of your handicap. Basically, you weren't an enemy I had to take seriously enough to use magic on."

"You piece of shiiiiiiiiit!"

"Well, now that the cat's out of the bag, let's begin after I get these out of my way." There was a dragging noise as the elder lich pulled a stiletto out of his head and threw it away. Clementine was still struggling as he removed the other, but it seemed even one of his hands far exceeded the strength of her entire body, and she couldn't budge in his embrace.

Once the stilettos were gone, the sinister red flames in his empty eye sockets turned to Clementine, who was breathing irregularly as she strained against him.

"Okay, let's begin."

Begin what? thought Clementine as the already intimate distance between her and the elder lich shrank even farther. In her ears was an unpleasant creaking noise.

When she realized what he was trying to do, she felt as though she'd been stabbed in the back with an icicle.

"You aren't...? You can't be...! Youuuuuuu!"

The noise was the shriek of her armor beginning to dent.

He's trying to crush me against his chest.

The elder lich should have been getting squashed against the armor as well, but he must have changed his body to be more powerful somehow. It was immovable and made her think of a thick wall.

"If you were weaker—"

The elder lich took a dagger out from somewhere. The blade was black, and there were four jewels set in the hilt. "I considered ending your life with this, but I figure there's not much difference between dying on a sword, getting snapped in half, or being crushed. You're *dead* no matter what."

Her whole body shuddered. Throughout his commentary, the pressure was gradually increasing. The strange weight on her chest was becoming oppressive. *Ping! Ping!* Unable to bear it, the plates of the adventurers she'd killed began popping off her armor and falling to the graveyard ground as if they were finally being interred. The first to go were the ones she had most recently acquired.

It got harder and harder to breathe. *This is awful.*

She hated the arm wrapped around her back.

She blamed herself for wearing light armor in order to increase her evasion and be able to attach the adventurer plates.

Having learned that swords had no effect on the elder lich, she began beating his face with her fists, half crazed. She was hitting so hard she was hurting herself, but she wasn't at leisure to feel the pain. Then, she drew her morning star and began frantically pounding with that, but she couldn't do it right and only ended up wounding herself.

It was easy to imagine the fate that awaited her. The choking breaths, the weight on her chest, and her breaking armor made it crystal clear what would happen.

"Don't struggle so much. If the position of my arm slips, it'll end too simply. You took your time killing *them*, so I want to take my time on you, too."

Clementine desperately continued her attacks. She tried pushing off of his head with her hand, scratching at him till her nails peeled back, biting him with her front teeth... None of it worked and the pressure continued increasing.

No matter how much she flailed, there was no escaping the jaws that were his arms. She still fought. Even as her breathing grew more difficult and her field of vision began to shrink, she fought for the chance to survive.

"*La Danse Macabre?*"

She couldn't even spare the effort to hear that quiet remark.

There was a gurgling sound, and Ainz was splashed with vomit and filth. Something dark flashed through the red flames in his vacant orbits.

Clementine, who had flailed and tried so desperately to escape, had devolved into something that could only convulse.

But Ainz didn't let up. On the contrary, he increased the pressure. Eventually Ainz felt the crack of a thick bone snapping against his arm. He let go of a body that was no longer even twitching.

Clementine's corpse fell to the graveyard ground with a thud, like a bag of garbage. Her face looked ghastly, distorted by pain and fear. Like a deep-sea fish that had been reeled in all at once, her innards were poking out of her mouth.

As Ainz took out his Bottomless Pitcher of Water to wash the vomit and filth from his body with its endless stream of fresh water, he spoke quietly to Clementine, who could no longer reply. "Oh, I forgot to tell you—I'm extremely self-centered."

5

Shrinking from his clothes that were sopping wet after their cleansing, Ainz sensed that something large was scampering his way. When he looked, it was Hamusuke, as he'd thought.

Hamusuke's combat ability was far inferior to Ainz's or Narberal's. If he'd have forced her to fight and she got hurt, it would have led to unnecessary expenditures, so he'd had her stand by a little ways away, but apparently she had come out once she could no longer hear battle noises.

Ainz was a little depressed he was able to read the subtle change in expression (*concerned for her master's safety*) on the super-giant hamster's cute face.

Having no idea her master was feeling that way, the giant hamster ran over surprisingly quickly and scanned the area. When her eyes met Ainz's—

"Blegh!" She keeled over belly up and continued shouting. "There's some kind of crazy monster here, that there is! Masterrrr! Masterrrr!"

Steeped in the torment of full-body weariness, Ainz held his head. Now that he thought of it, he had never shown Hamusuke his real face. But he couldn't leave it like this. When he looked out at the wall in the distance, he saw there were some adventurers battling his wraiths. He wanted to think they couldn't be overheard at this distance, but he couldn't say for sure.

"…This is like a bad comedy routine. Would you cut it out?" Ainz scolded in his dignified tone.

"Oh? That magnificent, valiant voice… Could it be…? You're my master, are you not?!"

"Yes, so could you keep it down?"

"What! Your appearance is far different from my most wild imaginings! I thought you possessed great power, but…now I will be even more loyal to you, that I will!"

"Uh-huh. More importantly, I'll say it again: Keep it down."

"M-master, you're so mean, that you are! I would like that you not dismiss my oath of devotion so casually, that I would!"

"Did you not hear what Lord Ainz just said, you fool?!"

A dent appeared in Hamusuke and she went flying.

Where she'd been standing up until a moment before, Narberal was slowly lowering her foot. "Lord Ainz, I don't believe there is any value in keeping such a stupid creature. May I grill her with lightning?"

"Don't. She's quite valuable to us in terms of reputation if we use her as the Wise King of the Forest. Even just taking her around with us live is beneficial. More importantly, Narberal, we don't have much time. Start looting these guys. Assuming the peacekeepers in the city will request us to turn everything in, we need to check for valuables first."

"Understood."

"I'm going into the mausoleum. I'll leave the cleanup to you."

"My lord! What shall I do with the corpses? Will we take them to Nazarick?"

"No. We need to point to them as the masterminds behind this incident. Just strip their gear."

"Understood."

"It hurts, that it does…"

Narberal heaved an exaggerated sigh and sent Hamusuke, who had returned, a chilly glare. "Pay more attention to anything Lord Ainz says than your entire existence. That is the duty of a minion. Even a creature like you counts as a minion—barely—so keep that in mind! If you don't, I'll promptly kill you."

Hamusuke shivered.

"Next time I'll punish you with magic, not a physical attack. In accordance with Lord Ainz's wishes, I'll cause as much pain as I can without killing you."

"I understand, that I do… Please don't look at me with such a scary face, that I ask… But I'm astonished by our master's new and powerful appearance, that I am. How magnificent!"

Narberal's expression softened just a bit. "Yeah. Lord Ainz is truly wonderful to behold. If you understand that, you might have a pretty good eye."

"I thank you, that I do. But if our master has a true form, do you have another form as well, hmm?"

"…I'm a doppelgänger; I just changed my face. See?" She took off her gauntlet to reveal a hand with only three fingers. They were longer than human fingers and looked just like inchworms.

"O-oh, I didn't know, that I did not."

"Why are you surprised? You're a part of the Great Tomb of Nazarick as one of its lowest-class minions now, so you can't let a little thing like that shock you. More importantly, why don't you help me loot these corpses?"

"Yes, ma'am! That I will!"

Nfirea was inside the mausoleum. When Ainz saw him, the red sparkles in his orbits grew dark. He was wearing some strangely transparent garments, but what Ainz was looking at was his face. A cut had been made straight across it, and the trails of hardened blood like reddish-black tears showed that his eyes under their lids had been sliced. It was clear he had been blinded.

"Well, blindness I can fix… Magic is so handy."

The bigger problem was his mental condition. He was standing stiff as a rod and hadn't reacted to Ainz's presence. Even if he couldn't see, he should have been able to tell if someone was standing right in front of him. Since he didn't, it meant he was being mind controlled. The question was, via what?

"It has to be this." Ainz was looking at the spiderweb-like circlet around Nfirea's head. There was nothing more suspicious around.

He casually reached out to remove it but stopped. Interfering before he understood what had caused this state was too risky. He faced the circlet and used a spell. "Appraise Any Magic Item."

In *Yggdrasil*, the spell would tell who made an item and what it did, and it worked in this world as well. Actually, it worked even better. Things he never would have learned in *Yggdrasil* popped into his head.

"…A Crown of Wisdom…I see. But hmm, considering what it does, this couldn't exist in *Yggdrasil*. I guess it couldn't be reproduced there?" he commented, impressed after acquiring general knowledge about the item. Then, he thought about what to do next.

The most important thing he considered was the argument for taking Nfirea to the Great Tomb of Nazarick just as he was. Getting control of a rare item and a rare talent was huge.

But he only wavered for a moment. "Deliberately failing at a job I already undertook would be a disgrace to the name of Ainz Ooal Gown. Crumble away—Greater Break Item!"

Ainz's spell shot at the circlet, and it crumbled elegantly into innumerable tiny sparkles. He gently caught the boy as he slumped over, then carefully laid him down and looked at his face. "All that's left is…to fix his eyes. I guess it'd be better to do that somewhere else, though…"

Stroking his bony chin, Ainz stood up. The undead he'd summoned hadn't been wiped out, but some of them had been destroyed. There was no doubt that reinforcements—*the meddlers*—would reach this place at some point. He had to recast his illusion and recreate his armor and swords before that happened.

And they had to finish looting. Ainz experienced a dark joy in the simple act of robbing all of a corpse's gear at once, something that hadn't been possible PK-ing in *Yggdrasil*.

As he thought to go help Narberal with that, she appeared at the entrance to the mausoleum with perfect timing. "Lord Ainz."

"What is it? Did you take all their stuff? Money, too?"

"Yes, it's about that. I found this." Narberal went into the mausoleum. She was clutching a black orb. It wasn't a very nice-looking stone—it seemed like the type of rock one could find on the shore of a river. It certainly didn't look valuable.

"…What is it?"

"It seemed very important to the hammerhead worm I was fighting. I don't know what it does…"

"I see…"

Narberal the NPC didn't know as many spells as Ainz, and most of them were for combat, hence her not being able to appraise the item.

Ainz took it and used the same spell as before. "Appraise Any Magic Item."

The red sparks in his eyes burned brilliantly.

"What…is this? A Jewel of Death? And it's an intelligent item?"

For having such a grandiose name, being "of death" and all, it wasn't such a fancy item. It augmented the user's ability to control undead and allowed them to cast a number of ghost magic spells so many times per day—neither of which powers held much fascination for Ainz. The downside was that it could control a human in possession of it, but Ainz and Narberal were protected against mind control and the jewel couldn't control subhumans or grotesques anyhow.

"This is a pretty meh item, but…" There was one thing about it that interested Ainz, and that was that it was intelligent. When he poked it, as if telling it to say something, a voice echoed in his mind.

"We meet for the first time, O great King of Death."

Ainz stared at the stone. This was a world with magic and monsters, so it didn't surprise him that something like this would exist. "Hmm. You really are intelligent, huh?" He deftly rolled the stone in his hand and then stared at it again, but it didn't seem like it was going to say anything. He wondered what the deal was but then had an idea. "I permit you to speak."

"I humbly thank you, O great King of Death."

That response reminded him of the ardent devotion of the Nazarick NPCs, and Ainz smiled faintly.

"I revere and worship your majesty's presence of absolute *death*."

Ainz was pretty sure he had all his auras turned off, so why was this item calling him the King of Death? Considering Ainz was undead, he figured it was flattery at best. "Go ahead."

"Thank you, Being of Profound Death. I thank all death that exists in this world that I should get to meet you, whom I worship."

For brownnosing, those were pretty serious words, and despite feeling self-conscious, Ainz puffed out his chest.

"And? Do you have anything to say besides flattery?"

"Yes. I am deeply aware how impertinent it is of me, but please, I beg that you would grant my wish."

"What is it?"

"I always thought I was born into this world to bestow death upon large numbers of people. But now that I have met you, O great King of Death, I realize the true reason: I was born into this world to serve you, your majesty."

"…Hmm…"

"O great King of Death, please accept my loyalty. And I humbly request that your majesty count me among the lowliest of your faithful servants." It was a sincere voice. Had the jewel had a head, it surely would have been bowed low.

Ainz curled his right hand and placed it near his mouth while he thought—about whether he should make it one of his subordinates or not, about whether he could trust it or not.

After a time, he slowly returned his gaze to the item. To be "safe," he should destroy it, but it seemed like a waste to destroy any more things that hadn't existed in *Yggdrasil*.

After casting some defensive spells on the orb, he went to the entrance of the mausoleum and called out to the giant hamster. "Hamusuke!"

"Master, what is it, hmm?"

"I'm giving this to you."

Ainz tossed the orb. Hamusuke nimbly caught it.

"Master, what in the world is this, hmm?"

"A magic item. Can you use it?"

"Hrm? …It seems I can, that it does! But how noisy it is! It clamors to be returned to you, master, it does."

Seeing Hamusuke like that, Narberal's eyes grew wide. "You would bestow it on a newcomer?!" Her slightly shrill voice showed how shocked she was.

"I took some precautions against detection magic, but I can't say for sure that it's a hundred percent safe; that's why I'm having Hamusuke hold on to it."

"Aha! Brilliant as usual, Lord Ainz. Not careless even for a moment, you make another admirable judgment call." Narberal indicated she understood, and Hamusuke, with a lump in her cheek pouch (slightly smaller than a human fist), made a dignified bow.

As Ainz was giving the two of them the order to withdraw, the red of his cape caught his eye. Feeling a bit playful, he grabbed the edge of it. "Once you're done looting, let's take Nfirea"—he flourished his cape—"and make our triumphant return."

Epilogue

Ainz pushed open the door of the inn where they'd stayed the other day. That instant, the place was swallowed up by perfect silence. Countless eyes were on him and Narberal, but no one got in their way. They stood before the innkeeper.

"Y...ou..."

Both his and the guests' eyes were all on the plates hanging from their necks.

Ainz made it short and nonchalant. "A room for two." He smirked. He tossed down the coins and silently took the key from the innkeeper.

Then, they went to their room where Ainz canceled all of his magic and returned to his true form. His mythril plate emitted a bright *ring* when it clinked his Nemean Lion. Up until just a bit ago, they'd been at the guild being debriefed about the previous day's incident. They'd been hurriedly awarded the plates there.

It went without saying that the silence in the inn had been caused by the plates. If a guy who arrived just a few days ago as a copper plate came back the next time with a mythril plate, it probably felt like he'd demolished the common sense they'd been building up all their careers. Their raw reactions did give him a sense of superiority, but he was also dissatisfied—because he was expecting they'd skip him all the way to orichalcum and instead he got one below that. How would everyone have reacted if his plate had been orichalcum?

Well, there was still a chance.

There were still only very few people who knew about the incident. And according to what he'd heard during his debriefing, their achievements were unbelievable and were really worthy of adamantite plates. The only reason they hadn't been given that was because they had no previous accomplishments, and the guild wanted to err on the side of caution, since the investigation was still incomplete.

In other words, internally at the guild they were viewed as adamantite-rank adventurers, of which there were only two teams in the entire kingdom.

He expected that, over time, the story of the fight in the graveyard and the name Momon would be known all over town. The guards who survived would surely talk. Everything was going so according to his plan that he chuckled to himself. It was more than a smooth start—it was perfect.

Ainz pinged his mythril plate with a finger, and then Narberal spoke up, curious. "What are you going to do with those two? You left it that you would contact them later about the reward, right?"

She meant Nfirea and Lizzy, the two apothecaries. Ainz had already made up his mind how to handle them. "Lizzy said she would give me everything, so I'm planning to have her take her grandson and go to Carne. I'll force them to make potions for me—no, for the Great Tomb of Nazarick."

"…Nazarick has ways to make potions. Why make those penis fish do it?"

"What I'm after is new ways to make potions."

Narberal looked at him vacantly without reacting, so Ainz explained, "The development of ways to create potions that didn't exist in *Yggdrasil* is important to work on, keeping in mind that our potion ingredients won't last forever. And we should probably work on combining techniques from *Yggdrasil* and this world to create new powers. It's entirely possible that we're six hundred years late to the game. Of course, we'll have to keep a strict watch to make sure no potions they make leave the premises, but…the way they were when I saw them, it probably won't be an issue."

Ainz had healed Nfirea's eyes, but perhaps because the mental strain was too great, the boy was still unconscious. Still, Lizzy was so deeply grateful her grandson was safe that she cried her eyes out and promised to pay the agreed-upon price.

"So I'll deal with them later. There are other things I need to do first."

Ainz cast Message to Albedo. Not contacting her despite receiving Entoma's Message was a pretty big slipup, but he hadn't had the time; he'd just have to get her to forgive him.

Then the Message connected, and the first thing she said was far beyond anything he'd expected:

"Lord Ainz, Shalltear has staged a rebellion!"

For a time, he couldn't understand what she'd said to him, but when he finally processed it, he vocalized his stupefaction:

"...What?!"

OVERLORD
Character Profiles

Character 5

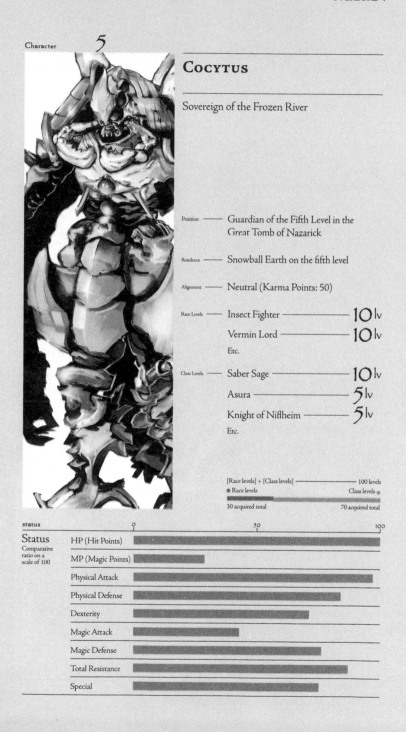

COCYTUS

Sovereign of the Frozen River

Position	Guardian of the Fifth Level in the Great Tomb of Nazarick
Residence	Snowball Earth on the fifth level
Alignment	Neutral (Karma Points: 50)

Race Levels

Insect Fighter	10 lv
Vermin Lord	10 lv

Etc.

Class Levels

Saber Sage	10 lv
Asura	5 lv
Knight of Niflheim	5 lv

Etc.

[Race levels] + [Class levels] ———— 100 levels
● Race levels   Class levels ●
30 acquired total   70 acquired total

status

Status

Comparative ratio on a scale of 100

	0	50	100
HP (Hit Points)			
MP (Magic Points)			
Physical Attack			
Physical Defense			
Dexterity			
Magic Attack			
Magic Defense			
Total Resistance			
Special			

DEMIURGE

Creator of the Inferno

Character　6

Position —— Guardian of the Seventh Level
in the Great Tomb of Nazarick

Residence —— The Red-Hot Shrine
on the seventh level

Alignment —— Extreme Evil (Karma Points: -500)

Race Levels —— Imp —————————— 10 lv

Archdevil —————————— 5 lv

Etc.

Class Levels —— Chaos —————————— 10 lv

Prince of Darkness ————— 10 lv

Shape-shifter ————————— 10 lv

Etc.

[Race levels] + [Class levels] ————— 100 levels
● Race levels　　　　　　　Class levels ●
35 acquired total　　　　　65 acquired total

status		0	50	100
Status Comparative ratio on a scale of 100	HP (Hit Points)			
	MP (Magic Points)			
	Physical Attack			
	Physical Defense			
	Dexterity			
	Magic Attack			
	Magic Defense			
	Total Resistance			
	Special			

Character

7

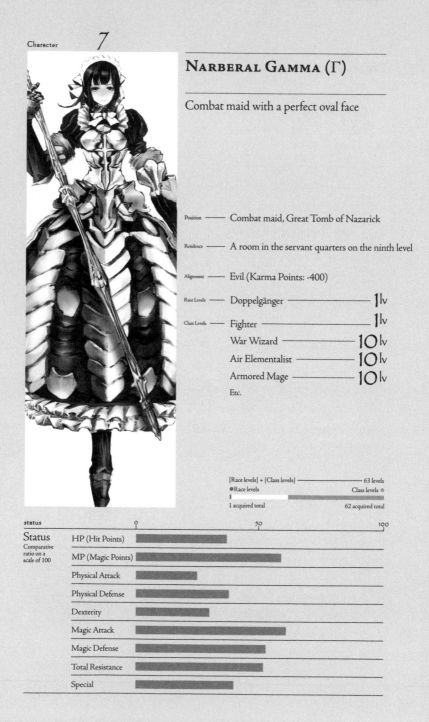

NARBERAL GAMMA (Γ)

Combat maid with a perfect oval face

Position	——	Combat maid, Great Tomb of Nazarick
Residence	——	A room in the servant quarters on the ninth level
Alignment	——	Evil (Karma Points: -400)
Race Levels	——	Doppelgänger ———————— 1 lv
Class Levels	——	Fighter ————————————— 1 lv
		War Wizard ————————— 10 lv
		Air Elementalist —————— 10 lv
		Armored Mage —————— 10 lv
		Etc.

[Race levels] + [Class levels] ———————— 63 levels
● Race levels   Class levels ●
1 acquired total   62 acquired total

status

Status

Comparative ratio on a scale of 100

	0	50	100
HP (Hit Points)			
MP (Magic Points)			
Physical Attack			
Physical Defense			
Dexterity			
Magic Attack			
Magic Defense			
Total Resistance			
Special			

Character   *8*

HAMUSUKE

Wise King of the Forest
("This name is a lie." –Ainz)

Position ——— Ainz's pet?
("I object to this." —Some female NPCs)

Residence ——— Ainz's room?

Alignment ——— Neutral (Karma Points: 0)

Race Levels ——— Unclear since none of
the same in *Yggdrasil*

Class Levels ——— Unclear since none of the
same in *Yggdrasil*
*Estimated level: 30 or a little above

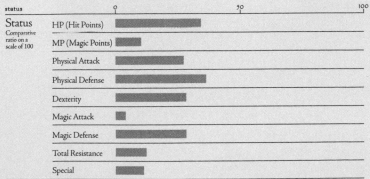

status   0   50   100

Status
Comparative
ratio on a
scale of 100

HP (Hit Points)	
MP (Magic Points)	
Physical Attack	
Physical Defense	
Dexterity	
Magic Attack	
Magic Defense	
Total Resistance	
Special	

Afterword

Long time no see, everyone. This is Kugane Maruyama.

Here is a story that happened while I was writing a battle scene. I was enacting a motion and my left hand smashed into a cup full of café au lait. Brown liquid splashed everywhere and tears welled up in my eyes. The only saving grace was that not a lot got on the bed and my manuscript didn't get hit... It might be fun for you to try to guess which scene was the one where I spilled my coffee, like, "This is about where it starts to smell like milk..."

That is the kind of challenge I faced while writing this, *Overlord, Volume 2: The Dark Warrior*. I hope you enjoyed reading it.

Perhaps you can recommend this story to someone who is sick to death of heroes saving girls? A protagonist could go save a boy now and then, right? It's gender equality! I do hope you like this protagonist even though he's crafty and only thinks of his own gains.

From here on, allow me to make some thank-yous:

To so-bin, who drew the fascinatingly beautiful illustrations. It's amazing how you get them to look even better than the pictures in my mind. The finished illustrations inspired me to rewrite a lot of the battle scenes.

Thanks also to Code Design, who made the wonderful cover and *obi* wrap. And to proofreader Osako for correcting so many hard-to-read sentences, thanks again. And to F-ta, my editor, sorry for all the trouble. And please give me way more red marks? (No, I get that not having any is better, but...) And to my friend from college, Honey, thanks again.

Most importantly, thanks to everyone who bought this book and everyone who sent me their impressions of the web version. I truly appreciate it. Your comments energize me.

Okay, so the next book...should be easier than this one...right? Looking it over, I don't get that feeling at all, but... Nah, if I can make something interesting, then I guess this amount of work is worth it... Okay, I think it's about time to wrap up the whining and say good-bye.

I'll do my best, so I hope to see you again in the third volume!

Well, then, see you.

KUGANE MARUYAMA
November 2012

Afterword by so-bin

Ah, youth— er, I'm old.

I was grinning the whole time I drew the picture for chapter 3. It's great to be young...

So-Bin

SHALLTEAR DOES THE UNIMAGINABLE AND REVOLTS. WHAT IN THE WORLD WAS GOING ON WHILE AINZ WAS GOING UNDERCOVER AS AN ADVENTURER?

How does the most
powerful guardian,
Albedo, respond to
her rival's betrayal?
Nazarick is destabilized
in Volume 3.

OVERLORD

Volume 3: The Bloody Valkyrie

Kugane Maruyama | Illustration by so-bin

Coming soon from YEN ON !